ACCLAIM FOR COI

"Second chances, old flames, and startling new revelations combine to form a story filled with faith, trial, forgiveness, and redemption. Crack the cover and step in, but beware—Mermaid Point is harboring secrets that will keep you guessing."

—LISA WINGATE, NATIONAL BESTSELLING AUTHOR OF
THE SEA KEEPER'S DAUGHTERS ON *MERMAID MOON*

"I burned through *The Inn at Ocean's Edge* in one sitting. An intricate plot by a master storyteller. Colleen Coble has done it again with this gripping opening to a new series. I can't wait to spend more time at Sunset Cove."

—HEATHER BURCH, BESTSELLING AUTHOR OF *ONE LAVENDER RIBBON*

"Coble doesn't disappoint with her custom blend of suspense and romance."

—*PUBLISHERS WEEKLY* FOR *THE INN AT OCEAN'S EDGE*

"Veteran author Coble has penned another winner. Filled with mystery and romance that are unpredictable until the last page, this novel will grip readers long past when they should put their books down. Recommended to readers of contemporary mysteries."

—*CBA RETAILERS + RESOURCES*

"Coble truly shines when she's penning a mystery, and this tale will really keep the reader guessing . . . Mystery lovers will definitely want to put this book on their purchase list."

—*ROMANTIC TIMES* BOOK REVIEWS

"Master storyteller Colleen Coble has done it again. *The Inn at Ocean's Edge* is an intricately woven, well-crafted story of romance, suspense, family secrets, and a decades old mystery. Needless to say, it had me hooked from page one. I simply couldn't stop turning the pages. This one's going on my keeper shelf."

—LYNETTE EASON, AWARD-WINNING, BESTSELLING
AUTHOR OF THE HIDDEN IDENTITY SERIES

"Evocative and gripping, *The Inn at Ocean's Edge* will keep you flipping pages long into the night."

—DANI PETTREY, BESTSELLING AUTHOR OF
THE ALASKAN COURAGE SERIES

"Coble's atmospheric and suspenseful series launch should appeal to fans of Tracie Peterson and other authors of Christian romantic suspense."

—LIBRARY JOURNAL REVIEW OF TIDEWATER INN

"Romantically tense, but with just the right touch of danger, this cowboy love story is surprisingly clever—and pleasingly sweet."

—USATODAY.COM REVIEW OF BLUE MOON PROMISE

"Colleen Coble will keep you glued to each page as she shows you the beauty of God's most primitive land and the dangers it hides."

—WWW.ROMANCEJUNKIES.COM

"[An] outstanding, completely engaging tale that will have you on the edge of your seat . . . A must-have for all fans of romantic suspense!"

—THEROMANCEREADERSCONNECTION.COM REVIEW OF ANATHEMA

"Colleen Coble lays an intricate trail in Without a Trace and draws the reader on like a hound with a scent."

—ROMANTIC TIMES, 4½ STARS

"Coble's historical series just keeps getting better with each entry."

—LIBRARY JOURNAL STARRED REVIEW OF THE LIGHTKEEPER'S BALL

"Don't ever mistake [Coble's] for the fluffy romances with a little bit of suspense. She writes solid suspense, and she ties it all together beautifully with a wonderful message."

—LIFEINREVIEWBLOG.COM REVIEW OF LONESTAR ANGEL

"This book has everything I enjoy: mystery, romance, and suspense. The characters are likable, understandable, and I can relate to them."

—THEFRIENDLYBOOKNOOK.COM

"[M]ystery, danger, and intrigue as well as romance, love, and subtle inspiration. The Lightkeeper's Daughter is a 'keeper.'"

—ONCEUPONAROMANCE.COM

"Colleen is a master storyteller."

—KAREN KINGSBURY, BESTSELLING AUTHOR
OF UNLOCKED AND LEARNING

MERMAID MOON

ALSO BY COLLEEN COBLE

SUNSET COVE NOVELS
The Inn at Ocean's Edge
Mermaid Moon
Twilight at Blueberry Barrens
(Available September 2016)

HOPE BEACH NOVELS
Tidewater Inn
Rosemary Cottage
Seagrass Pier
All Is Bright: A Hope Beach
Christmas Novella (e-book only)

UNDER TEXAS STARS NOVELS
Blue Moon Promise
Safe in His Arms

THE MERCY FALLS SERIES
The Lightkeeper's Daughter
The Lightkeeper's Bride
The Lightkeeper's Ball

LONESTAR NOVELS
Lonestar Sanctuary
Lonestar Secrets
Lonestar Homecoming
Lonestar Angel
All Is Calm: A Lonestar
Christmas Novella (e-book only)

THE ROCK HARBOR SERIES
Without a Trace
Beyond a Doubt
Into the Deep
Cry in the Night
Silent Night: A Rock Harbor
Christmas Novella (e-book only)

THE ALOHA REEF SERIES
Distant Echoes
Black Sands
Dangerous Depths
Midnight Sea
Holy Night: An Aloha Reef
Christmas Novella (e-book only)

Alaska Twilight
Fire Dancer
Abomination
Anathema
Butterfly Palace

NOVELLAS INCLUDED IN:
Smitten
Secretly Smitten
Smitten Book Club

OTHER NOVELLAS
Bluebonnet Bride

MERMAID MOON

A Sunset Cove Novel

COLLEEN COBLE

THOMAS NELSON
Since 1798

Published in Nashville, Tennessee, by Thomas Nelson. Thomas Nelson is a registered trademark of HarperCollins Christian Publishing, Inc.

Thomas Nelson titles may be purchased in bulk for educational, business, fund-raising, or sales promotional use. For information, please e-mail SpecialMarkets@ThomasNelson.com.

Library of Congress Cataloging-in-Publication Data

Coble, Colleen.
Mermaid moon : a Sunset Cove novel / Colleen Coble.
    pages ; cm. -- (A Sunset Cove novel ; 2)
ISBN 978-1-4016-9028-1 (trade paper)
1. Family secrets--Fiction. 2. Murder--Investigation--Fiction. I. Title.
PS3553.O2285M47 2016
813'.54--dc23
2015029201

Printed in the United States of America

16 17 18 19 20 RRD 6 5 4 3 2 1

For my family who gave me wings. Love you!

ONE

The Silver Pelican jewelry store in Bangor, Maine, was Mallory Davis's final stop, and she put on a bright smile. The place smelled of money—expensive perfume from the last customer and the rich scent of new carpet. Every other jewelry shop in town had only been willing to take her pieces on consignment, but she needed the cash now. She'd been a bit hesitant to come here because this was the most expensive store in town, and she was sure the owner would take one look at her suit, stylish ten years ago, and send her packing.

The sun glittered on her twenty pieces of sea-glass jewelry spread across the top of the glass display case. The presentation under it sparkled with diamonds and sapphires on black velvet.

Mallory nudged her favorite bracelet with one finger. "This one is white gold instead of the usual sterling silver. I mixed pink tourmaline with darker pink sea glass to create the piece."

The owner, in his forties with a paunch and bald head, picked up the bracelet and looked it over. "Very nice craftsmanship, Mrs. Davis. The quality is exceptional. The pink and green moon from the tourmaline is quite unique. And I really like the mermaid on it. How much do you want for these?"

She tipped up her chin and forced a confidence that was at

odds with the fluttery sensation in her stomach. "I need five hundred dollars for it. I have five of them ready here in my briefcase. And did you see these earrings?" She pointed out another offering. "The tourmaline makes them so distinctively Maine. These are two hundred dollars."

He nodded. "My customers are always asking for quality tourmaline pieces, and I find it hard to keep up with the demand when they want jewelry created in Maine." He pursed his flat lips. "I'll take everything you have here, plus all the mermaid-moon bracelets. Write me up an invoice and I'll give you a check right now. I think I can take most everything you make off your hands."

Hiding her elation, she took a surreptitious glance at her watch. Haylie would be out of school in half an hour. "Of course." She pulled the jewelry pieces out of her case along with an invoice pad.

She wanted to do a fist pump in the air. Her mortgage was a week late, but she could pay it electronically as soon as the check cleared.

The back of her neck prickled, and she resisted the urge to turn around. For the past week she'd had the uneasy feeling that someone was watching her, but try as she might to convince herself it was from the stress of her finances, she couldn't help swinging her head around to look. And saw nothing out of the ordinary.

She was letting her imagination run wild again.

But her joy bubbled to the surface when she remembered she'd done it. This was the beginning of good things for them.

Fifteen minutes later she thanked the proprietor and exited into the dreary gloom of an early-spring day. Tugging her jacket higher at the neck, her smile widened as she hurried to her blue Toyota. She pulled out her phone and dialed her best friend, Carol Decker.

Carol had been Mallory's rock when Brian died in a small plane accident two years ago. She lived in the house next door and ran Haylie around when Mallory had errands to run or needed to work on her jewelry designs. At fifty-five, she was twenty years older than Mallory and had never been married, but she was warm and cuddly as a new kitten.

Carol answered on the first ring. "How'd it go?"

"He bought everything I've got!" She turned the key and started the engine. "I need to pick up Haylie. It took him forever to write out the check." Before she pulled into traffic, she stared at the check for $3,500. "We can eat this month. And I can get the mortgage caught up."

Carol laughed. "I'd say you just shot the wolf at the door full of buckshot, then had him stuffed and mounted."

"Good riddance. I never want to see that mangy monster again." Mallory stopped at the light and noticed the engine running a little rough. "I need to get this clunker looked at. It's going to die on me before too long."

"I think it needs the spark plugs changed."

And she had the money to do just that. Mallory saw the time. "Holy cow, is it really two thirty? I'm going to be late."

She gunned the Toyota as soon as the light changed and drove as fast as she dared. The school was a good fifteen minutes away if traffic was moving.

"Haylie will be fine if you're five minutes late. Don't stress."

Easy enough for Carol to say. She didn't have children. "I've got to run. Talk to you when I get home."

She dropped her phone back into her purse, then drummed her fingers on the steering wheel as traffic stopped at another light. The clock on the dash flipped another minute closer to two fifty. The light changed to green and she shot through it.

Kids milled around the schoolyard as she pulled to the curb. She scanned the area for Haylie's red jacket.

Her breath caught in her throat when she saw her fourteen-year-old daughter talking to someone in a gray van. Wasn't that the same gray van she'd seen parked outside the house last week? That definitely had not been her imagination.

She threw open her door and ran toward her daughter. "Haylie!"

Her daughter looked up, her dark-brown eyes wide. The van's tires squealed as it peeled away from the curb. Mallory tried to see the driver as it sped past, but the windows were tinted, and she couldn't see more than a shape inside.

She reached Haylie and grabbed her arm. "I've told you never to talk to strangers."

Haylie rolled her eyes. "He was only asking if I knew some-one. I told him I didn't. Chill out, Mom."

Mallory gritted her teeth and swallowed the rebuke wanting to burst out. "He could have grabbed you and taken off."

Haylie shifted her khaki backpack to her shoulder. "Why do you have to make such a big deal out of everything?" She took off toward the car in an angry stride.

Mallory sighed and followed. Her daughter had no idea just how unsafe the world could be, how quickly life could go from perfect to shattered beyond repair. One mistake and the world could change. She knew that only too well.

She turned and stared after the van. Something bad could have happened because she'd been late. She had to be extra vigilant.

Her purse vibrated and she dug around for her silenced phone. *Dad* flashed on the screen and her smile vanished. Things had been tense between them for so many years, and she wished for the umpteenth time that she could find a way to turn back the clock.

Haylie waved to her from the passenger seat, and Mallory turned her back to her daughter's impatient face. "Hi, Dad." She forced a light note into her voice.

Only silence answered her. Was that the distant sound of a boat engine? "Dad, are you there? I hear gulls, but I can't hear you." She detected a faint gasp, and her fingers tightened around the phone. "Dad?" Was he having a heart attack? He'd put on twenty pounds this year, all around the middle. He was a heart attack waiting to happen.

Pulling the phone from her ear, she saw full bars. The problem wasn't on her end. "Dad?"

A choking sound vibrated in her ear, then his shaky voice whispered across the miles. "Love you . . . always. Find . . . Mother." A rattle sounded as though he needed to clear his throat and couldn't. "Tell . . . Haylie. Love her."

"Dad!" Her chest squeezed as the import of his words hit. He must be delusional. Her mother had been dead for fifteen years. "Where are you? I'll come right now."

"Should have . . . known better." The words were barely a whisper. A long sigh eased through the phone, and something clunked.

Pressing the phone tighter to her ear, she heard only the sound of the gulls, the lap of waves, and the *putt-putt* of the boat motor. "Dad, talk to me!"

He was on his boat, but where? She spoke his name again and waited. Nothing. Had he fallen? Maybe the clunk was the phone dropping to the deck. She didn't want to hang up, not while the connection held. How could she find him?

Wait, she had a family tracker app on her phone. Just for fun, she'd connected her dad's phone with hers. Still maintaining the connection with her father, she flipped over to the app and located his phone. It was near Folly Shoals. He must have been delivering the mail.

She went back to the phone call. "Dad?"

She got the *wa-wa* sound of a disconnected call in her ear.

A number popped into Mallory's head and she punched it in, then walked farther away so Haylie couldn't hear what was going on.

A deep male voice answered on the second ring. "Game Warden O'Connor."

Her chest tightened at the familiar voice. Had she really called Kevin O'Connor? "Kevin, it's Mallory. Dad's in trouble. Can you go check on him?"

There was a slight hesitation. "Mallory?"

His cautious tone told her all she needed to know about his feelings. "Hurry, Kevin. I-it sounded like he was dying." She gave him the coordinates.

"I'll call you."

"Give me two hours. On my way." She hung up and called her dad back again.

Only the gulls answered.

Claire Dellamare lifted her face to the wind and let it toss her hair as she inhaled the briny scent of the sea. Luke Rocco turned off the boat's engine, then threw the anchor overboard. The rocky crags of Mermaid Point, a westward promontory of Folly Shoals Island, rose to their left and blocked a bit of the sun glaring in her eyes. She could just make out the metal roof of Breakwater Cottage where Edmund Blanchard lived. He was a familiar sight around the Downeast as he delivered the mail by boat.

She turned to smile at Luke. "Why are we stopping here? I thought we were going to check out the orca pod."

Luke's good looks never failed to thrill her. With his nearly black hair and dark-brown eyes, he could have been a pirate in the old days. Finding him at the beach six months ago had been her lucky day, and knowing he loved her was a little bit of God's grace given to her.

"We are. There was something else I wanted to talk to you about first."

Her stomach plunged at his somber expression. "Walker?"

He rose from his seat at the controls. "No, Dad's fine. He's taken the news that I'm selling the cranberry farm better than I expected. I think he's weary of the battle, too, and he knows I can't keep up with the farm and my duties in the Coast Guard too. He's got other things on his mind now." A ghost of a smile lifted his lips. "Like dancing attendance on Dixie."

Claire had to chuckle. Seeing Walker start to date again after all those years as a widower had been a hoot. He was like a teenager. "You scared me there for a minute. So, what's wrong? You look so serious."

He reached into his pocket and withdrew a box. "This is a momentous moment."

A ring box.

Her breath caught in her throat, and her heart rate pumped into overdrive as he dropped to one knee. *It was happening now. Right now.* Her lungs compressed, and she stared into his handsome face and the eyes she loved so much.

He opened the little velvet box, and a beautiful marquis ring set with diamonds and tourmaline sparkled in the bright Maine sunshine. "I can't imagine my life without you in it, Claire. Will you marry me? I love you more than I can say."

A lump formed in her throat and her vision blurred. They'd been through so much together. Things that should have shoved them apart, not brought them together. "I . . . I love you too. And of course I'll marry you. Today, tomorrow, anytime you say."

He rose and slipped the ring on her finger. She threw her arms around his neck, and his lips came down on hers. It was the sweetest kiss they'd ever shared, warm and passionate with promise and commitment. She closed her eyes and clung to him. If she didn't open her eyes, maybe she could make this moment last forever, like a secret treasure only the two of them found.

When Luke broke the kiss, she murmured a protest and tried to pull his head back down. His grunt of surprise made her lids spring open. "What's wrong?"

He was frowning as he looked toward the pier at the breakwater below the point. "That's Edmund's boat, and it seems to be drifting aimlessly. And the game warden is just about to it. I think something's wrong. I should go see if there's anything I can do to help Kevin." His radio squawked with a request for aid from the Coast Guard. "That's Kevin's voice."

The boat bobbed in the waves about a mile off Mermaid Point. And she saw no sign of Edmund. "Let's help."

TWO

Edmund's boat floated aimlessly in the choppy waves toward the rocky shore off the island of Folly Shoals. Kevin consulted the GPS on his boat console and throttled back the engine. His boat slewed sideways and came to a stop beside the blue-and-white mail boat. Mallory's call had set all Kevin's alarms ringing, and the sharp *kee-arr* of a tern overhead added to his unease.

He tossed an anchor overboard, then tied up his boat to the mail boat and stepped aboard. "Edmund?" He moved toward the bridge, past the bay where Edmund had stacked the freight for delivery to Folly Shoals. The atmosphere aboard ship had a stillness, as if the boat held its breath along with him. Sheer imagination, but he couldn't shake the feeling of dread that curdled his lunch of lobster bisque in his belly.

He raised his voice above the wind whistling outside the windows. "Edmund, it's Warden Kevin O'Connor."

It felt odd to identify himself as a game warden instead of his first name. He'd looked up to Mallory's father for as long as he could remember. The whole area knew Edmund well. A lobster-man from a family that had fished these waters since the 1800s, Edmund was one of those men who had forgotten more about the sea than most men ever knew. He'd given up lobstering after his wife died and had gone to mail boat delivery instead.

A sharp coppery scent mingled with the smell of sea and kelp, and under all of it, a slight aroma of something sweet and perfumy. Kevin's steps faltered as he recognized the stench of blood. He curled his fingers into his palms and ducked to enter the bridge doorway.

He saw Edmund's boot first. Then his outstretched hand, and lastly, his head with a spreading pool of blood under it. He stepped over the chart map lying on the floor, then knelt and touched the older man's neck, searching for a pulse. No sign of life. Edmund's flesh was cold.

Kevin swallowed hard and retraced the steps to his boat to call the Coast Guard. Edmund had a radio on the *Mermaid*, but Kevin didn't want to contaminate any evidence. The bleeding head wound could have come from a bad fall, but until the investigation was completed, he didn't want to be accused of messing up a crime scene. After reporting his discovery, he used his cell phone to call the sheriff and the state police.

His cell phone began to play "The River" by Garth Brooks. Mallory. No way did he want to be the bearer of such bad news, but he couldn't ignore his duty. Or the way his heart still leapt at the sight of her name.

Inhaling, he answered the call. "Warden O'Connor."

"Kevin?" Mallory's voice quivered with a thread of terror. "Did you find Dad?"

He turned to stare at the island cliff rising toward the drifting clouds. An eagle's nest caught his attention, and he counted four small heads as he tried to decide how to phrase his answer. Should he be blunt or try to put her off?

He couldn't lie to her. "I found him, Mallory. I'm sorry, but there was nothing I could do."

At the sound of her choked cry, his free hand curled into a fist. He'd give anything to spare her this pain. She'd lost both her parents now, and he still cared about what she faced, even if he hadn't seen her in fifteen years. Soft weeping vibrated in his ear, and he waited until her sobs tapered off.

"The state boys are on their way and so is the sheriff. The Coast Guard will be here any minute."

"What happened? H-heart attack?"

"I don't know for sure yet." Details could wait until he saw her in person. She didn't need to know about the blood, not yet. "What's your ETA?"

"About an hour. You're still with him?"

"Yeah."

"Good. I'll be there as fast as I can. Where will they take him?"

A couple of orcas swam by the boat, and he watched their trajectory toward Sunset Bay. Even though he didn't want to, he had to come clean. "Probably to the coroner's."

She gasped. "There will be an autopsy? Why would they do that? You don't think it was a heart attack?"

"He had some kind of head wound. It might have been from a bad fall, but the coroner will have to make that determination."

"A fall?"

The phone went silent in his ear, and he pulled it away a moment to make sure the connection hadn't dropped. Cell service was sketchy out here. "Mallory?"

"I'm here, just thinking. Dad said something odd when he called me. He told me to find my mom. I thought he was delusional since Mom is dead. What if he was trying to tell me a woman had hurt him?"

"You're stretching, Mallory. Why would he mention your mom when it couldn't possibly be?"

"Maybe he was confused and it came out wrong."

"Let's wait and see what the coroner says. I'm sorry though, Mal." The old nickname slipped out before he could stop it, and he cleared his throat. "I mean, I know this is going to be hard for you and Haylie. Is she with you?"

"Not yet. I left her with my friend. Carol will drive her up in a couple of days." Her words choked off on a sob. "For th-the funeral, I guess."

"Is there anyone I can call for you?" As far as he knew, Edmund only had a sister, Blanche, who lived near Bucksport. She and Edmund hadn't gotten along for as long as he could remember.

"No, thanks though. I'll give Aunt Blanche a call. C-can you meet me at Dad's? I don't think I can go in there by myself."

"Yeah, of course. Text me or call when you hit Folly Shoals, and I'll meet you at the ferry dock." He hung up as he heard a boat approaching. Maybe by the time Mallory arrived, he'd have some answers.

Turning, he recognized Luke Rocco with his girlfriend, Claire Dellamare, who also happened to be Kevin's cousin. Raising his hand, he stepped over to help Luke tie off his boat.

Carol's Explorer reeked with the pungent odor of the pepperoni pizza in the take-out box on the backseat. She found it hard to

13

keep her mind on Haylie's chatter from the passenger seat. When Mallory had called with the bad news and to ask her to pick up her daughter, Mallory told her not to tell Haylie. It seemed wrong to keep her grandfather's death from her. Poor kid loved her grandpa. He was the only male influence in her life, though she didn't see him as often as Carol thought she should. The old man should have just let go of the past.

"So is it okay?"

Haylie's words finally penetrated the fog encasing Carol's brain. "Is what okay?"

Haylie exhaled in a sharp *whoosh*. "If I have a couple of friends over tonight? It's Friday."

"Oh, honey, I don't think that's a good idea with your mom gone. We have to pack and join her in Folly Shoals."

"But I'll miss Alisha's birthday party tomorrow! She actually invited me, and I can't miss it."

Fourteen going on eighteen. Carol's glance took in Haylie's determined expression. When did kids start growing up so fast? Mallory had her hands full most of the time. Even just two years ago Haylie had only cared about what her mother thought. Then she started middle school, and suddenly the only ones with anything important to say were a group of five friends on the swim team who had more money than sense. If it weren't for Haylie's grandpa, she wouldn't be taking those expensive swim lessons. Did the girl know how close her poor mom skated to the edge financially?

Carol pulled the car into the drive of Mallory's modest cottage in a cul-de-sac. "You'll have to talk to your mother."

"Can I borrow your cell phone?"

Carol handed it over and grabbed the pizza box from the backseat. "Don't be too long. The pizza will get cold."

Haylie's head was already down as her fingers tapped their way across the phone's screen. "I'll be right in."

Shaking her head, Carol got out and dropped her keys into her pocket as she approached the front door. When she unlocked it and stepped inside, she heard a sliding noise like a tennis shoe slipping across the tile. Was someone in here or was she imagining it? She stopped and tried to hear over the pounding of the blood in her ears. There. It came again, then she heard a *snick.*

"Hello?" Her voice quavered.

She shouldn't stay here. The pizza box fell from her nerveless fingers, and she whirled toward the door. She caught a flurry of movement, and a man with a ski mask over his face rushed at her from the kitchen.

She gasped and reached for the doorknob, but he grabbed her arm and whipped her around to face him. "You're not the Davis woman. Where is she?"

Think! She slipped her hand into her coat pocket. "She's not here."

"No joke, Sherlock." His fingers tightened on her arm. "Where is she?"

Before she could talk herself out of it, Carol jammed the key into his hand with all her might. The moment his grip loosened, she tore loose and threw open the front door. She exited the door screaming at the top of her lungs.

The next-door neighbor was driving by in his pickup. It screeched to a halt. He came running up the walk toward her. "Carol, what's wrong?"

She pointed. "An intruder. He grabbed me." Her insides matched the shake in her voice.

"Get in your car and lock it. Call the police." He jerked out a hunting knife from a sheath in his boot, threw open the door, and charged through the front door.

Carol rushed to her car and practically fell inside. She locked all the doors, then grabbed her cell phone out of Haylie's hands.

"Hey!" Haylie tried to grab it back.

Turning her back on the sulking girl, Carol called 911 and reported the break-in. "Yes, I'll stay on the line until officers arrive." Haylie's eyes were huge when Carol glanced back at her.

The neighbor exited the house and shook his head. "The back door is standing open and there's no one inside."

A police car screamed down the street toward them and parked out front. Two officers approached Carol's car. Still shaking, she got out. She told them everything she'd seen, but she had no description other than he was about six-two with broad shoulders. They checked out the house, too, but found nothing.

The younger officer with kind blue eyes rejoined them. "I don't think you should stay here, miss. The lock on the back door is broken. We'll hang around until you gather some things together."

The shock wore off enough for Carol to mull over the intruder's words. He was looking for Mallory. This was no casual break-in. She told the officer what the man said. "I'd better take Haylie to Folly Shoals to join her mother. I'll grab her things."

She felt safer with the officer beside her, and she quickly stuffed Haylie's clothes into a bag. There was no time to waste. Mallory needed to know what was going on here.

THREE

Mallory stood on the bow of the ferry from Summer Harbor and studied the buildings dotting the hillside of Folly Shoals. It had changed little in the fifteen years she'd been gone, but it was like she was seeing it for the first time. Colorful buoys hung on porches and outside the homes like strange lawn ornaments, and the soft hues of the houses blended together with barn-red buildings in a pretty mosaic enhanced by the fading light of later afternoon. From the sea, it was hard to make out the peeling paint and leaky windows she knew existed in the old structures.

Boats of every size bobbed in Sunset Cove as it curved in toward the town. Beyond the cove, the town spread out through the trees and rocky uplift of sea cliffs. A weathered gray dock poked into the blue water, and a red fish house flanked it to the right. The Hotel Tourmaline was grand, and its gray stone walls and mullioned windows surveyed the cove like the masthead of a great ship.

They would be docking soon. She zipped back to her car and prepared to drive off the ferry. Kevin would be here shortly in his boat to transport her to the house. She could drive, but the twisty gravel road out to Breakwater Cottage would take forever to navigate.

After the ferry docked, she parked in the lot, then got out to stroll the sidewalk along the water where a lobster shack and sandwich joint catered to diners. When she had time she wanted to check out the hotel, but she didn't want to run the risk of missing Kevin. Most of the shops were closed because it was after five, but she paused to peer in a few windows. The jewelry shop might be interested in her work, so she made a mental note to check back.

"Mallory," a male voice called behind her.

Luke Rocco strode toward her with a beautiful woman on his arm. He'd gone to school with Kevin and her, and he'd been a staunch ally during her darkest period.

"Luke!" She stepped to meet him, and he grabbed her in a bear hug.

"So sorry about your dad." He smelled of sea and wind with the pleasant tang of his cologne under it all.

She returned his hug and lifted her cheek to accept the kiss he planted there. "You heard already?"

"I was there. Claire and I were just offshore when Kevin arrived. I'm with the Coast Guard, you know, so I went to see if I could help."

Her eyes filled at the sympathy in his voice. "Thank you. I still can't quite assimilate it." She stepped back from his embrace to make sure his girlfriend didn't take offense. "Kevin is supposed to meet me here. Have you seen him?"

Luke shook his head and pulled the pretty blonde forward. She reminded Mallory of someone. Kate, she reminded her of Kate Mason.

"This is Claire Dellamare, my fiancée. As of this afternoon."

His white teeth flashed in his tan face. "I was proposing when we saw Kevin."

"Congratulations. You've got a great guy here in Luke." Mallory liked the other woman at first sight. Maybe it was those big blue eyes and the adoring way she looked at Luke.

"I think so. I've heard a lot about you from Luke. Like the daredevil way you used to swing out over the rocks on ropes and the late-night smelt fishing." The smile in her eyes faded. "But I'm sure sorry about your dad. Is there anything we can do?" She held up a bag in her hand. "I heard you'd headed here without packing so I grabbed a few toiletries for you."

"How incredibly sweet of you." Mallory's fingers closed around the plastic bag. "I came without so much as a toothbrush."

"I got a toothbrush, toothpaste, deodorant, shampoo, conditioner, and soap. As well as a few other girlie things. I hope it's what you like."

"It's perfect. Thank you so much."

Her insides froze when she saw Kevin walking toward her. He hadn't changed, not a bit. That same shoulders-back, head-up stride that ate up the feet between them quickly. His warm brown eyes were the color of chocolate swirled with caramel, and his thick brown hair glimmered with red highlights in the sunshine. At six-four he towered over most men.

His eyes never left her, and he lifted a hand in greeting before stopping in front of her and stuffing his hands in his pockets awkwardly. "Mallory, it's good to see you."

The formal words were like a fishhook in her heart, and she well remembered the last traumatic day she'd seen him. They hadn't spoken again until she called him for help, and she suspected he still hadn't forgiven her.

Mallory leaned into the salt-laden wind in the bow of Kevin's boat and stared at the approaching cottage that had been the Blanchard home for five generations. Had it really been fifteen years since she'd last seen the two-story structure and the cove where she'd learned to swim? She was cold clear through, and it was more than the brisk spring wind that chilled her.

She and Aunt Blanche were all that was left now. Her aunt never had children, so there wasn't even a cousin to share in her grief. Her gaze went back to the home where she'd grown up.

Breakwater Cottage stood on Mermaid Point. A stone breakwater curved around the point and provided a calm spot for the pier. The weathered shingles had withstood countless nor'easters, and the hundred-year-old metal roof was as sound as the day it was put on.

Kevin nudged his boat to the dock. She'd managed to avoid looking at him too hard. Everything about this situation made her uncomfortable, but it was her own fault. That mistake she'd made in calling him when she was panicked couldn't be undone now. It had been kind of him to meet her in Folly Shoals.

She leaped out of the boat to tie it off before he could help her, then walked up the rocky hillside to the house. A pile of lobster traps, thick with barnacles, were stacked on the southwest side of the yard, and a boat her father had been repairing lay upended beside them.

A boulder formed in her throat as she realized she was watching for her dad to come through the screen door. She would never see his smile again. The pain nearly doubled her over, and she paused to catch her breath.

She would never make him proud of her now, never rub out the stigma of her shame.

Kevin touched her arm, and she looked up at him. His bulk, swathed in the green game-warden uniform, dwarfed her five-foot-two frame. With shoulders as broad as the beam of a dinghy, he turned female heads all too easily. His eyes were filled with concern as he stared down at her. The wind had blown a thick lock of dark-brown hair over his wide forehead, and he stood too close for comfort.

Her arm tingled where his fingers pressed against her skin, and she pulled away hastily. "I'm all right. Everything just crashed in on me again." She set off for the front door.

Her father never locked the house, and she opened the weathered red door. The familiar scent of pipe tobacco wafted up her nose as she stepped into the foyer. It had been so long since she'd been here, too long. The pale-yellow walls showed a few more chips in the plaster, and she stepped into the living room. The plaid sofa her parents had bought in the seventies still held its spot to the left of the fireplace. Her gaze went to the green leather recliner facing the fireplace. The indentation of her father's body remained in the cushion, and she resisted the impulse to step over and put her hand on the seat.

Kevin's cell phone rang and she jumped. She listened to him reply in monosyllables to whoever had called. Was it the coroner? She bit her lip and clasped her hands together. She needed answers to what had happened today. She'd pressed Kevin for information when she first saw him, but he'd been reluctant to say anything more until he heard back from the sheriff.

She should have insisted he take her to where he'd found her father's body.

He ended the call and pocketed his phone in his dull-green jacket. "That was the sheriff. He says he thinks a swell struck the boat and your father fell and hit his head."

She eyed his flattened mouth and tense jaw. "What aren't you telling me, Kevin?"

Indecision flickered in his brown eyes. "I've been mulling over why I felt uneasy on the boat. Some things were out of order. The radio was off. Edmund never turned off the radio. I smelled perfume, too, a lady's perfume. His chart map was on the floor, and he was always so meticulous about his maps and equipment. It somehow felt . . . ransacked, though that's probably too strong of a word."

She caught her breath. "You think he struggled with someone? Maybe an attacker hit him over the head? Did you tell the sheriff?"

He shook his head. "Whoa, slow down. It's more of a gut feeling than any evidence I can point to. What am I going to say to Sheriff Colton? 'Hey, did you notice how messy everything was?'"

"But he's saying it's an accident! What if it's not? And Dad said to find my mother. What if that's why you smelled a woman's perfume? He was confused because he was dying, but mentioning my mom must mean something."

"Maybe." He looked unconvinced.

She stuffed her hands into the pockets of her jacket and turned away from him. If he wouldn't help her, she'd figure it out herself. "I want to see the boat."

"I'm not sure that's a good idea."

The sympathy in his voice made her eyes sting, and she fiercely blinked the moisture away. There was no time for tears, not yet. "I'm going to look at it no matter what you say."

His heavy sigh sounded behind her. "I'll take you. But the sheriff probably won't release it until tomorrow. I'll pick you up at nine."

She turned back to face him. "Thank you. I have to know what happened."

"I want to know for sure too. But be prepared, Mallory. It's not a pretty scene."

"I know." She couldn't think about it now. "I'll walk you out. Thanks for picking me up in Folly Shoals."

"Happy to do it. I still consider you a friend, even though . . ." He blinked and turned toward the doorway. "See you tomorrow. I'll pick you up here, and you can drive your car home in the daylight."

The opulent interior of Hotel Tourmaline was almost enough to make Julia Carver stand taller in her two-inch pumps. This was the kind of hotel she loved, rich and luxurious. Everywhere she looked, she saw reminders of the tourmaline the hotel had based its name on—from pale-pink walls to tourmaline stones embedded in the marble floors. It took only moments to navigate the spacious halls until she stood in front of a glass door marked Boyce Masters, General Manager. She saw an empty room with several chairs lining the pale-pink walls. Her fingers closed around the polished brass doorknob, and she started to turn it.

A deep voice spoke behind her. "You must be Ms. Carver. I'm Boyce Masters."

She faced him. His six-foot height towered over her five-foot-two frame. His brown hair was graying at the temples. She glanced at his broad shoulders and upper arms and guessed he worked out daily in the hotel gym.

She held out her hand. "Julia Carver, Mr. Masters. Pleased to meet you."

His hand was cool and dry as he shook hers. "This way." He stepped past her and held open the door.

The faint aromas of a clean male aftershave and copier toner lingered in the room. She followed him past another doorway into a spacious room. A huge bank of windows looked out onto the rocky Maine coastline with its thick tree cover.

He indicated the chairs that faced his desk. "Pick a seat." He pulled out a black leather chair opposite her and settled into it. "What can I do for you?"

"This is your off-season, and I have need of a room for at least three weeks, no more than five. I wondered if we might come to an arrangement about cost."

He raised a brow. "Three weeks? That would take us to mid-May, so I think we can accommodate you. It wouldn't be our largest or most luxurious room, but it should be comfortable."

She squashed the frown that wanted to form on her face. Large and luxurious was what she'd been after. "Fine. How about three hundred a week?"

A line settled between his eyes. "I was thinking more like five hundred."

She rose and picked up her bag. "I can rent something in Summer Harbor and take the ferry much less expensively."

"Four hundred."

Pausing, she studied his expression. She'd probably pushed him as far as he was going to be shoved. "That will work. I appreciate it."

She glanced at his left hand. No ring. So far she quite liked Mr. Boyce Masters. Julia and Boyce. The names sounded nice together.

She gave herself a mental shake. Once she took care of her little "problem" here, she'd be long gone.

25

FOUR

He hadn't expected seeing Mallory again would leave him so shaken. Kevin hung his hat and coat on the hook in the entry. The low murmur of Kate's voice mingled with that of his eight-year-old daughter. He'd lost his nanny when she married, and his cousin Kate had offered to fill in while he searched for a replacement.

"Sadie, Kate, I'm home." His leather recliner by the flickering fire beckoned, and he dropped into its comforting support before leaning down to pull off his boots. His brain felt fuzzy and disoriented, but he wasn't sure if it was because of finding Edmund's body or from seeing Mallory again.

Footsteps pattered down the steps and across the hall, then his daughter burst into the room like an energetic kitten. Her blonde hair curled to her shoulders, and she wore pink princess pajamas. She was growing up too fast, and her sweet face already showed the promise of head-turning beauty, much like her mother's. He'd have to threaten the boys away all too soon.

"I'm here, Sadie," he said when she tipped her head to one side to listen for his breathing.

The familiar pang struck him at her sightless eyes. He reached out and snagged her hand as she neared, then pulled her onto his lap, relishing the little girl scent of strawberry shampoo.

She nestled against his chest and reached up to run her small hand across the evening scruff on his cheek. "You're late, Daddy."

"I thought she'd be in bed before you got home." Dressed in jeans and a bright-blue sweater, Kate stepped into the room with Sadie's golden retriever, Fiona, on her heels. Kate was about thirty and as beautiful inside as she was outside. She'd had a rough time the past few months with a blood disorder, but thanks to a bone marrow transplant from her twin sister, she had recovered. The only remnant of her ordeal was her short blonde hair.

"Sorry I'm so late."

"You know I never mind. Sadie and I played Go Fish. There's chili in the Crock-Pot." She moved past him and knelt to throw another log into the fireplace.

Fiona's nails clicked on the oak floors as she came to lean her head against Kevin's thigh. He ran his fingers through the dog's silky coat. Fiona was four but showed no sign of a gray muzzle, thanks to the raw food diet Kevin fed her. He wanted the pooch to live as long as possible for Sadie.

"What took you so long?" Sadie asked, still nestled on his lap.

Kevin shot a warning glance toward Kate. "Just work. It's way past your bedtime."

"We don't have school tomorrow."

"Oh, right, I have a teacher conference. But it's still pretty late. You'd better go brush your teeth and get ready. I'll come along and tuck you in."

She wrinkled her nose but slid off his lap, reached out for the dog, and went down the hall toward the bathroom with Fiona in the lead.

As soon as he heard the distant sound of water running, he turned to Kate. "Edmund Blanchard is dead. I found him on his boat."

Kate's large blue eyes widened. "Oh no! Heart attack?"

He shook his head. "He fell and hit his head. Mallory got a call from him as he was dying. She contacted me to go check on him. It looks like there was a struggle on the boat."

"Murder, then? Is Mallory on her way here?"

"Already arrived." When the interest on Kate's face sharpened, he held up his hand. "And yes, I've already seen her. I'm going to take her to the boat tomorrow to assess things. The sheriff is calling it an accident though, so I don't know how much help we'll get if we decide someone attacked Edmund."

"Was it hard to see Mallory again after all this time?"

At the sympathy in her voice, he rose and went to throw more wood on the fire. "It was fine. She looked the same."

But did she really? Gone was the free-spirited girl he'd known, and in her place was a beautiful woman with wisdom in her dark-brown eyes. What was she really like now after fifteen years? He quelled his curiosity. Nothing could change what she'd done.

"Is she at her dad's house?"

"Yeah." He folded the lap robe on the floor and put it on the back of the sofa. "You might go see her. She'll need some support to deal with this."

"I'm not sure what kind of reception I'll get, but I'll give it a try. What about her daughter?"

He rubbed the back of his neck and went to pull the drapes, then paused to look at the yard bathed in the glow of the security light. "She'll be here in a day or two. She's with a friend."

"She's about fourteen, isn't she?"

Like Kate didn't know. The two had been great friends in high school, and though they'd parted ways after things went down so badly here, he knew she'd kept up on Mallory's situation. She was the one who had told him when Mallory's husband had died.

Kevin went back to his chair. "You tell me."

She twirled a strand of blonde hair around her finger. "Okay, busted. Haylie is fourteen."

"Have you tried to mend the rift since she left?"

Kate released her hair and went to grab her coat from the back of the sofa. "I've called her a few times but have never gotten her."

"Did you leave a message?"

She shook her head. "I didn't have the nerve. The last argument was pretty bad. I figured she'd check caller ID, and if she wanted to talk to me, she'd call back. She never did."

He walked her to the door. "Thanks for staying with Sadie."

Her gaze searched his. "Watch yourself, Kevin. You're way too vulnerable where Mallory is concerned."

He gave a jerk of his head in answer and shut the door behind her. No need to warn him. He'd already erected his walls long ago.

The wind moaned around the eaves of the cottage, and Mallory tightened the belt on her fuzzy robe as she studied the contents of the refrigerator. There was nothing a normal person would want to eat. She tossed out a carton of curdled milk and several baggies of dried-up sandwiches. Her father rarely ate at home, preferring to join his buddies for a sandwich and coffee at one of the local dives in Folly Shoals.

She tipped her head. Was that a knock at the door? She spared a glance at the clock on the range. Eight o'clock. It was a little late for someone to come calling. She curled her fingers into her palms and sidled to the door. Peering through the peephole, she saw the back of a woman's head.

She unlocked the door and opened it. "Can I help you?" When the woman turned around, Mallory took a step back and inhaled. "Kate. What are you doing here?"

The full moon gleamed on Kate's dark-blonde hair, and she lifted the two plastic sacks in her hands. "I figured there was nothing in the house to eat. Can I come in?"

Mallory wasn't steeled for this conversation, but her stomach growled, reminding her that she hadn't eaten in eight hours. "Of course." She stepped aside and allowed the other woman to enter. "This is very kind of you. The kitchen is this way."

"I remember." Kate followed her and set the sacks on the stained green countertop by the fridge. "There are turkey slices, bread, cheese, yogurt, guacamole, eggs, bacon, and baby carrots."

Even after all these years, Kate remembered some of Mallory's favorite foods. She pushed away the stab of guilt. "I'm starving. Want a sandwich with me?"

"I ate already. You go ahead though." Kate shucked out of her navy peacoat and draped it across a wooden chair at the battered table. She sat at the table and folded her hands.

Mallory wasn't sure what to say as she quickly made a sandwich and shook some potato chips onto an old melamine plate. "Coffee or something to drink?"

Other than her close-cropped hairstyle, Kate hadn't changed much since Mallory last saw her. About five feet five, her striking blue eyes dominated her heart-shaped face. Her makeup was tastefully done, and she wore no rings.

Kate stared back. "Done looking?"

Mallory's cheeks went hot. "Sorry. It's been a long time. You look good. Not married, I see."

Kate eased out a rueful grin. "The best guys all moved away after high school. Well, except for Kevin."

Mallory gave a jerky nod as she settled into the chair on the other side of the table. The elephant in the room wasn't going away without talking about it. "Look, we might as well get it all out in the open. I didn't treat you very well. I'm sorry." Even now, the apology seemed too little too late, and her guilt over the way she'd treated all of them only added to the blood on her hands.

Kate shrugged one shoulder. "You were dealing with your mom's death."

Mallory swallowed. Her throat was thick, and she took a bite of her sandwich. The bread was dry on her tongue. "But that was no reason to cut all of you out of my life that way. You were only trying to stop me from making a mistake. You were right, of course. I never should have married Brian."

That was a hard truth to admit. Brian had seemed like a safe haven at the time, but marrying him hadn't been fair to him.

Kate stared down at the table. "This is the first time you've been back in all these years? I mean, I haven't heard you visited or anything."

Mallory nodded. "Being here brings it all back. And seeing Kevin again . . ." She took a quick sip of her coffee. "I shouldn't have run off after Mom's death. Maybe Kevin and I would have married. Everything might have been different."

"Maybe things turned out the way they were supposed to. It's hard to second-guess it all now." Kate studied Mallory's face. "You haven't forgiven yourself, have you?"

Mallory set her cup back on the table. "I'll never forgive myself. Dad made it clear he never did either. When he called me this morning, it was the first time I'd talked to him in a month. I was a colossal failure as a daughter."

"I'm sure your mom didn't feel that way. She loved you so much."

Her eyes burned at the sympathy in Kate's voice. "I've dealt with it. I had no choice. I'm sure every time he talked to me, he remembered. Just like I did."

"You hadn't seen him at all?"

"Oh sure, we saw each other. After Haylie came along, we met up in Bangor a couple of times a year. It was always a little tense though. Disappointment typically filled his eyes."

Kate's lips flattened and she narrowed her gaze. "I bet you'd never treat Haylie like that."

Mallory forced down another bite so she didn't have to answer. She had deserved every ounce of her father's condemnation. The expression on her mother's face the last time they'd been together wasn't something she would ever forget.

FIVE

Mallory felt lighter somehow as she walked Kate to the door. The dim chandelier in the entry provided little light in the gloom of the moonless night. "Thanks for coming. It was good to see you."

Kate zipped up her jacket. "Maybe we can do lunch when the funeral is over? I'd love to meet Haylie."

Mallory reached for the doorknob, but as her fingers closed over the cold metal, a crash reverberated through the house. "What on earth? That sounds like it came from upstairs." She headed for the steps that led to the second floor. Kate followed on her heels. As Mallory turned the corner toward the three bedrooms, a cool sea breeze touched her skin. Was a window open?

Her father's bedroom door stood open. She reached inside and flipped on the light. The warm glow from the overhead fixture illuminated a room she hadn't seen in years. It smelled like her dad—a mixture of Old Spice and clove gum all mingled with pipe tobacco. Mom hadn't let him smoke his pipe in the bedroom, but he'd probably done whatever he wanted in the years since her death. A queen-size bed dominated the small space, and a bedside stand held a clock, two bottles of pills, and a dogeared paperback.

Her heart squeezed. Now her dad would never be able to forgive her.

She tore her attention from the picture of her mother that hung over the bed and looked at the window. The wind blew the blue curtains almost straight out from the wall. "The window is broken. That must be what we heard, but how could it just shatter like that?"

Kate stepped past her and bent down. "It didn't." She turned with a large stone in her hand. "This came through the window." She pushed back the curtains to reveal a large hole in the window. "We need to call Kevin. Someone did this deliberately."

"But why? Only a few people know I'm here yet. Or that Dad is dead."

"Did your dad ever say he was afraid or that someone was annoying him?"

Mallory wanted to remind her that conversation with her father had been strained at best, but she just shook her head. She reached out and took the rock from Kate. The moisture on the rock chilled her skin. "It's wet. Someone just picked it up from the beach."

"We probably shouldn't have been handling it. I wasn't thinking." Kate reached into her purse and pulled out her phone. "I'm calling Kevin."

Maine game wardens were usually first to respond to any kind of crime report. They were law enforcement in most of the remote areas. While Kate spoke to her cousin, Mallory wandered over to stare at her mother's picture. Trim and tanned, Karen Blanchard would have been about forty-three at the time, but she looked more like thirty. She stood on her lobster boat with a smile as bright as the sunshine gleaming down on her light-brown hair. She'd loved the sea. Her family had been lobster fishermen ever since the first lobster had been caught off the coast of Maine. Dad usually worked with her, but he hadn't been feeling well the day she died.

When the waves overturned the boat, had Mom remembered Mallory's last hateful words? She wished she could believe her mother had forgiven her.

"Kevin's daughter is already in bed, so my sister, Claire, will go over and stay."

Mallory whipped her head around to face Kate. "Your sister? What sister?"

Kate's eyes held pain. "I forgot that all happened while you were gone. We found out I had a twin who was taken from our home when we were five. We were reunited a few months ago, but that's a complex story for another time. Claire lives here now and is going to marry Luke Rocco. You remember Luke from school, don't you?"

She nodded. "Super nice guy. And I met Claire earlier today. Such a sweetheart. How wonderful that you found each other." Mallory looked back toward the window. "Call Kevin back and tell him to wait until morning. This rock isn't going anywhere. I could just shut the bedroom door to keep the wind from the rest of the house. I hate to disrupt everybody's evening."

"He's used to calls at night. We all are."

Mallory's attention was caught by a piece of paper partially under the bed. She took a step closer, then knelt and picked it up. There was no reasonable explanation for the dread that chilled her hands as she unfolded it and held it up to the light.

The bottom of the sea is so cold.

She gasped and the paper fell from her fingers.

Kate grasped her arm. "What is it?"

Mallory stared at the paper on the floor. She didn't even want to touch it. "A-a warning, I think. It's a little cryptic." She told Kate what she'd read. "I bet the note came loose from the rock. Look, there's a broken rubber band." She pointed toward the window. "We shouldn't touch it in case there are fingerprints on it."

A surge of heat flooded her chest, and she curled her hands into fists. "This proves someone killed Dad."

"Not necessarily. Maybe someone was trying to mess with him." Kate frowned. "What could it mean?"

Mallory glanced back at her mother's picture. "I don't know. Dad said to find Mom, but she's been gone for years. Nothing makes any sense."

If Dad had been murdered, his killer wouldn't have thrown this through the window. Maybe Kate was right, and Dad hadn't been murdered at all.

With the evidence bagged and plastic taped around the broken window, Kevin accepted Mallory's offer of coffee. He was cold clear through to the bone after trekking around the house and seashore in an icy, drizzly rain. Standing in the warm kitchen felt like a welcome sauna.

He curled his frozen fingers around the hot cup and settled in an old green chair at the kitchen table. "Kate gone?"

Mallory sat across the table from him, and she nodded as she took a sip of her coffee. "She wanted to get to your house so Claire could go home."

He noted the dark circles under her eyes. It had been tough to tear his gaze away from her from the moment she arrived back in his life. Her glossy dark-brown hair was even longer now, reaching below her waist, and there was a quiet maturity to her he hadn't seen before.

He picked up his cup again. "It's been a rough day for you. I was hoping you'd get a chance to go to bed early."

She lifted a wan smile toward him. "I probably couldn't sleep anyway. And you've had a rough day as well. Finding my dad, then running out here so late. That must be hard with a child."

He nodded. "I sometimes wonder if I should make a career change. It's definitely a challenge, but I can't bring myself to do anything else. And Sadie is okay with a nanny."

He glanced around the kitchen. It had been a long time since he'd been here. He and Mallory used to sit and drink hot cocoa at this table with her mother, who had been one of those really cool moms. She knew how to talk to Mallory's friends, and her humor and insight had helped steer him in the direction of his present career.

"I miss your mom." The words were out before he realized he'd spoken. "Sorry, that was callous."

Her smile seemed real this time. "No, it's okay. I like to talk about her. I couldn't for a long time. The guilt was just too much. But she was a good mom, wasn't she? She talked you out of going to California for college, and you decided to go to the University of Maine. Your dad wasn't happy." Her smile faded and she looked uncomfortable. "How are your folks, by the way?"

"Let's not talk about them." Hearing about his parents would just make her look sadder, and he wanted to see her smile again. "Remember when I brought that orphaned raccoon over to show her? She helped me feed it and just casually remarked that I would make a great game warden. I hadn't even thought about it until then. I was going to be a doctor like my dad wanted."

"She was an excellent judge of character." She slid a sidelong glance his way. "You were always her favorite."

Until he'd betrayed her trust. His chest hurt at the memory of the pain in Karen's eyes when she'd found out what they'd done. "Sorry isn't a good enough word for how I feel about her death, you know. You're not the only one who's carried guilt all these years."

She set her coffee cup, reddish-orange with a moose on it, down on the table. Her dark-brown eyes bored into him. "I was so mean to you, and I'm sorry. I'm sorry I left, and I'm sorry I never returned your phone calls." She inhaled sharply. "And I'm especially sorry I married Brian. That was a big mistake."

He stared back at her, remembering all the times he'd left messages for her, all the cards and notes he'd sent. When he heard she'd married Brian a mere three months after she left Folly Shoals, he'd rushed right out and started dating DeAnn just to mask the pain. Stupid, stupid, both of them. But they'd been young, so young. It seemed like another life. And DeAnn had been so fun and vivacious. She made him feel like he was the only man in the world. Until he wasn't.

The unspoken reason for Mallory's and his breakup lurked under the surface like a great white, unseen but still menacing. He wasn't going to go there. Not yet.

"What made you marry Brian so quickly?" He blurted out the words, spelling out a question he'd carried for fifteen years.

It was better than his other questions. He cleared his throat and took a gulp of hot coffee to avoid saying anything else.

Her lashes swept down and masked her eyes. What was she thinking? The years and the pain he'd caused made it impossible to ask. Did she ever think about the baby?

Her lids opened again and she stared at him. "After Mom died, I couldn't bear the condemnation I saw everywhere I looked. Not just my dad, but people in town too. They all knew how much I'd shamed her before she died. I had to get away, and Brian offered a way out. I know it sounds cold and calculating, but he had money and status. I took one look at his big summer cottage on the Atlantic and thought if I married well, I could make up for the embarrassment. It didn't work out that way."

Shame. They both still carried it, but it wasn't for the reasons she'd stated.

"What do you mean about it not working out that way?"

She looked down at her hands. "Brian never felt secure in our marriage. He sensed I didn't love him like I should, and it made him more demanding. W-we didn't have a very happy time of it. When Haylie came along, I prayed things would get better, but they never did. Not really. I threw myself into my jewelry, and he grew more distant and consumed by his investment business."

He couldn't keep his lip from curling. "So you got all you wanted. Money and prestige."

She gave a wry laugh. "Not a bit. He made some bad investments, then let his insurance lapse. The last two years have been pretty lean." Her chin came up and her dark eyes narrowed. "But it's looking up now. I'm making a name for myself with my sea glass and tourmaline jewelry. The watermelon tourmaline is so typically Maine."

"You always did love sea glass. I think we went looking for it on nearly every date. I'd love to see some of your designs."

She pulled her necklace out from under her blouse and showed it to him. "I have a signature design."

He touched the honed piece of watermelon tourmaline, a beautiful blend of soft pink and green. "A sea-glass mermaid on a tourmaline moon. Didn't your mom used to tell you a story about that?"

"She did. Mom used to say a pink moon was the time when mermaids had the most power and tried new things. I know now she made it up, but I still like the symbolism." Mallory rubbed her head and grimaced. "Anyway, I'm hoping the big sale I made this morning will turn things around for us, but it's hard to think about that now."

"I didn't realize he'd left you and Haylie in such bad circumstances." And what would he have done if he'd known? Their relationship was over the second she left town. He could never trust her after what she did.

He cleared his throat. "About that note on the rock. I'll have both items tested for fingerprints and DNA, but I'm not hopeful of finding anything. Tomorrow when I pick you up, I'll look again for footprints. I found one and took an impression, but I'm not sure if I missed anything in the dark."

She tucked a lock of long hair behind her ear. "What do you make of what the note said? Kate and I wondered if someone was trying to make Dad think Mom's ghost was taunting him."

"I can't see something like that rattling your dad. He would have laughed it off."

She nodded. "It's a pretty obscure thing to say. And what

would be the point? You don't think the message was for me, do you? I don't think anyone even knows I'm here."

He grinned. "You know how fast news travels here. The minute you showed up in Folly Shoals to meet me, everyone in three counties would have known it an hour later."

Her lips curved, and he'd forgotten how much he loved to see that smile. It always held a little mystery, as though she knew more than she was saying.

She took another sip of her coffee. "Too true. I wasn't thinking. So the message could have been directed at me."

"If it was, whoever threw it didn't know the house. That was your dad's room, not yours."

Her smile came again. "And you should know. You used to throw rocks at my window until I climbed down onto the kitchen roof and slid down the tree to meet you." Her cheeks colored. "Forget I said that. We need to find a way to move past our painful history."

"That wasn't so painful. At least until you fell and sprained your ankle. Getting caught by my dad—now *that* was painful." He rubbed his backside. "Remember the time he caught us catching smelt in the stream instead of the lake during the smelt run? Now I bust offenders for doing that. He made us clean out the fish house." She didn't return his smile, and his grin faded. "I'd better get home. Thanks for the coffee." He put his cup in the sink.

Maybe it was better not to go back. He wasn't quite sure what kind of future relationship they could even have with their history. And it was probably a moot point. She'd be heading back to her life in Bangor once the funeral was over.

He started toward the door, and she put her hand on his arm. "Would you mind looking around the house with me before you go? I just feel unsettled."

"Of course." He followed her toward the stairs.

Anything to delay his departure just a bit. He wasn't any too eager to leave her here alone.

SIX

The last time Mallory had been in her bedroom had been when she was twenty. Posters of Orlando Bloom covered the pale-pink walls she'd painted herself. Her graduation tassel hung from the pink lamp shade beside her bed and touched the top of the framed picture of her with Kevin at the prom. They both looked impossibly happy.

It was an eternity ago.

She averted her eyes and stared around the room. "Something feels off."

Kevin advanced into the room and knelt to peer under the bed. "The spread looks rumpled, like someone sat on the end of the bed. Have you been in here?"

"No. My luggage is still in the living room." There was a spot on the bedside table that held no dust. "My diary used to be there, but I haven't seen it in years. Something book-sized was there though, see the imprint? Maybe Dad took it. It's hard to say if he's been in here." A cool breeze touched her face, and she went to the window. "The window is up and the screen is broken."

Kevin joined her and touched the edge of the screen. "It's been cut."

She curled her hands into fists. "Someone could have climbed onto the kitchen roof below and reached here."

"I know."

Of course he knew. He'd done it often enough after she sprained her ankle. He'd settle on the roof and they'd talk for hours. Her parents never caught them.

She pulled out a small chest from under her bed. "The lock is broken. Dad wouldn't have had to break the lock. He knew where the key was." Lifting the lid, she put her hand to her throat. "It's empty."

"What was in there?"

"Report cards, my birth certificate, picture albums, letters from you, old journals."

The frown between his eyes deepened. "Why would anyone want to steal that kind of thing?"

She clasped herself and shivered. "I have no idea, but it gives me the willies."

"I'm not sure you should stay here alone. Someone has been in here, someone other than your dad."

His concern sent a frisson of heat through her midsection. "I'll be fine. I'll lock up when you leave, and Carol will be here the day after tomorrow with Haylie."

The warmth in his brown eyes intensified. "I don't like the thought of you being alone out here. It's remote. I have a spare room at my house. Why don't you come home with me?"

She started shaking her head as soon as she saw the direction he was heading. If being around him casually was painful, being with him in a more intimate setting would be pure torture. "I'll be fine, Kevin, really. I've got a handgun in my purse. Legal, of course."

He grinned. "And you know I have to see your permit since you brought it up. It's my job."

"My bag is in the kitchen." After a last glance around her room, she started for the hall.

He stopped outside her bedroom door. "What if you slept in another room tonight? I could nail this door shut so no one could get in via the roof. This is the only bedroom with that kind of outside access."

"I wouldn't want to sleep in Dad's room, but there is a guest room."

"Let me take a look at it."

She watched as he walked around the bedroom and looked out the window. It was a nondescript room painted off-white with a cream bedspread and old furniture. As far as Mallory knew, her aunt was the only one who had ever spent the night in this room. A pang struck her when she remembered being with her mother when she'd bought the bedding for this room.

Back in the hall, Kevin pointed to the door. "It has a lock on it, so it would be the best one to use. You have a hammer and some long nails?"

"Dad probably has some in his tool belt in the shed. The key is hanging by the back door."

She trailed him down the stairs to the kitchen. While he went to the shed, she pulled her gun permit from her purse along with her small .38 and laid them on the table.

He returned with her father's worn leather tool belt in his hand. His gaze went to the permit and gun. "You know how to use this?"

"I'm a crack shot. I've gone to a practice range every month for the past six months."

A frown crouched between his eyes. "Why?"

She sighed and ran her hand around the back of her neck. "I don't know. I had this weird feeling someone was watching me." She attempted a watery smile. "Besides, isn't a good Mainer supposed to have a gun?"

His frown turned to a glower. "You ever see anyone?"

She shook her head. "I think it was just nerves after Brian's death. It doesn't matter. At least I'm armed."

His expression partially cleared, and he nodded. "I'll fix the door."

She didn't go with him and listened to his heavy tread up the stairs. When the hammering commenced, she drifted to the window and looked out into the dark backyard. The thought of being alone now that she knew someone had been in the house terrified her, but she wasn't about to admit it. What would it be like to stay at Kevin's and meet his little girl? Did he ever think about his other child?

She quickly steered her thoughts away. Their situation hadn't changed just because her father was dead. The past was insurmountable, and they'd both moved on with their lives. Going back wasn't an option.

The house echoed with recrimination after Kevin left. Mallory walked through the silent rooms remembering so much. Too much. Pausing in the hall, she stared at a family picture. Her fifteen-year-old self smiled into the camera. Her mother had her arm draped around her, and her father embraced them both.

They'd just gotten back from a boat trip up to Nova Scotia, and she remembered that happy week with a fierce ache.

Turning from the wall of memories, she retraced her steps to the living room and reached for the remote. Before her finger touched the power button, she heard the *putt-putt* of a boat motor. The back of her neck tingled. No one came into the little cove unless they were bound for the cottage.

The sound of voices filtered through the walls. Her pulse kicked when she recognized Haylie's voice. She and Carol weren't supposed to come for another day or two. Mallory unlocked the front door and stepped onto the porch. The lights on the boat bobbed in the surf by the dock, and she saw her daughter's face, pale in the wash of light, by the boat's stern.

Mallory rushed down the steps and hurried down the hillside to the water, arriving as Carol and Haylie stepped off the boat and onto the dock. "What are you two doing here? I didn't expect you tonight."

The cold spring wind carried the strong scent of seaweed with it, and the incoming tide lapped at the pilings. She stared at the water taxi's pilot but didn't recognize the grizzled face under a cap. The man hefted three suitcases onto the dock beside them. Carol thanked him, and he touched his cap before starting the engine.

Haylie tucked a strand of dark-brown hair behind her ear, then picked up a bag by her feet. "Someone broke into our house, Mom. Carol flew into a panic, and here we are. And I'm missing the biggest party of the year." Her voice dripped with outrage.

Mallory struggled to assimilate the news. "Someone broke into our house? Did they take anything?" Luckily she'd already sold all the pieces of jewelry she'd created, but she would hate to have to buy all new supplies.

"They didn't take anything that I could see, but you can check later." Carol, bundled up in a black coat, lugged two suitcases with her as the boat engine revved and the craft moved away from the dock. She set down one suitcase at Mallory's feet. "I didn't think it was safe to stay there." Her gaze flickered from Haylie to Mallory and she mouthed, *Later.*

Eyeing her friend's pale face, Mallory nodded. "Let's get inside out of this wind." She picked up the suitcase. "What's in this?"

"Clothes for you. You took off without anything to come here. A policeman waited while I grabbed some of Haylie's things as well as some clothes from your room. We stopped at my house to pack a bag for me too."

Haylie set her jaw and picked up a suitcase. "I could have stayed with Jenna. I don't know why I had to come."

Carol grabbed another suitcase. "I'm starving. I was too upset to eat when we stopped at a drive-through on the way."

"I can make you a sandwich or some eggs." Mallory led the way to the house, half dragging the heavy bag up the hill by its handle, then carried it inside.

The warmth inside was a blessed relief. Where was she going to put everyone? Her old room was off-limits with the door nailed shut. The old sofa was comfortable, so Mallory could sleep there. Once she got the window fixed, she could have bars installed as well and move back into her old room.

"You can take my dad's room, Carol. The window is broken, but we can tape cardboard over the hole. Haylie, you can have the guest room. It's the last door at the end of the hall."

Her daughter heaved a sigh. "I'm going to bed. Can I borrow your cell phone, Mom? I want to text Alisha."

Carol gave her a stern look. "I told you I don't want anyone to know where we are."

Haylie's lips flattened and her eyes filled with tears. "I'm not a prisoner!" She sent an appealing glance toward Mallory. "Mom?"

This was more than a simple break-in. "What's going on, Carol?"

Carol shrugged off her coat, then ran a hand through her tousled brown hair. "Maybe Haylie needs to hear this. She's going to drive us crazy otherwise. A guy grabbed me, Mallory." She clasped herself and shuddered. "But the scariest part was that he was after you, not anything in the house."

Mallory blinked, and her vision wavered as the blood drained from her head. She felt faint and sank onto the sofa. "I don't understand. What made you think he was after me?"

"He grabbed my arm and said, 'You're not the Davis woman. Where is she?'" Carol's throat clicked as she swallowed. "H-he looked like a hired thug or something. His eyes were like nothing I've ever seen. Like he had no soul and wouldn't think twice about wringing my neck. Or yours."

Mallory touched her throat. "What is going on?"

"With your dad's murder, then this, I knew we had to get away. Fast."

Haylie's brown eyes widened, and the color drained from her cheeks. "Grandpa was murdered?" She dropped onto the sofa beside Mallory and leaned against her. "Mom, what's going on?"

She slipped her arm around her daughter's narrow waist. "I wish I knew, Haylie. But we're together, and we're safe."

For now. Nothing made sense though. Her family didn't come from money or have anything of value. She resisted the urge to call back the water taxi and run far away. But that would do no good. Someone had killed her dad, and someone was looking for her. Her grip on her daughter tightened as she remembered the man in the van at school.

Was that the same man who had broken into the house?

SEVEN

At the sound outside her window, Carol bolted upright in the bed. There it came again, and a shudder made its way up her spine, even though she recognized it as an owl. Or at least she thought it was. She wasn't used to so much wild-life. Only her love for Mallory would bring her this far out of civilization.

She slipped out of bed and padded barefoot down the hall to the kitchen. Her belly cramped with hunger, and she opened the refrigerator door. Some yogurt would hit the spot. The light glared on overhead and she winced.

Mallory stood in the doorway by the light switch. "You scared me."

"Sorry." Carol held up a container of yogurt. "I'll share."

Mallory's nose wrinkled. "I'm full, thanks. I'll have some chamomile tea. Want some?"

"Sure." Carol watched her move to the stove and put water on to boil. "This is all so overwhelming, Mallory. Just a few hours ago we were flying high after you sold all that jewelry. Now here we are with you running for your life. Is there something about your past you've never told me? This doesn't add up."

Mallory pulled down mugs from the cabinets. The cups were

as chipped as the paint on the green cabinets. Her movements were careful, and she still hadn't answered Carol.

Carol leaned against the Formica counter. "Mallory? What's going on?"

Her neighbor turned then, her face pale in the fluorescent lighting. "I don't know, Carol. Right now I'm remembering Brian's death in that plane. It was supposedly an accident, but what if it wasn't? We have no way of knowing, and I don't know what is true or false any longer. If you'd asked me this morning if there was anything dangerous in my life, I would have laughed. The only danger I've ever faced is from my own stupid decisions. But now I'm second-guessing everything that's happened lately. I'm so confused." She raked her long hair back from her face.

Carol put tea bags in the mugs. "So you don't know why anyone would be looking to harm you?"

"Not a clue. But I have to stay and find out, don't you think?"

Carol had wandered all her life, looking for a place where she fit, looking for the family she never had. The minute she'd met Mallory she'd known the bond between them could never be broken. She'd found that missing piece she'd yearned for. How did she keep Mallory and Haylie safe?

She'd do anything to protect them. "At least here you have a support system and people who know you. Back in Bangor, that guy could break in again, and he was terrifying."

"You'll get a chance to meet some of my friends tomorrow." Mallory yawned. "We'd better get to bed. I want to wake up early and watch the sunrise. Go for a run too."

Carol looked her over. "I've never known you to run."

"I think I'm finding myself again."

Carol stared after her as she went up the stairs. Could a place really matter so much?

The Hotel Tourmaline bustled with activity, but that was the way Julia liked it. Few people noticed her moving around. She cut across the gleaming marble floors in the reception area and went up the service elevator to the ballroom. The elevator still held the aroma of the Italian food the servers had carried up for an anniversary lunch an hour ago.

When she stepped onto the second floor, the wide carpeted hallways were silent, though she could hear the distant rumble of a vacuum on the other end as the cleaning crew tidied up after the reception last night.

An equipment cart rattled by and one of the housekeeping staff exited the main ballroom pushing the cart piled high with platters. She smiled and nodded as she passed. Julia waited until the noise of the clanging trays faded before she strolled past the rooms lining the halls.

If she could get a cell signal in her small room, she would have taken this call there, but a quiet corner here would have to do. Boyce had been right when he'd warned her about the size of the room. The thing he hadn't mentioned was that it was clear at the end of a long hallway and had no cell reception. She found a smaller meeting room with the lights out and went to the window. Holding her phone up to the sunlight, she checked her bars. Three bars should be good enough. It would have to be.

Her pulse pounded in her ears as she found Ian's number and called it. On the second ring his deep voice answered.

"It's me," she said.

"You're late. I told you to call at eleven."

"I had to wait until there was an empty room to use. Cell service is spotty here."

"Bunch of hicks," he muttered.

She leaned against the wall. "What was so important that a text wouldn't do?"

"I wanted a real update. No lies. You're real good at lies, Julia, and I don't trust you."

"That's rich, coming from you. I'm not the one who murdered a woman. I'm helping you out, remember?"

"I have no illusions about why you're doing this. It's not for me but because you want to go to Washington."

She didn't bother denying his accusation. "I told you I'd handle this. There's no reason to escalate it. Back off and let me take care of it."

"I don't like putting all my eggs in one basket, and I wasn't sure you'd be able to get hold of the papers."

She frowned and wished he were here in front of her. "You were always too impatient. I've got it all under control."

"You told me you could deliver without anyone else getting hurt, but I'm still not so sure. We need to wrap this up in a week."

"Three. I haven't even made contact yet." Even three weeks would take a miracle. Two months and maybe she could get this wrapped up. "You forget that I'm saving your butt. I'd like a little appreciation."

He went silent on the other end. "This is mutually beneficial. What about the old guy? What happened to him?"

Her fingers tightened around the cell phone. "I didn't mean to hurt him. His death was an accident."

He made a huff that she took for agreement. She'd rather he didn't know she'd had to kill the old geezer.

How had she lived so long without this view of the sea and the feel of the pebbles under her sneakers? Catching her breath after her run along the water, Mallory stood at the edge of the water and looked at the sun coming up over the whitecaps. The cold stones under her soles were worn smooth by the action of the waves, and she saw a glint of green sea glass among the rocks. She stooped to pick it up and ran her fingers over the rounded edges.

Still in fuzzy red pajamas and a robe, Carol yawned and stretched beside her. "What are you doing up so early? And it's *cold* out here, cold enough to give an Eskimo chilblains."

"Wimp. It's just brisk."

Carol gave a mock shiver. "Brisk like a blizzard."

Mallory rarely got cold, especially when she had an opportunity to stand here mesmerized by the power of the sea. "You would have missed the sunrise. I used to watch the sun come up with my mom every morning."

The sun threw out bands of purple, orange, and gold as the fireball slowly rose above the water. If only her mother were standing here with her. All the regrets in the world couldn't change things now.

Carol tightened the belt of her robe. "It sounds like you've missed living here. Why didn't you ever come back to stay?"

"People have long memories here." She stared across the ocean toward the Schoodic Peninsula and could barely make out a hint of land. To the northeast would be Beals Island, then Jonesport, and on up the coast to Lubec and the Canadian border. It felt as though she'd never left. This place was in her blood, in her soul. "I'd love to just pack up and move back. I love it here. Haylie would have a fit about leaving her friends though."

"So do it. She's not even in high school yet. You're the mom and she'll adjust."

That was one of the things Mallory loved about Carol. She spoke her mind and advised her the way her own mother might have.

"You still haven't told me why you left." Carol picked up a stone and threw it into the waves where it disappeared in the sea foam. "You've hinted at trouble with your parents, but that's old news by now. There's nothing to keep you from being part of this life again. Heck, I might even move too. It's so wild and free out here. Plus, you can have lobster whenever you want. What's not to love?"

"I got sick of lobster as a kid. We had it just about every day." She smiled at the memory. "It took a long time to realize how lucky I was." She saw Carol shiver. "Go on back inside. I'm going to take another little run along the beach. I'll be in soon."

"You don't have to tell me twice." Carol turned toward the granite steps cut into the hillside from the beach. "I'll have coffee and breakfast ready."

Mallory inhaled a lungful of sea air, then broke into a jog. The pebbles ran away from her sneakers, and her breath began to quicken with the run. How many times had she run along this shoreline? Too many to count. Had she deprived Haylie of the privilege of growing up here? Mallory had thought a life away from the lifeblood of the sea would be better, but she'd been so wrong.

Was Carol right? Maybe it wasn't too late to go back, to face down her past and build a new life here. The people who made a living from the sea were the best—hardworking, strong as granite. It was the grit she'd learned from this place that had kept her from giving up when things got rocky.

Haylie needed that in her life. Maybe it wasn't too late.

EIGHT

Kevin tied off his boat at the dock below Breakwater Cottage. It was a beautiful April morning with the thermometer hovering near fifty-five, almost balmy by Maine standards. A few daffodils poked through the rocky soil along the path to the house, and as he neared the steps, he heard voices. He frowned as he glanced at his watch. It was barely eight. Who would have arrived this early?

He approached the door with stealth, then relaxed when he heard an unfamiliar female voice telling Mallory she was starving. The voice sounded young, like an adolescent. He rapped his knuckles on the door and heard light footsteps coming toward the entry.

Mallory was in sweats with her long, dark hair falling around her face. Her brown eyes widened when she saw him. "Is it eight already? I'm late. Come in and I'll get changed. Carol and Haylie arrived last night."

"I thought they weren't coming yet."

"So did I."

As she explained the reason for their arrival, he felt his danger barometer rise ten notches. "The guy actually mentioned your name?"

She nodded and leaned close enough for him to catch a whiff of vanilla from her hair. "I didn't mention it, but some guy in a van was talking to Haylie at school when I arrived to pick her up yesterday. He tore off when I interrupted. What if he'd intended to grab her?"

"You don't have any idea what the guy could have wanted?" His brain searched for reasons. "Any loan sharks after you?"

Pink flooded to her face. "I hate debt. The only thing I owe on is the house. My mortgage payment was a week late, but I paid it this morning. I've wracked my brain trying to make sense of it and can't. Come meet my daughter and Carol."

He'd always loved her brutal honesty. He followed her through the house to the kitchen where the tantalizing aroma of bacon hung in the air. A young girl in pink pajamas sat at the table. She turned alert brown eyes his way. If someone had compared her picture with Mallory's at that age, they wouldn't have been able to tell the difference. She was petite with small bones like her mother, and her dark hair was tied back in a careless ponytail.

Her gaze brightened as it swept over his uniform. "You're a policeman? Maybe you can convince my mom it's safe to let me use her cell phone. She said you could decide."

"Game warden." He looked at Mallory. "Did you tell her about the break-in here and the rock?"

Mallory's eyes narrowed in warning, and she shook her head as if asking him not to say anything else, but he ignored her plea as he glanced back at Haylie. "She shouldn't be sheltered from the truth. She's fourteen, old enough to know."

Another woman, probably in her fifties with green eyes and dark-brown hair, turned from the stove. "There was a break-in here too?" Her brows rose.

"This is Carol Decker," Mallory said, her voice resigned.

"Someone riffled through Mallory's old bedroom, and someone threw a rock through one of the bedroom windows. With a threatening note attached to it."

Carol waved the spatula in her hand. "So the intruder already followed her here?"

"I'm not sure. They could be unrelated. It's possible the break-in and the rock had something to do with Edmund's death. Until we know for sure they were directed at Mallory, it's best if no one knows where you are. So no text messages from here to anyone."

Haylie burst into tears. "It's *boring* here, and you're telling her to keep me a prisoner!" She got up from the table and rushed from the room.

Mallory heaved a sigh. "Sorry. Teenage angst is painful. You really think it's unsafe to let her text her friends?"

"At least for now. I don't like all these incidents, especially the one at your house."

Carol carried a plate of bacon and a bowl of scrambled eggs to the table. "You hungry?"

"Thanks, but I already ate. What can you tell me about the guy you saw?"

Carol hunched her shoulders. "Not much. I only saw his eyes through the ski mask. He was a big guy though, and those eyes were downright scary." She set the food on the table and spooned eggs onto her plate.

"Did you get the name of any of the responding officers? I can call to get an update." He faced Mallory. "I also heard back on the rock we recovered from your dad's bedroom. No prints or DNA."

"Just like you thought," Mallory said.

Carol transferred some bacon to her plate. "I'm sure the police officers told me their names, but it was all a blur." The chair scraped on the linoleum as she pulled it out and sat.

"I'll just call the Bangor police department then." He removed his phone from his jacket pocket and went into the living room. His call was routed to the detective in charge of the case.

"DuBois," a gruff voice barked.

"Game Warden O'Connor from over by Summer Harbor. I'm calling about the break-in at Mallory Davis's home. Her father's home here in Folly Shoals was also broken into, and I thought we should be sharing information in case they're related. Especially since her father died yesterday."

"Murder?" The detective's tone sharpened.

"The sheriff thinks it was accidental, but I'm not so sure. Did you find any evidence at the scene?"

"The back-door lock was broken. We secured the scene but found no evidence. I sent a man back over there this morning, and the place had been ransacked overnight. We'll need Mrs. Davis to take a look and see if anything is missing. It was clear they were looking for something though. The cushions on the sofa and chairs were ripped open and so were the mattresses. Every book in the house was on the floor, and all the drawer contents were dumped out. Not sure what to make of it."

Kevin imagined the scene and winced. "Did the neighbors see anything?"

"Unfortunately, the woman who lives across the street from Ms. Davis is on vacation, and the guy on the other side of Mrs. Davis's home is elderly and can't hear. He was in bed by eight and didn't know anything had happened until an officer showed up to ask questions. A guy in a passing vehicle heard Ms. Decker scream and ran inside, but the intruder was gone by then."

Kevin told the detective all he'd found here, then rattled off his number. "I'd appreciate it if you kept me apprised of anything that happens there. I'll do the same with you."

He ended the call and pocketed his phone. With the items missing from Mallory's bedroom, he suspected what was happening here was related to whatever was going on in Bangor. He just prayed he could keep Mallory and her daughter safe.

The sea spray hit Mallory in the face as Kevin's boat skimmed the waves. Gulls squawked and swooped low overhead. She raised her face to the glorious spring sunshine and felt her sadness lift a bit. She couldn't do anything to bring back her father, but she could try to find out what happened to him.

Kevin throttled back on the motor and pointed toward Summer Harbor where boats dotted the inlet. "Your dad's boat is in slip fifty-five. The sheriff agreed to meet us there. He wants to make sure we don't mess up any evidence."

She stared at the boat. The name *Mermaid* stood out in red lettering. "That looks like a different boat."

"Edmund got a new one about six months ago."

As Kevin stopped his boat a few feet away, she studied her father's new boat. The craft was a fifty-five-footer with a second deck, and its red, white, and blue paint looked pristine. Where had he gotten the money for something this new and large? The contract job of delivering the mail to the islands wasn't very lucrative.

Kevin reached over and tied the two boats together, then boarded her father's boat. He reached across and held out his hand to her. She accepted his assistance and stepped onto the rolling deck of the mail boat, then quickly let go of his hand. His touch still caused her insides to quiver like a jellyfish. She stole a glance at him, but he didn't seem as rattled by her touch as she was by his. In fact, if anything, he was a little standoffish and remote, but she couldn't blame him.

She shoved her hands in the pockets of her jacket and looked around the *Mermaid*. It didn't feel like her father's boat either. She was used to his old thirty-foot one with its patched spots and old upholstery. This one still smelled new. There were no stains on the carpet or the seats.

Kevin caught at her arm when she took a step toward the cabin. "We'd better wait here for the sheriff."

"Is there blood?" She wanted to be prepared for what she might see.

"Some. He had a head wound. You sure you're ready for this?"

"As ready as I'll ever be." She nodded toward a familiar bulky figure in the back of a skiff. "Here's Danny."

At six-seven, Sheriff Colton's stature was hard to miss. And his fiery-red handlebar mustache and weathered skin caused him to stand out anywhere he went. Once upon a time he'd played for the Celtics, and he was a hero to most everyone in the area.

He tied up the skiff, then climbed the ladder to the deck. His big hand came down on Mallory's shoulder. "Sorry about your dad, Mrs. Davis. He was a good man."

Her eyes welled at the sympathy in his voice, but she managed not to let the tears fall. "Thank you. I appreciate you letting me take a look at the scene."

A frown creased his forehead. "Kevin here said you were insistent. I hope you're prepared. I'm not going to pull haul with you. You can see it all if you're set on it." He jerked his head toward the cabin. "This way."

She swallowed hard and followed him. A gull landed on the railing and surveyed her with beady black eyes as if to see if she could go through with this.

Kevin caught her arm when she stumbled a little. "Careful."

She ducked under the doorway and into the cabin. The coppery scent of blood hit her in the face, and she flinched. It took all her fortitude not to turn and run back into the salty air. Kevin gripped her arm again, and she wanted to thank him, but any words in her mouth dried up when she saw the stained carpet.

There was a lot more blood than she'd expected. The bloodstain was two feet in diameter, and in her mind's eye, she saw her dad lying there. A shudder worked its way up her spine, and Kevin pulled her against his chest.

"Steady," he whispered in her ear.

Inhaling, she allowed herself to rest against his bulk for a moment. Being around him had always made her feel safe and protected. She took a tighter hold on her emotions. "I'm all right." She pulled away from his embrace and approached the reddish-brown pool. It still looked damp. She looked away from the blood and assessed the rest of the cabin. Her father's chart map was on the floor.

She stepped to the radio. "You said the radio was off when you found him? So he never tried to send a distress call."

"It was off, and I've never known him to turn it off." Kevin turned to the sheriff. "I smelled perfume too. That's gone now, of course, but did you notice a scent when you were first here?"

Danny's bald head swung back and forth. "Not that I noticed."

Mallory caught a glint of something shiny under the captain's chair and knelt. "There's a bracelet here."

"Don't touch it," Danny said.

"I didn't." She peered closer. "It looks like a woman's tennis bracelet. Those look like diamonds."

Danny extracted a bag and gloves from his pocket. He pulled on the latex gloves, then transferred the bracelet to the bag. "I'll have it checked out. Seems expensive."

Mallory rose. "Does this alter your belief that he accidentally fell and hit his head? I think someone was here."

"Even if he had a lady friend on the boat, that doesn't mean she killed him. Your dad was a strong fellow. I think a woman would have a hard time inflicting a killing blow on him."

"If she wasn't to blame, why wouldn't she call it in if he fell and was injured? He called me and seemed to be alone. Wouldn't she have telephoned for help?"

Danny pulled off his gloves. "Let's not speculate, Mallory. She may have been on the boat on a different day. We'll see what the lab comes up with."

So he wasn't changing his call on her father's death. She exchanged a long look with Kevin. His brown eyes narrowed, and she knew he wasn't satisfied with what they'd found either.

There was only one thing she could do. Fulfill her father's contract to deliver mail and dig some of this out for herself. From as far back as she could trace, her ancestors had lived here. She was a true Mainer, and people would talk to her. It would be easy enough to take over the route. In this area it was notoriously hard to find contractors willing to deliver the mail.

And the job might lead her to what happened aboard this boat.

NINE

The island of Folly Shoals rose from the ocean offshore the Schoodic Peninsula. Three miles in diameter and ten miles long, it boasted a variety of landscapes from low-lying cranberry bogs to soaring sea cliffs and evergreen forests. The cool wind tried and failed to get through Kevin's Red Sox Windbreaker.

The bow of the boat rode the sea spray and waves toward shore. He glanced at Mallory who sat straining forward with her gaze narrowed. Lost in thought, she stared toward the island as if seeing something beyond the sea cliffs.

"I'm sorry about your house." He'd taken her to check out her house in Bangor before bringing her home. The police had met her there, and she'd confirmed nothing appeared to be missing.

"Thanks. What on earth could the guy have been looking for?"

Every item in every drawer and closet had been tossed to the floor. "I wish I could say it was kids just vandalizing the place, but that wouldn't explain the man who grabbed Carol and asked where you were. I'm beginning to wonder if your dad had possession of something the guy wants, and he thinks you have it."

"It makes no sense at all."

The wind blew her long hair in a swirl around her face, and her cheeks were pink from the chill. Being around her was already setting his teeth on edge. She'd run off, deserting him after he'd stood up to his parents for her. Though a callus had replaced the pain, he wasn't sure he'd ever really forgiven her for what she'd done. Or even could.

She lifted her chin and sniffed the air. "I've missed the scent of the sea. There's nothing like it."

He was so used to it that he hardly noticed anymore. "So who's Carol?"

A smile tipped her full lips. "Carol is my best friend and next-door neighbor. She jumps in to help whenever I need her. Which seems too often lately."

"What does she do?" He squinted at the horizon and gauged how best to head into the waves and round the point.

"She runs social-media campaigns for companies. Since she works from home, she's usually able to help me out at a moment's notice, but I try not to abuse that."

"She's not married?"

"No. She was engaged for a while last summer, but she found her fiancé at a strip joint with a woman in his lap."

He winced. "Creep."

"That's what I told her. She dumped him and said he was just the latest in a long list of losers and that she was done looking. She hasn't dated since then, as far as I know." Mallory stood and shaded her eyes from the glare off the water.

They were passing near Winter Harbor, a small town where they'd spent a lot of time back in their dating years. The white clapboard buildings looked quaint and charming by the sea, and up close the town lived up to its image.

His cell phone trilled, and he grabbed it from his jacket pocket. Someone from the hotel was calling. "Warden O'Connor."

"There's a rabid fox in the garden, Warden." The man sounded rattled. He wasn't a Mainer, but a flatlander with a slight Southern accent.

He tried to place the voice and failed. "At Hotel Tourmaline?"

"Yes, sorry. This is the manager, Boyce Masters. Can you come right away before it bites someone?"

"I'm just docking at Folly Shoals. I can be there in about fifteen minutes."

"What am I supposed to do with it in the meantime?"

"What makes you think it's rabid?"

"It's snapping its jaws and foam is dripping from its mouth." The manager's voice held distaste.

Kevin winced at the description. "Sounds rabid. If you have someone knowledgeable about wildlife, have him wear thick leather gloves and try to throw a net over it. If not, just keep your guests indoors. I'll be there as fast as I can."

"Just hurry."

Mallory rose and went to lean against the bow's railing. "Trouble?"

"We've had a rash of rabid foxes lately. Raccoons too. Pay attention whenever you're outside and keep a close eye on your daughter."

She shivered. "I hope you've warned your little girl too."

"I did." He watched her in the morning sunlight. The tug at his heart took him by surprise. She shouldn't have the power to move him this way, not after all this time. He wasn't sure he could get used to running into her. The sooner she left, the better.

She turned away to stare toward the harbor. "I made a decision this morning. I'm going to take over Dad's mail delivery and see what I can find out."

His gut clenched. "That could be dangerous, Mallory. Let me see what I can find out. You need to stay out of it."

She whipped around with her chin in the air, a stance he quickly recognized.

He held up his hands. "I'm not trying to boss you around, but this is my job, not yours. You've got your daughter to worry about. You can get back to your normal life, and I'll call you when I get to the bottom of what happened."

"What normal life? Until we get to the bottom of this, I'm not sure we're safe anywhere." Her brown eyes flashed. "It sounds like you're trying to get rid of me, Kevin. Do I make you that uncomfortable?"

"Of course not, but what happens if you put Haylie in danger by poking around? You aren't thinking this through."

Her eyes grew luminous, and a fat tear rolled down one cheek. His throat tightened. Tears made him feel helpless. He gripped the wheel and steered toward the dock. She stared at him, then turned to face the shore.

Her tense back told him he hadn't dissuaded her. "The funeral is the day after tomorrow. I'd thought you'd go back to your life then."

"Sorry to disappoint you. The entire town may feel the same way, but I'm staying."

Great, just great. He should probably switch the topic. He'd never persuade her. "How's your aunt holding up with the news about your dad?"

She crossed her arms over her chest. "Stoic as always. She

says she's not coming to the funeral. Typical. She's hidden in the house for years. I'm done hiding out in shame. That's part of the reason I'm staying."

"Not coming to her own brother's funeral?" His mind churned. If he got Blanche to the funeral, she'd be quick to tell Mallory what a crazy scheme she had planned. If Mallory wouldn't listen to him, maybe she'd listen to her aunt.

The gray stone walls and mullioned windows of Hotel Tourmaline peered down on its Downeast Maine location of wind-tossed waves and rocky crags like a great castle or manor in Ireland. As Kevin approached with Mallory, a valet, dressed in black slacks and a white shirt, stepped forward to open the door of the grand entrance, which was decked out in gleaming brass and glass. Kevin thanked him and asked where he might find the manager. The valet directed him across the pink marble floors to the hotel office.

Kevin paused before the gleaming wood door. "If you like, you can get some coffee while I take care of this, or you're welcome to come with me." Silverware clinked to their left, and the aroma of lobster bisque wafted their way.

Before Mallory could answer, the door opened, and a balding man in his fifties nearly barreled into him. His salt-and-pepper mustache was trimmed to military precision, and he wore a navy suit with black shoes polished to mirror perfection.

His hazel eyes widened. "Warden O'Connor, you're here. I'm Boyce Masters. This way." He didn't wait for an answer but took off at a brisk clip toward the hall leading to the back garden.

Kevin shrugged and followed with Mallory at his side. "This might not be pleasant," he whispered. "Stay back."

"Kevin O'Connor, you forget who you're talking to. If you recall, I had a pet skunk in the tenth grade."

He grinned. "And if *you* recall, that didn't turn out so well. Someone had a bedroom that reeked of skunk spray for weeks."

She smiled back with a glint in her dark eyes. "That wasn't my fault. The dog got hold of it. You told me baby skunks couldn't spray."

"I was wrong."

"Can I write down that confession?" The mirth in her eyes evaporated, and she gasped. "Oh, Kevin, I think it's rabid."

Masters held open one of the double glass doors, and Kevin's gaze landed on the fox trapped under a wire lobster trap. The animal lunged and bit at the wire like it thought it could bite through anything. Foam dripped from its snarling mouth, and garbled sounds he'd never heard from a fox came from the enraged animal. The mangy fur confirmed his suspicions.

He exited the hotel behind Mallory. "Who put the trap over it? I'm surprised anyone was brave enough to get close."

A woman moved from the shadows. "I did."

Her age could have been anywhere from midforties to midfifties, and she exuded a calm competence with her neat gray suit and pumps. Her brown hair was swept into an updo, and her blue eyes looked back at him with a quizzical expression, as if she thought he should have known she was perfectly capable of handling anything life threw her way.

"Good job." Kevin unwound his backpack from his arm and unzipped it to peer at the contents.

The animal would have to be sedated for him to move it.

The way it had its teeth clamped on the wire, he could probably use a needle instead of the gun. He selected the long hypodermic needle and approached the fox as it snarled and chewed on the metal. Small paws snagged the wires, too, so he could aim for a leg. The fox didn't seem to notice him as he knelt and prepared the injection.

He pulled on leather gloves, then moved closer and jabbed the needle into the animal's paw. It barely flinched, but its snarls increased for several frenzied minutes until it began to quiet down and list to one side. It finally collapsed.

Kevin glanced at the manager. "You have a box? I have one in my boat, but I won't bother getting it if you have one."

"I asked the staff for one." The woman produced it from behind one of the benches.

He took it and thanked her. "You weren't frightened by the fox?"

She shook her head. "I grew up near Canada, and foxes are pretty common. As are bears, chipmunks, eagles, and wolverines. Not much scares me. What will you do with the fox?"

"It will be tested for rabies, but there's no question in my mind that it's rabid. It will be put out of its misery." He glanced at Boyce. "Any reports of it biting anyone?"

"Not to my knowledge. It just showed up here this morning, and Ms. Carver reported it. She had it contained by the time I got off the phone with you." He sent an admiring glance toward the woman.

Ms. Carver's smile was self-deprecating. "Anyone would have done the same." She held out her hand to Mallory. "Are you all right? You look a little faint."

Kevin hadn't thought to check on Mallory, and when he

turned to look, she did appear a little green as she took the woman's hand and sank to a stone bench. She'd always had a soft spot for animals and would even take spiders out of the house to release them. He shouldn't have said the animal would be put down, but if she knew how much torment the poor creature was in, she wouldn't want it to suffer.

He knelt beside her. "You okay, Mallory?"

Was it his imagination or did Ms. Carver stiffen? He directed his attention back to Mallory. "Let me get you home for lunch. I'll drop you off and take care of the fox."

"I'll treat you all to lunch. I insist." Boyce held open the door. "It's the least I can do."

Kevin helped Mallory up. "I wouldn't say no to that lobster bisque of yours."

TEN

Silverware tinkled around Claire and her sister, Kate, as they sat at a corner booth in Hotel Tourmaline's elegant Oyster Bistro. The big window overlooked the sparkling blue waters of Sunset Cove, and Claire admired the view as she took a quick sip of her iced tea.

Kate's blue eyes, so like her own, regarded her over the top of her glass. "So, what did you think of Mallory?"

"I liked her, though we didn't get to talk much before Kevin showed up. You can see she's strong. And speaking of Kevin, what is up between them? You would have had to take a machete to cut through the tension between them. And that doggone Luke refused to say a word. He just said it was old history. Men!" Claire's ring caught the light, and she paused to admire it. Engaged. It didn't seem real. The happiness that bubbled up inside her was hard to contain.

Kate wiped the beads of moisture from her glass. "They were going to get married, and she backed out and left town. Her mom died, and I think it just took the heart out of her. I suspect Kevin's dad had something to do with it too. He blamed Mallory for Kevin's decision to go into the warden service. He had his heart set on his son becoming a doctor."

"Kevin doesn't strike me as the kind of man who would let himself be led around by the nose by a woman."

"Unlike Luke?" Kate's teasing grin shot her way.

"Kate Mason! I do *not* lead him around by the nose." Claire couldn't stop her smile at the thought though. Luke was crazy about her, and he didn't care who knew it. "I called my mom to tell her. She had a million plans by the time we hung up. I think any hope of a simple wedding is toast. And she informed me she knew this was coming and bought us a house ages ago. Luke was a little put out until he found out which house it was. I guess he's always loved the property."

"I knew your mom would make a fuss. You're her only child. She'll go all out."

Claire's smile faded. "Any word from your mom or your uncle?" She still couldn't call them *hers*. Not after what they'd done.

Kate picked up her tea again and didn't look at her. "I haven't talked to them in a couple of weeks. It's been too hard to see them in prison. I still love them in spite of everything."

A pain clenched Claire's chest, and she reached over to take her sister's hand. "I'm sorry, Kate. Let's talk about something else. Like the wedding. Or the house we're going to live in! It's a clapboard Colonial, three thousand square feet, and in the middle of a hundred acres. It needs a lot of work, but that will just make it ours. We both *love* it."

"It was good of your mom to get it."

Claire pulled out her phone to show the pictures. "I'm going to hire a contractor and designer to redo it, so I thought I'd stay here at the hotel while it's being redone. That way I'll be close and won't have to take the ferry over every day. You don't mind, do you?" She'd been staying with Kate since she came back to Downeast Maine, and the two had been recapturing the lost years.

"I knew I would lose you sooner or later. A few weeks early won't matter." But Kate didn't smile in spite of her light words. She looked over the pictures of the old Colonial house. "It's lovely, Claire. I'm so happy for you."

"I'll come over for lunch with you at least three times a week. I promise." She gave Kate's hand a final squeeze, then leaned back as the server brought their fish tacos.

A woman standing in the doorway to the restaurant caught her eye. She seemed like the kind of woman who had attracted attention from men all her life and knew it. In spite of the tiny lines around her eyes, she was stunning, dressed in a slim suit that accentuated her slim figure. Her French roll emphasized the delicate bone structure in her face.

"Who are you looking at?" Kate twisted around to see. "Do you know her?"

"I've seen her before, but I can't place her. I feel like I should know her though." Claire shrugged and dug into her fish taco. "It will come to me." She squinted. "Isn't that Mallory and Kevin with her and the hotel manager?"

Julia could barely stop a smile from forming as Boyce directed them to a booth in the corner of the restaurant. What a stroke of luck to be involved with that rabid fox business. It was early in the season. By June, every table would be occupied during mealtimes, though she wouldn't be here to see it. Her goals had to be accomplished way before then.

And what luck that she'd met Mallory nearly as soon as she'd stepped foot on Folly Shoals. The young woman was prettier than she'd expected and looked nothing like her father or mother. Nearly black hair glistened in the sunlight streaming through the big bank of windows behind the table and fell to below her waist. Her brown eyes were so dark they were almost black. The contrast with her pale skin was striking.

Mallory glanced around the room. "I'll have to bring Haylie here. She would love it."

The pink granite floors continued into the dining room, and the chairs had been newly upholstered in burgundy. Smiling servers, offering beverages and taking orders, moved among the few vacationing guests eating lunch.

Boyce motioned for the server. "Haylie's your daughter?"

"Yes, she's fourteen but looks and acts eighteen, I'm sorry to say. Kids grow up way too fast."

Julia noticed the way the handsome game warden watched Mallory. The man was smitten, and who wouldn't be? Petite and small-boned, beautiful Mallory was the kind of woman who had any man yearning to take care of her. Julia had been a woman like that once herself. Even now at fifty, she turned an older head or two. She wanted to tell Mallory to enjoy her power while she had it. A blink of an eye and that fresh beauty would be marred by wrinkles around the eyes and mouth, and skin that was just a little tired.

She eyed the warden again. Mallory could do worse than the tall, broad-shouldered man beside her. His calm, competent manner was that of one who had seen a lot of hard knocks but had learned to let most things roll off his back. Julia was a good judge of character most of the time, and this one seemed like a good guy, better than most, and she'd seen plenty of the bad ones.

But Julia had more important reasons for her joy at getting to know more about Mallory than speculating about budding romance. After they placed their orders, she leaned forward. "So, you've always lived on Folly Shoals? This is my first visit here."

Mallory smiled and nodded. "Until I was twenty. I left the island, and yesterday was my first time back in fifteen years." Her gaze shifted to the linen-covered table, and she ran her finger around the rim of her water glass. "My father d-died, and I came at once."

Julia reached across the table and took her hand. "Oh, my dear, I'm so sorry." Her heart pounded in her ears at the effort to keep her expression pleasantly sympathetic. The man had deserved to die though. Too bad Mallory didn't know what he'd done, how greedy he'd gotten.

"Thank you."

Julia removed her hand. "I think I heard something about your father's death. He fell and hit his head on the boat?"

"We really shouldn't be discussing an open case," the game warden said.

In her lap Julia curled her hands into fists. What was the meddling warden's name? Kevin. That was it. Kevin O'Connor. "Of course." She sent a brilliant smile, designed to disarm, toward him. His wary expression eased, and she turned back to Mallory. "So I expect you'll go home after the funeral?"

Mallory glanced sideways toward Kevin. "No, actually, I'm staying. I'm going to fulfill Dad's mail contract until it runs out in September." Her chin lifted as if defying anyone to argue with her intentions.

Julia's chest squeezed hard at the news. She'd hoped that after the rock through the window the woman would go back to her regular life and forget all about this place. She might have to escalate her efforts. "You'll stay at your father's?"

"Yes. My daughter is here, too, and my best friend. I'm eager to show Haylie what a summer is like on the coast. I haven't been lobster fishing in ages. Not since . . ." Her voice trailed off and she glanced at the warden, then looked back impassively.

The server brought steaming bowls of lobster bisque in bread bowls, and Julia fell silent. If she was able to pull off her plans, maybe everyone would walk away. But she wasn't hopeful.

ELEVEN

The small church in Folly Shoals held a lot of memories for Mallory. She slipped into the front pew with Haylie and Carol before the rest of the mourners arrived. Light filtered through the beautiful stained glass windows that arched nearly to the cathedral ceiling. The red carpet had been replaced with a more subtle blue gray, and the padded pews were new too. Her Sunday school class had been in a small room in the basement, the faint musty smell overpowered by the strong scent of crayons and fabric softener. It was where she'd first met Kevin and where he'd slipped her that first love note when she was fifteen.

She focused her attention on the casket, which had replaced the Communion table. Masses of flowers dripped over the casket's edge, and pictures of their family played in an endless PowerPoint display on the overhead screen. Even in podunk Maine, technology had found its way to the church. Inhaling, she prayed for strength to face the day.

Carol touched her hand. "You okay?"

"I'll be all right. The worst of it is that there's no family left."

"What about Aunt Blanche?"

Mallory shook her head. "She doesn't drive, and she hasn't

been out of the house in years. When I called to tell her, she told me she'd be praying for me. I knew then she wouldn't be here."

A shaft of light pierced the dimness of the church when the double back doors were propped open, and people began to enter the church to pay their respects. She rose and smoothed the skirt of her navy suit, then went to stand by the coffin. If her father had been murdered as she thought, maybe his killer would come today.

She accepted hugs and condolences as the townspeople flowed down the aisle and moved past the coffin. Toward the back of the church, she saw a familiar set of shoulders towering over the rest, and her spirits lifted even as her pulse blipped in her neck. She'd known Kevin would come. Then she saw the woman behind him.

Ignoring the others ahead of her, Aunt Blanche came toward her. The shapeless black dress she wore billowed out from her lanky frame like a pirate's sail above her startlingly red shoes. Her mostly white hair flowed onto her shoulders in a curtain. As long as Mallory could remember, her aunt had never cut her hair, and the uneven ends gave her an unkempt appearance. Her husband's death during the Vietnam War had sent Aunt Blanche into a depression from which she'd never emerged. She kept a reclusive lifestyle, but when Mom was alive, they'd made the trek as a family to visit her once a month.

Watching her now brought a sharp ache as Mallory realized how much she looked like Dad.

"Mallory." Her aunt embraced her with a waft of strong, flowery perfume emanating from the folds of her dress.

"I didn't think you'd come." Mallory found it hard to talk past the constriction in her throat. She shifted her focus to Kevin as he stopped and shoved his hands in his pockets a few feet behind her aunt.

Aunt Blanche straightened, and her hands fell back to her side. "Your game warden wouldn't take no for an answer. He showed up three hours ago and bullied me into getting dressed. I wanted to come, of course, but well . . ." She tossed her head so her hair fell away from her angular face.

Mallory's gaze met Kevin's. "You convinced her?"

He shrugged. "You needed someone here with you. Carol's great, I'm sure, but at a time like this, you need family."

"I did. Thank you." She looked back at her aunt. "And thank you. I felt so alone before you got here." And Kevin had cared enough to ensure her aunt came. Why had he done it?

Her aunt's gaze flickered past her to the coffin. "Edmund would have approved of a closed casket. It's so barbaric to stare at a poor dead body. That's what convinced me, you know. Not that your game warden didn't have a glib tongue—he did. But when he told me you had opted for a closed casket, I knew you'd grown up to be a woman of taste and wisdom. I wanted to see if I was right."

She stared deeply into Mallory's eyes, and Mallory stared back. What did Aunt Blanche see? A failure who was struggling to earn enough to stay afloat? A flighty daughter who killed her own mother? She waited to see condemnation creep into her aunt's pale-blue eyes, but instead she saw only approval and pride.

The pride shamed her. Didn't Aunt Blanche remember what she'd done?

Mallory broke the intense scrutiny. "You haven't met my daughter, Haylie." Ignoring the slight shake of her daughter's head when she gestured to her, she motioned for Haylie to join them.

Haylie's lips flattened and a frown crouched between her eyes, but she slid off the pew and approached them. Mallory put her hand on her daughter's shoulder and gave a warning squeeze. *Be nice.* She willed Haylie to hear her unspoken command, and the girl stiffened as if she'd caught the import of that tight grip.

"Haylie is fourteen and is a terrific swimmer. She just made the swim team. Haylie, this is Aunt Blanche, Grandpa's sister. She hasn't seen you since you were five, so you probably don't remember."

Haylie looked back at her great-aunt. "Aren't you the one who made the gingersnap cookies? They were awesome. And you had a cat named Puddles."

Aunt Blanche tucked a white strand of hair behind her ear, revealing a large gold hoop in her lobe. "Puddles is still around, too, though she's not so quick to catch mice now. What's your best event? Your mother was an ace freestyle swimmer, but she couldn't do a decent butterfly to save her life. I won the state event back in my junior and senior years."

"That's my best event, too, but I'm working on my butterfly."

While Haylie chatted with her aunt about swim times, Mallory moved closer to Kevin. "I can't believe you got her here. Thank you."

"I thought she'd be good support for you."

She couldn't look away from those warm brown eyes. She wasn't sure their history could ever really be over.

"What's this I hear about you taking over Edmund's mail delivery?" Blanche demanded. "You've got talent with your jewelry, and Kevin tells me you just made a big sale that will really establish your name. Seems foolhardy to throw it all over just to poke around."

Mallory glared at him, and his face colored a bit, though he didn't meet her gaze. So that's why he'd gone to fetch Aunt Blanche. He brought in reinforcements.

"None of us want you hurt," he said. "I'll look into this. So will the sheriff."

Why was he so set on getting rid of her? But the bigger question was, why was she so determined to stay? It was much more than finding her father's killer. It was about finding herself again, but that would seem silly to her aunt and to Kevin. Luckily, she didn't have to answer to either of them.

She put her arm around Haylie and took her aunt's hand. "The service is about to start. Let's get seated."

Mallory had a fistful of gorgeous sea glass after a day strolling the rocky shoreline with Haylie and Carol. She should have been tired, but she was too wired to sleep so she decided to see what she needed to do to start delivering the mail. The knob to Dad's mailroom turned easily under her hand. She opened the door and flipped on the light. Strange. He'd always kept the room locked.

Carol followed her into the small, cramped room overflowing with metal filing cabinets. "Tell me what we're looking for again."

The place hadn't been painted in years, and the tan paint was even dingier than Mallory remembered. The old wooden desk, as big as a dinghy, took up most of the northwest wall. Envelopes, pencils, file folders, and wire baskets covered every bit of the surface. She frowned when she saw all the envelopes on the worn wooden floor too. Someone had ransacked the place.

"It looks like somebody emptied the baskets of mail on the desk and floor. Someone was looking for something." Mallory stepped to the desk and stared at the jumble of envelopes, then flipped open a green file folder. Empty. She riffled through the other folders. "Every folder is empty. Dad never would have left it this way."

Carol pulled open a filing drawer. "This is empty too. I think all the files are here on top of the cabinet."

"This just proves that whatever happened to Dad might have had something to do with the mail delivery. I've been approved to fulfill his contract with the post office. There should be a mail schedule around here somewhere."

Carol pushed her brown bangs out of her eyes and shook her head. She was already in her pajamas, blue fleece ones, and her bare feet peeked out from under the too-long pajama pants. "It will take all night to put this room back together."

"You don't have to stay up. I'll work on it."

"I'll help for a while. I'm not sleepy yet. This is a little scary. What could someone be looking for?"

"I don't know, but I'm going to find out."

"Should we call the sheriff about this?"

"Probably, but I don't feel up to dealing with more questions tonight. He already knows we've had a break-in." Mallory took out her phone and snapped several pictures from different angles. "He'll be able to see what it looked like before we cleaned it up. I think we should organize the mail first. Dad typically used the metal trays to sort it for the various islands."

Mallory sat on the cracked plastic seat of the office chair and scooped a space clear so she could set the trays out. She grabbed a pile of envelopes and dropped them in the baskets by location. Folly Shoals, Swan's Island, and Frenchboro.

Carol knelt to scoop the envelopes on the floor into a pile. "So, tell me about tall, yummy, and handsome. The chemistry between you was as thick as the fog out there tonight."

Mallory's pulse blipped, and her chest felt hot as she wheeled around in the chair to face Carol. "Until a week ago, I'd convinced myself I hardly remembered Kevin. He was part of a past too painful to talk about or remember." Her throat thickened and she swallowed. "But maybe it will help to talk about it. W-we were engaged." She rubbed her forehead. Not now. She couldn't go there right now. She took a deep breath, then exhaled slowly. "I'll tell you about it another time."

Mallory turned the chair back around and felt paper against her foot. This was going to take forever. She rose and pulled the chair out so she could crawl under the desk. There were half a dozen envelopes on the floor by the back left castor. After scooping them up, she started to back out but whacked her head on the drawer above her. She heard an odd click, then the drawer dropped down and she had to duck to avoid it hitting her in the head.

"What on earth?" she muttered.

"What's wrong?" Carol crouched down to peer under the desk at her.

"I think it's a hidden drawer." She rotated so she could sit down and face the chair and Carol. From this angle, she could see into the desk if she had enough light. "There should be a flashlight in the top filing cabinet by the door. Can you grab it?"

Carol nodded. She returned and crouched down to hand the flashlight to Mallory, who flipped it on and shone the light into the recesses of the hidden drawer.

"There's a thick sheaf of papers here." She pulled them out, then crawled out from under the desk. The dust tickled her nose and she sneezed.

She tried to tamp down her excitement. It might be nothing, but why would her father have hidden these papers unless they were important? Sitting at the desk, she unfolded the papers and began to read. "These are just my adoption papers. They're interesting because I've never seen them before, but I don't think they matter now."

"You'd mentioned you were adopted. Have you ever thought about finding your birth mother?"

"After Mom died I thought about it a lot, but I couldn't do it."

A thousand times she'd tried to imagine what that search might look like. Would she find other siblings or maybe just a mother who didn't care? It was too dangerous to contemplate.

"Don't be such a ninny, Mallory. I've never known you to be a coward. It might be time to look for her. You never know what kind of blessing she might end up being to you and Haylie."

Mallory sat back and looked at the papers. "I don't really want to know about her. She gave me away. That said it all."

Carol winced. "That's a sweeping statement. At least she didn't abort you, and she could have."

"True." Her father had said for her to find her mother. Could her birth mother have something to do with this?

TWELVE

The dull roar of the ocean hitting the rocks was a background noise Mallory barely noticed as she spread the papers out on the desk. She hadn't yet touched the packet of letters under the folded sheet that spelled out the details of her adoption. "The names are blacked out, and even the year. October 11 is the date of the final approval though. Mom told me I was two weeks old when they got me so that would make the year 1981."

"They were lucky to get an infant. That's not so easy. What did your mother say about it?"

"We didn't talk about it a lot. I mean, I always knew I was adopted. I don't have a conscious memory of when my parents told me."

"What's going on?" Haylie stood blinking sleepily in the doorway.

Oh boy. Mallory turned to face her daughter, who wore Mallory's fluffy red robe. "Hey, I thought you were sleeping."

Haylie's hair was tousled, and she pushed it out of her face as she stepped into the mail room. "I couldn't sleep. It's too quiet here, and then I heard you talking." She pushed papers out of the way and sat on top of the desk. "Are you finally going to look for your birth mom? I thought you didn't want to find her."

"I didn't, but maybe it's time. According to Mom, my birth mother was an unwed mother without a means of support who loved her baby enough to want a better life for her."

Haylie's brown eyes narrowed. "You sound cynical, like you don't believe it."

"I think you do what you need to do in life even if it's hard. If she'd really loved me, wouldn't she have kept me? I can't imagine giving you away." Mallory smiled at her daughter, who was looking more and more confused and lost. "It's not a big deal, Haylie. Really, you don't need to be upset that I'm looking."

"What if finding them mixes everything up? I mean, you always said this is your real home. That you didn't need to know more."

"And I don't. And in case you're worried about yourself, you know all that's really important. You're Daddy's daughter and mine. You know exactly where you came from. You've grown up in Bangor, you have lived in the same house all your life, and you have great memories of your father."

"You're old, Mom. Why haven't you wanted to find out about your real parents?"

Old. Maybe she was in her daughter's eyes, but she still felt like she did the summer she was twenty. She forced a smile. "I know my real parents. My birth mother and father are unimportant, really."

Carol looked back at her steadily. "I don't buy it. I think knowing you were given up for adoption is another reason you're so afraid of failing."

There was no real way of answering her friend. Mallory couldn't deny she hated to fail or that she edged too close to perfectionism most of the time. Had it started with knowing she'd been given away? Maybe.

Haylie sat on the floor and folded her legs under her. "Well, I think you should find your birth parents. What if they have a lot of money and can help out, Mom? I'm not a kid. I know money has been tight and you're struggling to keep the house. Maybe your real parents would want us now."

Mallory held up her hand. "Don't put yourself into my shoes, honey. They didn't even know about you. And if they wanted to get to know us, they would have found us. It's not that hard these days."

Carol began to stick pencils in a cup. "You don't know that, Mallory. What if you were hidden really well? Or what if they'd kept track of you all these years? There's no way of knowing how they feel."

She rubbed the back of her neck. "I may have no choice if I want to find out what happened to Dad." Mallory pulled the packet of plain white envelopes banded together with a fat rubber band toward her. "These letters were with the adoption papers. I'm not sure why."

The stack of letters was innocuous enough. They shouldn't have made her heart pound in her chest, but they did. Her hand hovered over them. She took a deep breath and tried to quench the fear choking her. Once she opened these, she might never be able to go back to the way things were. Knowing about her past might reveal things that could destroy the life she knew now. Was she ready for that kind of upheaval?

"Mallory?"

Carol's voice calmed her, and she picked up the packet and

unwrapped the band. "There's no return address." Fanning through the letters, Mallory shook her head. "Not on any of them. This is the most recent postmark."

"Maybe you should read the oldest first," Carol suggested.

Mallory nodded and set the stack aside and pulled out the single paper from inside. "This one is postmarked April 1986, so I was five. Looking at the postmark, it probably arrived a day or two before my fifth birthday." She cleared her throat and read the letter aloud.

Dear little one,

I like to imagine you walking the shore with your new mama. Do you love the water? I think you must love the sea and already know how to swim. Your mother says they've named you Mallory. I've called you Audra for years in my heart, so it's hard to get used to the idea that you have a different name. I like Mallory though.

I miss you very much, and I think about you every day. Your mom says she has told you that you're adopted. No matter what, I never stopped loving you. And I never will. You were the most precious little baby I'd ever seen. When you looked up at me with those dark eyes and curled your fingers around mine, I didn't think I could do what had to be done. But I had to.

I hope you like the stuffed cat I sent. Happy birthday!

Love,

Your other mother

Mallory's vision blurred, and when she looked up she saw tears on Carol's and Haylie's cheeks too. "I remember a stuffed kitty. I never remembered where it came from."

"How are you going to find her?" Haylie asked.

"I don't know." Mallory folded the note and put it away. "I guess I have to try. It feels wrong though, like opening Pandora's box."

But did she even want to find the woman? A cauldron of emotions—pain, curiosity, rejection, determination—swirled through her gut. Once it was done, it couldn't be undone.

Kevin slid a plate of bacon and pancakes across the table to his daughter, who smiled up at him and pulled it toward her. Her fingers moved along the spoon until she had it in her grasp firmly enough to feed herself.

"What are we going to do today, Daddy? Can we search for sea glass?"

It always amazed him to watch her run her fingers over the sand to find sea glass. Her fingertips knew the difference between sea glass and any other flotsam tossed onto the shore by the waves. "It's supposed to be sixty today so we could do that."

His cell phone chimed with a call as he reached for the ice drawer to give Fiona a couple of cubes. "Good girl." He glanced at the phone and gave a sigh. Adelaide again. "Game Warden O'Connor."

"He's at it again." Adelaide Wilson was an eighty-five-year-old widow who lived in downtown Folly Shoals. Her apartment was above Libby's Sweet Shop and across from the fire station. She walked three miles every day and was a common sight with her red felt hat and walking stick. Kevin had changed her tire for her once, and ever since, she thought he was the only Maine warden around.

She viewed every event happening on Folly Shoals as her personal duty to report to Kevin, and she posted everything on the game warden's Facebook page. If no one responded to her within half an hour, she called Kevin. That meant at least five calls a week from her.

"Who's at it again?" Kevin rinsed his hands and glanced out the kitchen window at a vole scurrying through last autumn's leaves. His remote cabin was miles from any town, and he loved living way out here, though he often wondered if he should move to town for Sadie's sake. Getting her to and from school or to a playdate was a constant challenge with his work schedule.

"George Paschal. He's running his ATV through Harry's woods again."

ATV use was forbidden on private land without the owner's approval. Harry Harner had all his land posted and was known to go ballistic over hunters, ATVs, and snowmobiles on his property. "Harry hasn't called."

"I doubt he knows, but I saw George with my own two eyes."

"I'll check into it, but Harry is the one who should be making this call." Kevin knew his rebuke wouldn't slow her down. Maybe she should have been a game warden herself.

"I'll let you know if I see him again."

The phone clicked in Kevin's ear, and he gave another sigh before putting it on the kitchen table. Tires crunched on gravel outside, and he looked through the window again to see Mallory's Toyota pull to a stop at the side of the house by the kitchen door. She must have taken the first ferry to the mainland this morning because it was barely nine o'clock. She and Haylie got out of the car and headed toward the door.

After the funeral two days ago, she'd given him the cold

shoulder, and he couldn't say he blamed her. The last thing he wanted was to run into her every time he turned around and be reminded of the past. And what did she think she was going to accomplish by poking into things? He was afraid she'd end up at the bottom of the sea.

"We've got company." With the dog on his heels, he opened the door. "I wasn't expecting to see you so early this morning."

"Haylie was going crazy cooped up in the cottage so I thought I'd see if you and Sadie wanted to take a drive up to Jonesport and do a little looking for sea glass."

Haylie peered past him at Sadie. "Mom promised ice cream. There *is* an ice-cream shop up that way, isn't there?" She tossed her head as if daring him to deliver any news but the one she wanted.

"Unfortunately, no. But we can grab some in Summer Harbor before we leave." The kid's attitude wasn't as pronounced as the last time he'd seen her, but it still raised his hackles. Would Sadie be that contrary as she grew? "Come on in. We're just finishing breakfast." He stepped aside so they could enter, then shut the door behind them.

He should have emptied the dishwasher this morning and loaded up the dishes. The kitchen looked even smaller with the stove covered with pans and flour spilled across the dark-gray counter and onto the gray ceramic-tile floor.

Sadie rose with her hand still on the oak table. "Who's here, Daddy?"

He glanced toward Mallory and didn't see surprise, only interest. Had he ever told Mallory his daughter was blind and had a seeing-eye dog? He didn't think so, but she might have heard it from her dad. "This is my friend Mallory and her daughter, Haylie."

Mallory stepped closer to his daughter and pulled something from the pocket of her jacket. "Hi, Sadie, I've heard a lot about you. I make sea-glass jewelry, and I brought you something. It's a mermaid-moon necklace." She held up a necklace, then pressed her lips together as if realizing what she'd just done. Reaching out, she took Sadie's hand and put the necklace into her palm. "It's really pretty, just like you."

"I love sea glass." Sadie ran her fingers around the edges of the necklace. "Thank you. Daddy said we could look for sea glass. I just like to hold it, but it must be fun to make jewelry." Her voice was wistful. "What's a mermaid moon? What does it look like?"

"My mother used to tell me a pink moon gave a mermaid power to overcome her troubles and make a new start. So the round piece you feel is watermelon tourmaline. It's a very soft pink and green like watermelon. The raised pieces of glass on it make up a mermaid. This one has two tiny pieces of ruby-red sea glass for her eyes."

Sadie ran her fingers over it. "It feels so pretty. Did you know sea glass comes from mermaid tears? Daddy said you lived at Mermaid Point. Have you ever seen a mermaid?"

"Mermaids aren't real," Haylie said in a lofty voice.

Sadie's face fell. "I know, but it's fun to think about them."

Mallory shot Haylie a look and mouthed, *Be nice*, then motioned to Fiona. "And who's this fine golden? Is she your dog?"

Sadie nodded. "This is my guide dog, Fiona."

Mallory's attention swung to Kevin, and he saw the amusement there. Their favorite movie had been *Shrek*, and he'd never admitted to anyone that whenever he spoke Fiona's name, he remembered snuggling on the sofa with Mallory.

Haylie's brown eyes widened. "I've never seen a real guide dog. She's beautiful. Is it okay to pet her?"

"Yes, she's not working at the moment. Once I put her vest on, she knows not to go to anyone's side but Sadie's."

Haylie petted the dog and crooned to her. "Can you see anything at all, Sadie?"

Kevin tried to mask his wince, then realized the question didn't bother Sadie at all. She'd probably heard it a thousand times at school. Instead of answering for his daughter, he shut his mouth and went to set his coffee cup in the stainless steel sink.

"I can see light and dark a little. I was born early and it just happened. But it's okay because I have Fiona." Sadie reached out, and her dog quickly bumped her hand with her head. "How old are you? I'm eight."

"I'm much older than you, nearly fifteen. I like little kids though. I babysit for the neighbor sometimes when she has to run to the store for a minute." Haylie leaned against the counter. "Can we go now? I want to do something fun."

"We could take the boat around to Jonesport instead of driving. It would be faster," Kevin said.

Mallory tucked a curl behind her ear. "I was hoping you'd ask. I have something I want to talk to you about."

He eyed her determined expression. "Let me get my boat keys."

THIRTEEN

Mallory took off her shoes and let her feet soak up the chill from the sand. The water was as blue as the Caribbean, but still cold this early in the spring. She'd missed this so much.

Jonesport was a charming village made up of saltbox homes weathering in the salt air. The town boasted a Coast Guard station, and a bridge crossed the beautiful blue water over to Beals Island. From their vantage point, she could see boats dotting the harbor of the offshore island. The bay was a beautiful curve of sand, and even now, she caught glints of sea glass in the rocks and sand.

She watched Kevin watch his daughter as Sadie moved confidently along the uneven terrain with the help of the dog. Haylie ran along with them, and the laughter of the children mingled with the squawk of the seagulls and the distant rumble of boat engines. They had the beach to themselves too.

Kevin cupped his hands to his mouth. "Don't go too far, kids. Stay where we can see you."

"She's amazing, Kevin. You've done such a great job with her. Her disability doesn't seem to faze her at all. What happened, if you don't mind me asking?"

He shoved his hands in his pockets, and a line formed on his smooth brow. "She was born blind. She was born so early that we didn't think she'd live. She had stage-three retinopathy. They tried laser surgery, but it didn't work. She's got a great attitude though."

Mallory's heart squeezed at the thought of not just watching a tiny infant struggle to live but then finding out she'd be blind. "I'm sorry, Kevin."

"We don't need your pity. She's bright and healthy otherwise."

His cold answer stung and she straightened. "That was compassion you heard, not pity. It's clear she's strong and can overcome just about anything. But it's not easy for her or for you."

His gaze finally met hers. "I didn't mean to bite your head off. I have to guard her against people who make her doubt her abilities, and it's gotten to be second nature."

"And you're not happy I'm staying." She stared him down and dared him to contradict her. His meddling with her aunt had proven how far he'd go to get her out of town.

His eyes softened, but he shook his head. "You're in over your head, and I'm afraid you're going to leave Haylie an orphan if you keep poking around. Let the sheriff and me do our jobs. You're better off picking up your life again and trying to put this behind you."

"Are you sure that's all it is? Ever since I got here, I've had the feeling you'll be glad to see the back of me."

His mouth flattened, and he put his hands in his pockets. "I don't want to talk about our history. Just go home and let me handle this."

"And how do you propose I do that when my house was broken into back in Bangor? The guy was looking for me, Kevin. He didn't steal anything, but if I'd been there, I have no idea what he might have done. Killed me, too, maybe. I can't run from this. I'm surprised you think I could."

What was his problem? Did he think she would cause him trouble of some kind? Did he still resent her so much that he begrudged her a life back in her hometown?

She lifted her chin and glared at him. "I don't need your help. I'm going to fulfill Dad's contract delivering the mail, and if I hear anything important, I'll pass it along to the sheriff. I'll try to stay out of your life." To her mortification, she felt the hot sting of tears, but she blinked furiously and refused to give in to her emotion.

What had she expected? That he would realize the moment he saw her that he hadn't put her behind him? Their relationship had been over fifteen years ago. Maybe she'd been naive to think they could at least be on friendly terms. Especially after the way she'd left him to face the gossip by himself.

He pulled his hands from his pockets and held out his hand. "Let's have a fresh start. I didn't intend to make you feel unwelcome. We can at least be civil." A muscle hardened in his jaw. "And maybe you do need to stay here and face whatever it is. Flush the guy out. Catching him might be the only way."

His words sapped the anger from her and she inhaled, then nodded. "Apology accepted."

"You said you wanted to talk to me about something. Was catching this guy what you wanted to discuss?"

A glint of royal blue caught her eye, and she stooped to pick up a piece of sea glass. "Not exactly." She rolled it in her fingers and watched two men plucking periwinkles from the rocks. She hadn't tasted the small snails in years. Her mom used to pickle them, and seeing the harvest brought a wave of nostalgia. Her mom used to call them wrinkles.

"Mallory?"

She looked up into Kevin's warm brown eyes. "I need a favor."

His eyes went wary. "Okay."

"I want to find my birth mother."

He blinked. "Whoa, where did that come from? Why now, of all times?"

"Dad said for me to find my mother. What if he was talking about my birth mother? Maybe she's connected in some way to this. I found my adoption papers hidden in his desk. Why would Dad hide them in a secret drawer? It seems strange."

"I'm hardly an expert on tracking down adoption records, but I might know someone who is."

"You don't think I'm crazy? This could be a rabbit trail."

He shrugged. "We have to examine every path right now. Nothing ventured, nothing gained." His gaze followed hers. "Want some wrinkles? They'd probably sell them."

"I wouldn't have the vaguest idea how to pickle them." But her mouth watered at the thought.

"It's time Haylie experienced real Downeast cuisine." He hailed the two men and walked toward them.

Mallory watched his broad back. His take-charge attitude was going to be an asset in her quest. As long as she protected her heart.

The blue sky overhead deepened the brilliant color of the ocean as Mallory headed out on her first mail run now that she had possession of her dad's boat. The sea spray left a salty taste on Mallory's lips that reminded her of the wrinkles Kevin had fixed for all of them. Her father's boat responded to the throttle with a surge of speed and a purr from the engine. Everything she'd learned about navigating a boat had come back to her in a flash once she was aboard. It was like riding a bike—impossible to forget. Where had he gotten the money for such an expensive craft? The question swirled in her head as she steered the boat toward the dock.

The bow hit the dock bumpers, and she quickly tied off, then grabbed the bag of mail and stepped onto the pier's weathered gray boards. Rocks embedded into the hillside served as steps up the steep slope to the blue building, its paint peeling from the sun and salt. There wasn't much mail to deliver to this island, about ten envelopes and a newspaper. The door stuck a bit as she tried to open it, but she jiggled the knob and succeeded in pushing it open. A woman standing by the coffeepot stared at her with a curious expression.

"I'm Mallory Davis, Edmond Blanchard's daughter." She held up the bag of mail. "It took a few days to get permission to take over Dad's mail route."

The woman's gray hair was atop her head in a messy bun with a pencil stuck through it. She wore small, round glasses halfway down her nose, à la John Lennon, and her plump figure strained the seams of the men's overalls. A discreet name badge on her ample chest read *Dixie*.

"Bless your heart, honey." Her accent was as thick as Georgia mud. "I'm so sorry about your daddy. He was a good man."

A lump formed in her throat as she pulled out the mail and handed it to Dixie. "Thank you." She followed Dixie to the battered wooden counter at the back of the twenty-by-twenty room.

Dixie went behind the counter. "Folks will be glad to get

their mail. It's been a week since our last delivery." There was no condemnation in her tone, just sympathy.

Mallory leaned on the counter. "Did you know my father well?"

The light in Dixie's eyes dimmed. "Not as well as I would have liked. I dangled the bait, but your daddy wasn't biting. Might have been because I was a flatlander. Even after twenty years here, the locals think I'll go back to Georgia any day. Plus, I think he never got over your mama's death."

Mallory barely suppressed a wince. "No, I don't think he did." Dixie's left hand was bare of rings. "Did Dad ever mention having an enemy? Was he afraid at all?"

Dixie's penciled-in brows rose. "Scared? Your daddy? Not hardly. He had a gimlet stare that would put the fear of God in anyone." She adjusted the pencil in her hair.

"Any idea where he got the money for that new boat?"

Dixie inhaled. "We've all yawed about it here on Walker's Roost. He went from that rickety old boat that used bumpers to keep it afloat to that shiny new toy he was so proud of. I asked him about it once, and he grinned and said his ship had come in. Investments, I reckoned."

Mallory pressed her lips together. Her dad didn't believe in the stock market, and he was as tight with his money as bark on a birch tree. She couldn't see him risking even a dollar on the market. "When did he get it?"

"You don't seem to know much about your daddy. The two of you have a falling out?"

"Not really. Just busy lives."

Dixie began to sort the envelopes into piles. "He launched that pretty new boat the Friday before Labor Day. I remember because I tried to get him to take me on a picnic on Labor Day, but my request fell as flat as a cake with no baking powder. That man was as cagey as Al Capone. But it worked out for the best. I got me a beau anyway. Walker Rocco."

"Luke's dad?"

"You know Luke?"

"Most of my life."

The more time she was with Dixie, the more Mallory liked her. She would have made a great stepmother. Had Dad ever dated? She'd never heard him talk about another woman.

She slid a business card across the counter to Dixie. "If you think of anything else, could you call my cell?"

The other woman picked it up and glanced at it. "Sea-glass jewelry, eh? You should comb the beach on the other side of Walker's Roost. It glitters so much with sea glass you'd think there was buried treasure there."

"I'll do that." Mallory turned to go.

"Oh, one more thing, honey. I just remembered something. I was cruising past Folly Shoals on my boat and saw your daddy standing out on Mermaid Point with a slick sort in a suit. They were both gesturing like they were arguing. I'd never seen the man before, and there was a fifty-foot yacht anchored in the cove."

"Did you see the name of the yacht?"

Dixie's forehead wrinkled. "It was *Wind* something. Part of the name was hard to read because there was a whale painted through it. The last letter was an *R*."

The possibilities were endless. "Could you tell if it was one word or two?"

Dixie shook her head. "I think it was two words, but I wouldn't swear to it. I'll admit I got as close as I dared, but I couldn't make it out."

"If you see it again, can you call me?" If the boat owner had anything to do with Dad's death, he was long gone, but Mallory tried to hold on to hope.

"Of course." Dixie scooped up a pile of envelopes and disappeared through the door to the back.

If Mallory only knew what state registration the boat held. She could search a database of names and find out something. Right now it was like looking for plankton in the ocean.

The giggling shrieks of the two little girls set Julia on edge as she lay on her belly in the tall weeds with their budding flowers of pink and purple. Mosquitoes swarmed her, and the annoying buzz in her ears made her want to scream. The scent of mud and weeds filled her nose. The countryside was beautiful when viewed from the climate-controlled interior of a Lexus, but this up-close-and-personal view was more than she wanted.

She brought the binoculars to her eyes and focused on the children. Mallory's girl was fourteen but looked older with her curvy figure. Kids matured so early these days. When Julia was fourteen, she was still playing board games and riding a bicycle. Haylie looked like bicycles were beneath her. But she seemed nice enough to the game warden's kid. A golden retriever barked and ran after a Frisbee that Sadie tossed across the grass, greening nicely in the sunshine they'd had the last few days. The dog fetched it and carried it back with her tail held high and her ears lifted.

"Good girl!" Sadie's voice carried on the wind.

Julia studied a row of shrubs closer to the girls. If she crawled she could get close enough to hear a little better. The trick was to do it without being detected. She swore under her breath as her right knee sank into cold, wet mud. The jeans cost the earth, and if the stain didn't come out, Ian was going to buy her new ones.

Creeping along on her hands and knees, she got to the line of shrubbery and peered through the space between two branches. It let her see all the way to Mallory's front door. Julia was closer to the sea here, too, and the breeze helped disperse the mosquitoes.

A woman exited the house with a yard chair. She was older than Mallory, and Julia tried to figure out who she might be. Nanny maybe? Though she couldn't see how Mallory could afford a nanny, and Haylie didn't strike her as a kid who would take kindly to being looked after when she thought she was so grown up.

Haylie glanced toward the woman. "Carol, did you ask Mom about taking us to the mainland? If I have to go to this podunk school, I want to join the swim team, and there's an organizational meeting for the summer team."

The woman, Carol, glanced toward the house, then back at Haylie. "I'm not sure it's wise to do anything extra right now when we're all trying to stay safe."

"You can't be serious. I can't give up my swimming. You have to convince her. If I stop swimming now, I'll never catch up. I want to make the Olympic team someday."

"You think your mom can really afford fancy swimming lessons? Even in Bangor she was barely making ends meet. I think you need to grow up, honey. You don't seem to notice how hard she works to make sure you have what you need. Give her a little credit. She's doing the best she can."

Haylie's hands balled into fists. "I have to swim!"

Spoiled brat, that's what she was. Julia was beginning to rethink her objection to taking the kid. Maybe it would teach her a thing or two.

A twig snapped beside her and she jerked around to look, then relaxed when she saw her stepson's right-hand man. "What are you doing here?"

Frank Richards crawled up beside her. "Helping out."

"I've got this under control." She never should have hired him. He was too much of a risk taker, too eager to show Ian how well he could do. Someone more impartial would have been better.

He squinted toward the house. "I think we need to get rid of the evidence."

"What?" She turned back and looked at the children playing in the yard. "Not with kids there."

"I can do it if you don't have the stomach for it."

Julia looked back toward the house. "Let's circle around to the side and see if we can hear anything inside the house."

Fourteen

Maybe he'd actually get through a Saturday without a call. Kevin parked his truck in front of Breakwater Cottage, then hopped out and opened the door for Sadie and Fiona. The dog's tail wagged, and he gave her a pat as she waited to assist Sadie to the house. Mallory had called him after getting back from the mail run today to tell him what Dixie said. He couldn't think of anyone fitting that description, but he had an idea he wanted to talk to her about.

Mallory and Haylie stepped out the screen door and onto the front porch. Haylie rushed toward him and Sadie, and at first he thought maybe she was warming up to him. Then she cast a glance back toward her mom and came close enough to whisper.

"Can you convince my mom to let me join the swim team here? She has me locked up like I'm in jail. It's like she's afraid to let me out of her sight. I'm going *crazy*."

He put his hand on her shoulder. "She has cause to be worried, Haylie."

"What can happen at swim team? I mean, come on, the place will be crawling with adults."

The kid had a point. "I'll see what I can do." She looked too much like Mallory for him to offer much resistance.

Her lips curved in a smile, and she took Sadie's hand. "Let's throw a Frisbee to Fiona. I'll throw the Frisbee toward your feet so if the dog misses it, you can find it."

"Okay." Sadie's sweet face lit with a smile.

Kevin watched them go with an odd ache in his chest. Haylie seemed to be looking for ways to help Sadie be more like a normal kid, and he was grateful. Most teenagers wouldn't have bothered.

Mallory lifted a brow as he reached her on the porch. "What was that all about?"

"Swim team." When she started to shake her head, he put his hand on her arm. "She has a point, Mallory. You can't keep her locked up. I know you want to protect her, but I know the swim team coaches. One is a big guy who used to be in the Marines, and the other is a no-nonsense woman who also teaches martial arts. Haylie'll be safe."

"You're all ganging up on me. Carol is trying to talk me into it too." She slanted a glance up at him. "You're sure she'll be safe?"

"As safe as at school. Loosen the apron strings, little mama."

Amusement sparked in her eyes. "Okay." She called Haylie over and told her she could go join the swim team. "When is the next practice?"

Haylie's ponytail bounced as she hugged her mother. "It's this afternoon. Thanks, Mom!"

Kevin winked at her, and she reached over and deposited a quick kiss on his cheek before rushing back to join Sadie.

Carol, dressed in khaki slacks and a blue Windbreaker, stepped through the door. "What's all the excitement?"

"Swim team. I finally said yes." Worry still creased Mallory's brow. "I hope I don't regret it."

"She'll be fine. I think I'll go play with the girls. My back

109

hurts from working at my computer all morning, and I need some exercise."

"Thanks, Carol," Mallory called after her, then smiled up at Kevin. "She's just making sure I'm not worrying while we're in my office. I've been going through things to see if I can find a clue to my birth parents. Come with me."

He followed her to the office. A big wooden desk, covered with bins of mail, took up most of the room. "Shew, it's stuffy in here. Mind if I open a window?"

She picked up some papers on the desk. "Have at it." She frowned. "Oh shoot, I need to run get my adoption papers out of the car. I took them to town to make copies because Dad's printer didn't have a photocopier."

Kevin struggled with the sticky window until he managed to get it up. "I thought you swore you'd never track down your birth parents. Are you sure you want to do this?" The salt-laden breeze lifted his hair and cleared the room of the stale odor from being shut up.

She started for the door and stopped. "I have to. Dad mentioned my mother, and it couldn't be Mom he was referring to. It has to be my birth mother."

She looked super cute today with her dark hair pulled back in a long braid. The dark circles were gone from under her eyes, and there was a flush of color on her cheeks. He averted his gaze. Any attraction he felt was just the lingering mist from when he was young.

"The first thing I have to do is find out her name. Then maybe I can track her down."

"That's one of the things I wanted to talk to you about. I know a private investigator in Louisville, Abby McKinley. Let me give her a call." He whipped out his cell phone and called up her number. Mallory leaned against the door frame, obviously interested in what he might learn.

Abby answered on the first ring. "Kevin, I haven't heard from you in forever. How's everything in my favorite state?"

"Nice now that spring is here. Listen, I have a job for you—finding my friend's birth mother. It's pretty important and may be tied to a murder." Mallory flinched at the word *murder*, and he realized he'd never called her dad's death a murder until now.

"Sure, give me the details and I'll see what I can find out this week. Those are usually pretty easy to track down these days."

"I don't know a lot." He gave her Mallory's name and birth date and the names of her adoptive parents.

"That should be enough to get started. This probably is none of my business, but has she had counseling? It's recommended these days to make sure an adopted child is ready for what she may find out. I mean, the parents could be convicts . . . they could be on welfare and eager for a handout from her. It might not be pretty."

"I don't think she has, but right now there doesn't seem to be much of a choice."

Abby let out a heavy sigh. "If I have any questions, may I call her?"

He gave her Mallory's cell phone number as he wandered over to the window. A flutter of movement by the shrubs bordering the yard caught his attention. Frowning, he leaned closer and saw someone disappear into the trees. The shadows were too deep for him to make out more than the person's baseball cap.

He ended the call and dropped the phone into his pocket. "Someone was watching the house."

Mallory's dark-brown eyes went wide, and she wheeled toward the door. "The girls!"

"They're fine. I can see them, and Carol is throwing a Frisbee with them. But I want to look around. Tell Carol to take them to town for ice cream and then on to swim practice. I'll see if I can track this guy. I'd like them away from here."

He strode after her to exit the kitchen door and hurry toward the grassy area where the children played. His boots sank in the soft ground, and he paused as he reached the row of shrubs.

It didn't take much of an investigation to see the impression where someone had laid on the ground and watched the house. The same person who had ransacked the office?

Mallory sent Carol away with the children, then ran to catch up with Kevin. She batted away bugs as she followed him. How was he even following the trail? She couldn't see anything in the short grass and weeds, but he was like a bloodhound tracking a scent as he climbed over rocks and through wild-blueberry barrens. His muscular arms flexed against his brown game warden shirt as he pushed branches aside for her.

He'd always been tall and strong, but the years had broadened his shoulders and chiseled his features even more. In his early twenties he'd been handsome. At thirty-five, he compelled attention in a way that went beyond mere good looks. Being around him was going to test her fortitude in ways she hadn't expected.

She forced her attention back to the ground. "Can you tell who it was?"

"Someone light—either a teenager, a small man, or a woman."

"Lots of open territory here." She stopped to wave away a cloud of insects.

He stopped at the top of the hillside looking down into the cove. "The granite steps lead to the water here. Whoever it was came by boat." He squinted in the bright sunshine. "Several boats out there, but they're too far to see anything."

The only boat she recognized was her dad's blue-and-white one bobbing at the dock.

He shoved his hands in his pocket as he turned back to face her. He opened his mouth, then stopped for a second. "You smell that?"

She started to say no, then the acrid scent of smoke came to her nose. "Smoke?"

"Fire!"

When he pointed, she saw flames licking the roof and spilling out the windows. She started back toward the house, but he grabbed her arm. "Wait. Let me check it out."

She lifted her chin. "I'm going with you." She shook off his grip and darted along the edge of the trees toward her house.

The structure was fully engulfed in flames. Even if the fire department arrived this minute, they'd never be able to save it. A weight pressed against her chest. Gone. Everything inside would be incinerated. Pictures, trophies, all the little mementos.

Her arms felt like lead and her legs didn't want to hold her. She fell to her knees in the damp grass and stared at the flames flaring high in the spring wind. Crackling, popping, and whooshing sounds of fire mingled with the sound of breaking glass and falling beams. How could it have spread so far so fast?

Kevin rushed past her, but an explosion of flames forced him back. The heat of it baked against Mallory's face until her skin felt tight. Her eyes burned, both from the smoke and the unshed tears she struggled to hold back. The smoke filled her lungs and made her cough. All her childhood memories were in this place. The flames consumed them in front of her eyes.

Kevin knelt beside her and slipped his arm around her waist, pulling her against him. Even the spicy scent of his cologne failed to push away the choking odor of smoke. She let her head fall to its natural place in the crook of his neck and allowed the tears to escape.

"I'm sorry, Mal." He pressed his lips against her forehead.

The familiar nickname and the kiss both gave her fresh courage. "Someone set this fire, didn't they? It went up so fast. There had to be an accelerant."

His chocolate-brown eyes narrowed, and he nodded. "I smelled gasoline."

She smelled it, too, then, a cloyingly sweet scent mingled with the smoke. "What if Haylie had been inside? Or anyone else, for that matter?"

"I think whoever it was knew Carol had taken the kids and left us here. I'm not sure what message they're sending either. What was the point of burning the house?"

"Maybe they think if I don't have a home, I'll have to leave." She pulled away and stood.

Rubbing at her stinging eyes, she stared at the house as several rafters groaned and collapsed. Glowing embers fanned into the air and blew toward them. Kevin pulled her farther away from the fire as the heat intensified.

What *would* she do now? Her father was a stickler for

insurance, but it would take months to rebuild. Where would she and Haylie live in the meantime? Going back to Bangor wasn't an option, not with someone after her. The only way to make all this stop was to find out who was targeting her. And why.

Kevin backed her away a few more feet. "I have a big house. You, Carol, and Haylie are welcome to stay with me."

"We could probably stay with Aunt Blanche too."

He shook his head. "An old woman isn't going to protect you. And the stress of having you all there would probably be hard on her. Besides, the travel would be rough. Don't be stubborn. We'll be chaperoned with Carol there."

The thought of staying at his house drew her—and scared her to death. If she was already feeling this pull toward him, how much harder would it be to see him every morning and every night? But he wanted to help her find whoever was behind all this. Not even the sheriff seemed all that interested, though maybe this act of arson would change his mind.

She stared up into Kevin's face, searching his expression for any sign of uncertainty. "I guess I don't have much choice."

He lifted a brow. "Don't make it sound like a death sentence. I don't think whoever did this is going to stop. At least with me, you'll have some protection."

"I don't even have my gun any longer. My purse was in the kitchen."

So was her phone and all their belongings. Haylie would be upset too. "We'll have to make a run to my house in Bangor and get some things."

"You're not going back there alone. I'll take you." His voice was grim. "And I've got a small revolver you can borrow."

"Thank you." Her gaze collided with his, and she thought she saw a hint of yearning in his face. Or was it wishful thinking? They'd both moved on long ago. She had to be careful not to read too much into his concern.

FIFTEEN

What was he thinking bringing Mallory here? Kevin tossed the last pillow on the bed and gave a quick look around the bedroom. He could hear Mallory's voice upstairs in Sadie's room as she got Haylie settled.

Sadie was thrilled to have Haylie sharing her room, but he suspected Mallory's daughter would be less happy. Carol's room was down the hall, and he'd put Mallory in his bedroom near Sadie. The thought of her in his bed nearly made him crazy, but he wanted to take the downstairs bedroom so any intruder would have to get through him first.

He shut the door and went back to the living room, where he found her going through a photo album of Sadie's first year. "She was cute, wasn't she?"

Looking up, Mallory closed the book. "She still is. And more than that, she's wonderful and well adjusted. I always knew you'd be a good dad."

The blood drained from his face at her reference, and the anger he'd kept in check for days flared out of control. "And that's why you were so quick to run off when you lost the baby?"

In long strides he made for the door. He never should have

brought her here. He stepped out into the cool breeze. The sunset gave a colorful show as it sank over the budding trees to the west. He inhaled and tried to grab the tail of his rage.

The door squeaked behind him, and he smelled the scent of her vanilla shampoo. "We have to talk about it, Kevin. I knew you were still mad."

He turned and, keeping his distance, leaned against the porch post. "What was so much better about Brian? You left here and married him practically the next day."

Her big brown eyes held an ocean of sorrow. "Everyone thought you only wanted to marry me because I was pregnant. I wasn't so sure myself."

"Don't give me that, Mallory. You were out of here like a shotgun blast. Were you afraid I'd never match Brian's income potential?" A bitter laugh escaped his lips and he set his jaw. "As it happened, you were right. But we're happy, me and Sadie, even if I'm not rolling in dough."

She looked away, but not before he caught a glimmer of moisture in her eyes. "It wasn't that at all, Kevin. I . . . I felt Mom's death was punishment for o-our sin. That I didn't deserve to be happy." She passed her hand over her forehead. "I was stupid, okay? When I look back, I realize how messed up my thinking was, but it's too late to fix it now."

"It's too late, all right." A movement caught his eye, and he saw the sheriff's big 4 x 4 pickup roll to a stop. "The sheriff's here."

Just as well. There wasn't much to be said about the situation. It was done.

The big sheriff unwound his long legs from under the wheel,

hiked up his belt, then headed toward the house. He pushed his hat away from his forehead and lifted a hand to Kevin when he met him at the steps. "Got a minute?"

"Of course." Kevin opened the door and stepped aside to allow him to enter. "Mug up?"

"Ayuh, I wouldn't say no." Danny's hazel eyes were sober above his flowing red mustache.

"I'll get some coffee."

The flush in her cheeks deepened when she saw the sheriff, and her expression went wary. "Sheriff Colton. Any news about the fire?"

The sheriff took off his hat, revealing his bald head, and turned it in his hands. "Looks to be arson, Mrs. Davis. Lots of gasoline in your dad's office. Any idea what the arsonist might have wanted to destroy in that room?"

She shook her head and went to sit on the blue-plaid sofa. "That was the mail room, but I'd delivered all the mail that had collected there."

Danny's eyes narrowed. "Makes me wonder if someone had hoped to prevent a letter from being mailed. First your dad dies and now this."

"So you believe me about Dad's death—that it wasn't an accident?"

"Maybe. This incident makes me wonder what really happened. I'm going to look into Edmund's death a little more." He stared down at her from his six-foot-seven height. "I hear you've been poking around yourself."

She crossed her jean-clad legs. "Who told you?"

"I ran into Dixie out on Walker's Roost this morning. She's

all exercised about this, so if she says to take a look at Edmund's death, I'm going to do it."

"I guess that makes me chopped liver." Kevin grinned to take the sting out of his words. At least he wouldn't have to buck Danny as they looked into this. "What can I do to help?"

"You get called to people's homes pretty much every day. Keep your ears open, ask if anyone knows if Edmund had mentioned anything. Someone has to know something."

Mallory clasped her hands over her knee and leaned forward. "Did Dixie tell you about the argument she saw between Dad and a guy in a suit?"

Danny shuffled his size-fifteen feet and took a sip of his coffee. "She didn't mention that. Just said you were suspicious that his death wasn't an accident."

Kevin watched Mallory as she told Danny about the argument. Every emotion showed in her expressive dark eyes and full lips. When she was twenty, there was never any question of what she was thinking or feeling, but since she'd returned, he noticed she held back. He wanted to smile at the way the old Mallory was showing herself now, even if it was dangerous to his equanimity.

"Any idea who the man might have been?" Danny asked.

Mallory rose and paced the floor. "Dixie had never seen him before, but I'd like to know where my dad got the money to buy that big boat. Dad was a simple man—a mailman. Since Mom's death he'd lived on about forty thousand dollars a year. Luckily, he owned the house free and clear, but that boat was easily two hundred thousand dollars. Where'd he get it?"

Danny stroked his red mustache. "That's a real good question, Mrs. Davis. It should be easy enough to find out how he paid for it. I'll get back to you on that."

"The guy was some kind of businessman from the way Dixie described him. What if he was a loan shark or something? Maybe Dad was gambling and made enough money to buy the boat, then lost it all and was in debt to that guy?"

Danny held up a big paw. "Come into the wind. I never knew your dad to gamble, did you?"

The animation on Mallory's face evaporated, and she shook her head. "He thought gamblers were the stupidest people on the face of the earth. But he was lonely. Maybe his views changed. I just don't know what to think."

At the pain in her voice, Kevin wanted to go to her side and slip his arm around her waist, but he forced himself to stay where he was by the garden window.

Danny clapped his hat back onto his head. "I'll make some inquiries about that boat, check with some bookies I know. I don't want you to worry. We'll get to the bottom of it."

Kevin blocked his exit to the door. "And what about the arsonist? That's worrisome on its own, Sheriff. Someone broke into Mallory's house in Bangor, and now someone has burned down Breakwater Cottage. It's not just about her dad, but about her." When the color drained from her face, he wished he'd kept his mouth shut. "Someone killed her dad, and I think that same someone is after her. We have to get to him first."

"Ayuh, and I plan to do just that."

Kevin curled his fingers into fists and stared at Mallory. "We'll keep you safe, Mallory."

Trust replaced the fear in her eyes. "I know you'll both do your best, Kevin."

Would his best be good enough? What if he hadn't been there today and the girls had all been in the house? The place went up so fast. They would have been overcome by smoke before they could get out.

The bed squeaked as Mallory sat on the edge of the mattress. She felt Kevin's presence in this house like the whisper of wind on her skin or the way the sun emerged from a cloud and caressed her arm with a hint of warmth. Everything in the house exuded his strength and compassion. If not for him, she'd have no choice but to return to Bangor and whoever waited for her there.

She'd known he hadn't forgiven her for what she'd done, but seeing his rage today had her rethinking her options. Maybe her dad's insurance would pay for her to stay at Hotel Tourmaline, but sorting it all out would take time, and she didn't have the money to stay there on her own. Kate didn't have room, not with Claire there right now. Aunt Blanche lived too far away. The options weren't good.

Carol shut the door behind her and held her finger to her lips. She winked at Mallory. "Well, that didn't turn out too badly. Nice digs, and I think I can stand to look at him over the breakfast table."

Heat settled in Mallory's cheeks. "If I'd had any choice, I wouldn't have come here." She told Carol about the argument.

Carol settled onto a straight-back chair by the door. "There is enough heat flowing between you two to rival molten lava. That kind of chemistry isn't something to ignore, and he's bound to still be mad. I can see a lot of love was there once, and I think it's still there. You moved on, but I don't think you ever got over him, not really. This will give you a chance to see what's still left."

"There is *nothing* left but bad memories. He made that clear." Mallory didn't want to talk about it. If she let herself linger on what used to be, she'd go crazy.

She rose and walked around the room, the wood floors cool against her bare feet. The pictures on the walls drew her attention. She studied one of Kevin holding an infant swaddled in pink. "Sadie's a newborn here. He's so proud."

"He's a good dad. You can tell she's his main focus. He's lived here all his life, hasn't he? What about his family?"

Mallory turned and went back to the bed. It was time for all of it to come out. "His family has lived here for generations. His dad was a game warden, too, but he never wanted Kevin to go into that field. His dad dropped out of medical school when Kevin's mom was pregnant with him. He always made Kevin feel that he'd ruined all the plans he had for his life."

Carol winced. "The things parents saddle their kids with."

She didn't want to go there. Mallory had enough regrets of her own. "Kevin was a whiz at science, all subjects really, but he won every state science award out there. His dad wanted him to go to med school."

"But Kevin didn't see it that way?"

"Exactly. He loved being outdoors, and he wanted to protect Maine's wildlife. He's happiest when he's walking the old trails and rescuing orphaned animals."

"He's a caretaker at heart. You can see that with how he is with his daughter. And how he is with you, too, really. He was Johnny-on-the-spot when he found out what had happened. That would have been a good trait in a doctor too."

"He would have been miserable cooped up in an office all day long." Very few people knew the truth. "Kevin was going along with it though, just to keep the peace. He started college here in Maine, and I started at a small community college. He came home to see me every weekend and never looked at another girl. We had plans for our future. He graduated college early, then got accepted to med school. Then I got pregnant."

Carol's green eyes went wide and she straightened. "What? Not Haylie?"

"No, no." Though she'd often wished that Haylie was Kevin's. "We were going to get married so he never went to med school. I tried to talk him into going, but I think he was glad for an excuse to do what he really wanted. I miscarried right after that, two weeks before our wedding. His parents hated me, and I felt Mom's death was a punishment. All I wanted to do was run. So after her death, I . . . I just up and left."

Carol put her hand to her mouth. "I'm so sorry, Mallory. What a mess. No wonder you didn't want to come back here. And Kevin didn't go back to school after you called off the wedding and left town?"

Mallory's eyes burned as she shook her head. "He said he didn't want to be a doctor anyway. He was accepted by the Park Service and trained to be a game warden."

What might have happened if she and her mother had never fought that morning? How might life have been different?

"There's more. It was my fault my mom died. We had a terrible argument when she found out Kevin and I weren't going to go through with the wedding. I said some terrible things to her. Told her if I were her real daughter, she wouldn't treat me that way." She swallowed the boulder in her throat. "Mom was so mad and upset with me that she forgot to check the fuel gauge on her boat. When it ran out of fuel, she was stranded in the crosshairs of the storm."

Carol touched her hand. "I'm so, so sorry. That has to have been hard."

"I keep thinking about her final moments when she knew she was going to die." Her voice broke. "I hope she knew I didn't mean any of it. She was the best mom ever." Mallory closed her eyes and called up her mother's face. How many times had she wished for a chance to make it right?

"What about his parents? I assume they were opposed."

"Totally opposed. They didn't speak to him before I left, and he didn't want to talk about them when I asked. I've heard through the grapevine that he hasn't spoken to his father in years. Kevin's younger brother, Mike, became a neurologist in Boston, so he's the favored child in his dad's eyes."

"Did you get along with them?"

Mallory thought of the years of tiptoeing around them and shook her head. "His mother always seemed a little jealous of me, and his dad was indifferent. That all escalated when Kevin told them he wasn't going to med school. They had to blame someone, and I was the easy target."

Carol twisted a lock of hair around her finger. "Does he see his mom?"

"Kevin meets her for lunch or coffee every couple of weeks, but he's never been back to the house. His dad has never even seen Sadie. Mike has three kids, and I guess that's enough for him."

Carol's eyes narrowed. "For someone who professed no interest in the handsome game warden, you know a lot of details. Who is the grapevine that kept you informed of all of it?"

Mallory looked away. "Aunt Blanche." She wasn't about to tell Carol how often she pumped her aunt for information over the years.

"What about his mom? If that were my son, I'd take a frying pan to my husband and straighten out his attitude."

"I'm not sure what the situation is there. Aunt Blanche could only repeat what she'd heard, and the gossip was mostly about Kevin's dad. Being a game warden, too, he is a public figure up here."

She stopped and thought again about the situation. With both of them working as game wardens, hadn't they run into one another on occasion? How was that handled? If the opportunity came up, she would have to ask Kevin.

Sixteen

The cell phone on the table next to Kevin finally penetrated the near coma he was in. He knocked his watch to the floor as he fumbled for it. "Game warden." His voice was hoarse.

"Adelaide Wilson here, Kevin. You need to go to Dixie's house right away."

"Dixie?" Righting the clock, he saw it was eleven. He hadn't been asleep all that long.

"She runs the post office on Walker's Roost. She posted on Facebook that there was an intruder in her yard."

He rubbed his head. "Oh, right, sorry, I wasn't thinking. She hasn't called me."

"I tried calling her and she didn't answer. I think something is wrong." Adelaide sounded even more upset than she usually was.

His feet landed on the floor. "I'll run out there, but it's going to be a good hour before I arrive so don't go calling anyone else."

"I won't. You're a good boy, Kevin."

He grinned. She was eighty-five if she was a day, and he didn't mind that she called him a boy. Some days he wondered where the years had gone. After jerking on his jeans and a sweatshirt, he grabbed his gun and headed for the door. A light was on under Mallory's door, but instead of disturbing her, he left a note by the coffeepot, then drove to the harbor and boarded his boat.

The stars were out in abundance as he rode the choppy waves and drank in the scent of the sea. Some days he wished his job involved a little less babysitting and a lot more action. He'd likely get there and find Dixie fast asleep. At least he hoped so.

He docked his boat and climbed the hillside to the post office. Dixie's house was behind the older building, and as he approached, he saw the porch light on and her front door standing open. The hair on the back of his neck prickled, and he unsnapped his holster and put his hand on the grip of his gun.

Mounting the steps, he peered through the open door but didn't see anyone. "Dixie? It's Game Warden O'Connor."

No answer. He pushed open the screen door and stepped into the entry. The house was small and a little ramshackle on the outside with clapboards that hadn't seen a paintbrush in at least twenty years. In spite of its exterior, the inside was neat and clean and smelled of lemon wax. The floors were old pine but shiny with care.

He moved through the house, checking both bedrooms, the kitchen, and the living room. No one was inside the place. Back outside, he went around the side of the house to the small barn that housed her goats. The things were nuisances, often escaping their pens. He'd lost track of how many times he'd come over to help her herd them back inside. The barn door hung open, too, and a dim bulb tried valiantly to illuminate the cavernous interior.

"Dixie?" He stopped and listened. Was that a groan?

He quickly stepped inside and called for her again. This time he heard the groan quite clearly from one of the stalls to his right. Still on alert with his gun at the ready, he stepped to the back stall, past the one that housed the goats. They milled restlessly and bleated as he passed them.

He saw Dixie's bare foot before he saw her. In a red nylon nightgown, she lay crumpled in some old hay. He knelt by her side and touched her arm. It was cold so he knew she'd been out here awhile. A horse blanket hung on the wall, and he grabbed it and spread it out over her. Did he dare turn her? He pulled out his flashlight and flipped it on.

A gash bled on her left temple, but he saw no other injuries in a cursory inspection. Her gray hair lay spread out around her. He gently rolled her over, and she winced at the light in her face, then opened her eyes. "Don't move, Dixie. It's the game warden."

"Warden." She rolled her head from side to side. "Hurts like a nettle."

"What happened?"

"There was a man." She swallowed and lifted her head a bit. "Don't just stand there eyeing me like a calf looking at a new gate. Help me up. I'm indecent." She tugged at the hem of her nightgown.

"I'm not sure you should move yet. Your head is still bleeding."

She made a shooing motion and sat up. "You're as bad as an old woman. I need some tea in my belly and some ice on my head. I'm going to the house. You can come along, or stand there looking silly."

Shaking his head, he helped her to her feet. "Let me carry you." He made a move to sweep her into his arms, but she smacked his arm.

"You'll do no such thing. There will be rumors flying that we're having an affair before you know it. Next thing I know,

Walker will throw me over." Her back erect, she marched toward the door, though she wobbled just a little.

Grinning, Kevin caught up with her. "There could be worse things said about me."

A hint of a smile lifted her weathered face. "You should be married. A tongue as glib as yours shouldn't be loosed on single women."

He chuckled as he glanced around the moonlit yard. There was no sign of whoever had struck her. He waited to ask more questions until they were inside her neat kitchen sipping hot tea and eating homemade chocolate-chip cookies.

He put down his cup. "Now tell me what happened here tonight."

She fixed him with a stare. "You'd better take good care of your lady, Warden. I think she's in trouble."

Kevin had gotten Dixie to the sofa and had pulled a beige afghan over her. She already had more color in her cheeks, and her eyes were bright and alert. She'd already wound her gray hair into a bun and stuck a pencil in it to hold it tight. He handed her a cold washcloth.

"I don't think you're going to need stitches. Once the bleeding eases off, I'll put some butterfly tape on it. But if you're dizzy at all or have a headache, you should go to urgent care."

She pressed the washcloth to her oozing cut. "You sweet thing, I'm not going to the doctor. I'm as healthy as my goats. I'd like another crack at that man though." She pumped her fist in the air. "I should have taken a shovel to his head."

He pulled the armchair closer to her and took out a notepad and pencil. "Can you tell me what happened and why you think this has anything to do with Mallory?"

"I couldn't sleep so I was playing around on Facebook when I heard the back door creak. It only makes that sound when it's opened so I knew someone was in the house. I shot out a message on Facebook and closed my computer."

Her hazel eyes narrowed, and she sat up a bit more. "I crept out of my bedroom and into the hall closet. Once I heard his steps go into my room, I went right out the door myself. I have a shotgun in the barn so I was heading for that when he caught me."

Imagining the scene made him wince. "He caught you in the barn?"

She nodded. "I was just reaching for the shotgun when he grabbed my arm and spun me around. His head was covered with a ski mask so I can't give you a description beyond the fact that he was about six feet tall and of average build. That's about as helpful as a hose in a rainstorm though, I know."

"He mentioned Mallory?"

She nodded and turned the cloth on her head over to the other side. "He asked what I'd told Mallory about him."

Kevin leaned forward. "What did he mean by that?"

"I think he's the same fellow who was arguing with Edmund that day out on Mermaid Point. I saw enough of his eyebrows through the mask to know he had gray hair like that guy. That's the only thing I can come up with. They were both too far away for me to identify him even if he hadn't been masked. But let me tell you, it sure made me wish I could have read the name of that boat."

"Me too. What did you tell him when he asked?"

"I told him I gave Mallory his name. He shook me like a rag doll, then threw me into the wall." She touched her head. "I reckon this was God's punishment for lying, but the fellow sure got my back up. I wanted to scare him."

Kevin sat back and frowned. "You might have put Mallory in more danger, Dixie. If this guy thinks she's after him, he's likely to intensify his efforts to get to her. He's already broken into her house in Bangor and burned down Edmund's house."

"I heard about the house. It doesn't seem possible that sweet old cottage could be gone. But the fire doesn't seem to have been set to try to kill her. She wasn't even inside."

"That's true. We don't know what this guy is after. I think it might have been to burn up whatever evidence he thought was inside the house." He picked up the first-aid kit beside him on the table and opened it. "Let's bandage that cut."

She didn't flinch when he sterilized the cut and bandaged it. "I'll run you to urgent care."

"I already told you I'm not going anywhere. If I need to I'll see the doctor tomorrow. Right now all I want to do is go to bed."

"What if he comes back?"

She swept her arm toward the door. "If you'll get my shotgun for me, I'll give him a reception he won't soon forget. I don't think he'll be back though. He could have killed me if he wanted to."

She had a point. "I'll get your gun. You go on to bed and I'll bring it to your room."

He waited to make sure she could navigate on her own, then slipped out the back door and walked across the moonlit yard to the barn, which was still faintly illuminated with the overhead light. The goats bleated at him as he went to where he'd found Dixie and grabbed the shotgun. As he started to return to the house, he noticed a card on the straw-littered ground and stopped to pick it up.

It was a business card for a restaurant favored by locals called Ruth and Wimpy's Kitchen. He'd eaten there many times, and it was always packed, thanks to its homegrown fare of lobster prepared in myriad ways and the hefty sandwiches they served. He pocketed it and carried the shotgun back to the house.

He found Dixie in bed with the covers pulled up to her chin. Her gray hair was spread out on the pink pillowcase. Her eyes were sleepy, but she didn't appear to be in any pain. After making sure the gun was loaded and ready, he propped it in a corner. "Sure you don't want to go to town?"

"I'm positive."

"You ever get over Hancock way? I found this." He pulled the business card from his pocket and showed her.

She wrinkled her forehead. "I'm lucky if I make it to Summer Harbor to the library every six months. I can't tell you the last time I ate anywhere but Dixie's Diner. Heck, I feed half the population of Walker's Roost every Saturday night."

He'd heard of the ribs she made for family and friends in her kitchen on Saturdays, but he'd never been able to accept an invitation. "I'll check out the restaurant, but it's probably a dead end. Call if you hear anything. And you can thank Adelaide Wilson for me turning up. She saw your Facebook post."

She rolled over on her side, and her eyes drifted shut. "It will just encourage her nosiness."

She might have a point. Kevin grinned and pulled the bedroom door shut behind him.

SEVENTEEN

Moonlight filtered through the bedroom curtains. Mallory had tried to read awhile, but even the latest Denise Hunter romance couldn't keep her attention from wandering down-stairs to where Kevin slept. She shut off her e-reader and swung her legs out of bed. She eased open the door and slipped across the hall to the bathroom to wash off her makeup. Wait, she'd forgotten her bag of newly purchased toiletries in the car.

Stopping in the entry, she listened for a moment to make sure no one was stirring downstairs. She didn't want her quick trip to her car to awaken anyone. Satisfied that everyone else was asleep, she tip-toed quietly down the stairs and unlocked the door to step onto the porch. A lump formed in her throat when she saw the pink moon. There were many nights when she was a child when she and her mom would sit on the hillside and watch for a splash of a mermaid tail. She'd been crushed when she found out mermaids were a myth, but old habits died hard, and she still had to look.

The porch boards shifted under her feet a bit as she went to the stairs and stepped down into the yard. The cold, wet grass chilled the soles of her feet, and she picked up the pace to her car.

She'd left it unlocked, so she reached inside and grabbed the bag on the passenger side.

As she quietly shut the door and turned back toward the house, the hair on the back of her neck prickled. An almost atavistic fear made her rush for the porch as if a monster lurked in the shadows.

She took the steps in two strides, then stood with her chest heaving. A hand came down on her arm, and she nearly screamed until she realized it was Kevin.

She pulled out of his grip. "I just lost two years of my life."

"Sorry. What are you doing out here by yourself?"

She held up her bag. "I wanted to wash my face."

The moon threw light and shadow over him and made his face look even more rugged. He was still fully dressed, and his gun was strapped at his hip. "I would have gotten it for you. Wandering alone out here in the dark isn't a good idea. Whoever burned down your house could be lurking around."

She gave an uneasy glance into the shadows. "I was fine."

His fingers closed over her arm again. "You have to be more careful." His manner was still distant.

She searched his gaze. "I . . . I thought I felt someone watching me out there." When he started that direction, she shook her head. "It was probably just my imagination after the stressful day."

Her words didn't deter him, and he bounded down the steps. "Get inside!" As he went, he switched on his flashlight and searched the shadows. His precise, careful motions showed her how good he was at his job. How many times had he conducted a sweep for intruders like this? Only it would have been at someone else's house, not his own. What had she done by coming here?

She started for the door, then stopped. She wasn't going anywhere. What if he needed her help? She pulled out her cell phone with her finger poised to punch in 911.

A few minutes later he emerged from the line of trees along the south side of his property and joined her on the porch. "I found a fresh impression in the grass by the woodshed. It looked like someone had been kneeling there recently." He took her arm and grabbed the screen door. "I want you inside. He could have a gun."

She let him propel her into the entry. Maybe she hadn't been crazy. She wrapped her arms around herself and shuddered. "I shouldn't stay here, Kevin. I've just put you and Sadie in danger. What if he burns down *your* house next? I should go."

"We're all going to be fine."

"What does he want? I don't understand any of this. I'm no threat, and I don't have anything someone would want. Heck, I can barely make my mortgage some months." She swallowed past the constriction in her throat and dropped her hands to her sides. "I'm going to find out though. I refuse to be terrorized." She slanted a glance up at him. "You trust your private detective friend to find out where my birth mother is, right?"

"I called her back and told her what was happening here. She promised to drop everything and focus on your problem. She hopes to have some preliminary information by tomorrow night. It might not be much, but maybe it'll be a start."

Mallory rubbed her head where pain had begun to flicker. "It probably has nothing at all to do with my birth mother. The lead Dixie gave me about that guy Dad was arguing with is probably where I should focus."

"Maybe someone else saw that man with your dad. We can poke around more tomorrow. For now, get some rest."

"Who can sleep knowing someone was watching us again tonight?"

He opened the door for her. "I'll stand guard."

Of course he would. That was the kind of man he was. Even if he hated her now, he'd protect her. She went past him and rushed to her bedroom before he could bring up the past again.

So much had happened that Mallory barely thought about the letters she'd found from her birth mother, but as sunrise lit her room, she bolted upright in bed as she remembered she hadn't lost them in the fire. They were in a packet under the passenger seat of her car.

The wood floor was cool under her bare feet as she got out of bed and pulled on a fluffy robe that Kate had brought over. The clock on the stand flipped to five, but she wasn't a bit sleepy now.

She wouldn't be able to go back to sleep until she had those letters safely inside. After sliding her feet into shoes, she opened her door and crept down the hall to the front door. The first gleams of sunlight streamed through the window. She unlocked the door and eased out. The last thing she wanted was to wake up Kevin.

The air smelled of dew, and the scent took her back to her childhood. When she was a little girl, her parents took her on a vacation every year, and they always left in the early-morning hours like this. She could still remember the excitement she had felt creeping out of the house before the sun began to peek over the horizon.

The grass drenched her feet as she hurried to her car and grabbed the manila envelope out from under the seat. With it safely in her hand, she breathed a little easier. It would have been a catastrophe if she'd lost it.

When she reached the front door, she heard a coughing sound and froze, but it was just a roaming coyote. She glimpsed a mangy coat and gleaming eyes. Kevin's warning about rabies made her hurry to get back inside.

She closed the door and ran smack into someone. The warm hands that came down on her shoulders made her shiver. "Kevin, I'm sorry. Did I wake you?"

His hands left her shoulders. "I was already awake. I didn't sleep much last night." His deep voice rumbled in her ear. "I didn't want to tell you earlier, but I got called out to a break-in."

She listened to him tell her about the man who attacked Dixie and the strange comment implying that Mallory was in danger. "So that man arguing with Dad must be important."

"Looks that way. I'm going to see if I can find the name of the boat. But what were you doing outside? I told you not to go out there by yourself."

"It's starting to get light so it was safe." She held up the manila envelope. "Some letters from my birth mother as well as the adoption papers. Luckily I'd put them in the car. I wanted to make sure they were okay."

He flipped on the hall light, and she blinked at the glare. "We might as well have coffee. Want some breakfast? How about you fix the coffee and toast, and I'll make you an omelet that will make you weep for joy."

His light tone lifted her spirits. Maybe he would let go of the strain between them. She smiled and punched him lightly in the side. "You're putting too much pressure on me to make good coffee. How can I compete?"

"I've made it really easy for you. I have Captain Davy's coffee and a Cuisinart coffeemaker. Even a child could make coffee that will make your eyes roll back in your head."

Giggling, she followed him into the kitchen and laid the envelope on the table before moving to the coffee grinder. As the aroma of coffee filled the kitchen, he piled the ingredients for the omelet beside the cooktop.

She eyed the box. "Cream cheese?"

"Just you wait. Cream cheese makes the omelet."

She watched his deft, practiced movements as he stood at the cooktop. His dark hair was spiky from sleep, and the muscles of his back and arms flexed as he flipped the omelet. Something long dead stirred in her again, and she wanted to flee. Or maybe what she really wanted was to move right into his arms and kiss him. There was danger in both scenarios playing through her head.

He raised a brow. "What? You're looking at me weird."

She turned away from his probing gaze and got two mugs from the cabinet. "Maybe it's because I'm trying to summon the courage to cry when I taste that omelet. I wouldn't want to disappoint you."

Her life had been spent disappointing people—her mom and dad, Kevin's parents. Since that first horrendous mistake when she was twenty, her life had been one mistake after another. Though she didn't regret her daughter, her marriage to Brian had been a disaster from the beginning.

"Cream?" Kevin waved the carton of whipping cream in front of her.

"Coffee without cream would be a sacrilege." She took the carton and poured a generous amount in each mug, then carried them to the table.

The packet of letters caught her eye and she opened the flap. "My birth mother sent letters starting when I was about to turn five."

Kevin carried two plates to the table and put one in front of her. "Have you read them all?"

She pulled out a chair and sat down. "I haven't had time." She removed the sheaf of letters and plucked one off the bottom. "I've read about ten so far. They are all written around the time of my birthday each year, and she just asks how I'm doing and assures me she thinks of me every day. It sounds like she sent a gift every time, though I don't always remember what she says she sent. My parents never told me where the gifts came from."

She took a bite of the omelet, and the taste of jalapeños, cream cheese, veggies, and cayenne hit her taste buds. The spicy heat bit her tongue and made her eyes water. "Wow, this is good. But it's *hot*."

He grinned and picked up his fork. "Told you it would make you cry."

"I think that was a cheat." She took another bite and looked at the letter. "This one would have been written about my sixteenth birthday."

It all seemed like a waste of time. The sweet lady in these letters wouldn't have hurt anyone, but her notes had succeeded in awakening the interest Mallory had stuffed away all these years. The thought of finding her birth mother terrified her and intrigued her all at the same time.

She sipped her last bit of coffee. "You going to go back to sleep?"

He shook his head. "I've got some paperwork to do. The girls will be up by six thirty to get ready for school, so I'll fix pancakes when I hear them stirring."

The chair scraped on the tile as she pushed back from the table. "I think I'll go shower." She needed a little time away from his distracting presence so she could think.

EIGHTEEN

The stench of burned pancakes was only barely discernible with the window open. Kevin dumped the contents of the skillet, wiped it out, and tried again. He needed to pay attention this time instead of trying to listen for the sound of Mallory's bedroom door opening.

"Daddy, what did you do?" Sadie entered the kitchen with Fiona on the lead. She was still dressed in her pink princess pajamas, and her blonde hair cascaded in a tangle down her back.

"You can still smell the burned pancakes?" He waved his hand in the air.

"I think I'll have cereal."

"I can make some unburned ones. With real maple syrup."

"I'd still rather have cereal."

"Help yourself." His inclination was always to wait on her, but he'd been told he was doing her no favors by not making her learn to do things on her own.

"Bowl," she told Fiona.

The dog led her to the counter left of the sink, and Sadie reached up. Her fingers felt along the edge of the cabinet door to the handle. She opened the door and found a bowl, then reached into the next cabinet and located the cereal. Kevin started to get the milk for her, then checked himself again. Waiting, he watched her sidle along the counter to the refrigerator and take out the carton of milk. A few moments later and her cereal was ready. Her triumphant smile made it worth the agony of watching. Cereal in hand, she turned and counted off the steps to the table, then set down the bowl and pulled out the chair.

He heard footsteps and turned to see Haylie wander into the kitchen. She was already dressed in jeans and a swim-team sweatshirt. Her feet were bare, and her wet hair hung down her back.

"Pancakes?" he asked.

She wrinkled her nose. "I only have toast or yogurt in the morning. I have to stay in shape for swimming."

There was something wrong in the world when a kid that young was concerned with staying skinny. He pressed his lips together and pointed the spatula at the refrigerator. "We have yogurt."

"Sugar-free?"

"Sweetened with Stevia."

She went to the fridge and turned with a frown on her pretty face. "These aren't fat-free."

He fixed her with a stare. "Your brain needs good fats. Eat it." He handed her a spoon.

She shrugged and took the small tub of yogurt to the table. "Mom can get me some of the kind I like."

He gritted his teeth and said nothing. Mallory was going to have her hands full with that one by the time she was seventeen. He poured maple syrup on his pancakes and carried the plate to the table. As he set it down, he heard the doorbell. The place was like Grand Central Station this morning. So much for a peaceful breakfast with all of them holding hands and singing "Kumbaya."

He nearly groaned when he saw his mother standing with Kate at the door. His glance slanted to Mallory's closed door, and he prayed she'd stay in her room a little longer. The last thing he wanted was to subject her to his mother's inquisition.

When he opened the door, his mother's smile faltered. "Did someone wake up on the wrong side of the bed?"

"Hi, Mom. Kate. You're out and about early. I was out on a call until the wee hours."

Kate sniffed. "Yum, we're in time for coffee. And is that the delectable aroma of burned pancakes?"

He grinned, his irritation washing away. "I'll dig the burned ones out of the trash if they smell that good. Come on in." Nothing for it but to face the music.

He led the way back to the kitchen and went to the coffeepot. Maybe his mother would think Haylie was babysitting for Sadie and he wouldn't have to explain.

"Grammy, are we going to lunch today?" Sadie asked. "Can my friend Haylie come too?"

"Of course, honey . . ." His mother's voice trailed off and she gasped.

He turned with coffee cups in his hands to see Mallory standing in the hall. His mother would jump to the wrong conclusion, like always.

The smile froze on Mallory's face, and she looked carefully from his mother to him. "Um, good morning." She had dressed in jeans and a red long-sleeved T-shirt, but her feet were bare and her hair was still wet.

"Mallory." His mother's voice was flat. "I'm sorry about

144

your father." Her mouth was pinched as she reached for one of the cups Kevin held. She carried it to the table and sat next to Sadie.

"Thank you, Mrs. O'Connor. I'm sure it's a shock to see me here, but there's a good reason." Mallory's voice was strained. "You might not have heard what happened yesterday. Someone burned down my dad's house."

"Oh no!" Kate took the other cup of coffee from Kevin. "You're all okay? Where's Carol?"

"She's in the shower. We're all fine. None of us were inside."

Kevin watched his mother's expression as Mallory told them what had happened. His mom always had a poker face and he never knew what she was thinking, but she'd never really liked Mallory. Just like Dad, Mom had blamed her for him dropping out of medical school. It wasn't fair, but there it was. Blaming someone else was always easier than looking squarely at truth.

His mom took a sip of her coffee. "So, are you heading back to Bangor today?"

Mallory poured herself a cup of coffee with jerky movements. "I'm not going back, at least not until I find out who killed my father. And who burned down our house."

"I see."

Mallory glanced at the girls. "Haylie, why don't you help Sadie get changed and then take her outside to wait for the school bus?"

For once Haylie didn't complain, and both girls left the kitchen with the dog. Kevin's gut tightened. He recognized the determined expression on Mallory's face. She intended to have it out with his mom, and he couldn't blame her. It had been a long time coming.

A sip of coffee laced with heavy cream bolstered Mallory. She settled across the table from Mrs. O'Connor. Kevin's mother had never made any secret of the disdain she felt for her, and seeing her so unexpectedly had reminded Mallory of the years she'd spent pursuing the impossible task of winning Candace's approval. She glanced at Kevin, and he shrugged as if to say this discussion was inevitable.

Kevin looked a lot like his father, same warm brown hair and eyes, same nose and strong musculature, but he had his mother's bone structure. On him it looked masculine, but on Mrs. O'Connor, the prominent cheekbones made her appear exotic. She was about fifty-five now, and she looked every bit of it with a fine map of lines around her eyes and forehead.

Mallory traced the curve of her cup with a finger. "Let's not pretend, okay? I know you were shocked to find me here. And probably upset. I wouldn't be here if there were any other choice."

"There's always a choice. You could have gone to the inn. Your father would have had insurance."

"I insisted," Kevin said. "There were three of them, and the inn is crazy expensive."

"There are motels too." Suppressed fury flickered in Mrs. O'Connor's narrowed eyes. "You're just getting back on track, Kevin, and now here she is. Messing with your head again, disrupting your life." She turned her head and glared at Mallory. "You ruined our family, Mallory. *Destroyed* it! None of us will ever be the same. And it's all your fault."

Mallory looked down at her hands and made no attempt to

defend herself. His mother couldn't blame her more than she blamed herself.

Kevin slammed his coffee cup onto the table, sloshing coffee onto its surface. "It's Dad's fault, Mom. He's a bitter man. None of this is Mallory's fault. You think she got pregnant all by herself? That would be a first. And while we *both* made a mistake, God forgave us. Don't you think it's odd that Dad can't? And it's clear now that you haven't either."

His mother's back was stiff enough to surf on. "She wrecked your life, Kevin. You would have been a doctor but for her."

Mallory's fingers tightened around her coffee cup. "Hey, I'm right here. You don't have to talk over my head. Did you ever once ask Kevin what *he* wanted? I knew when we were sixteen that he didn't want to be a doctor. He just wanted to please you both. Do you really think he would have been happy stuck in an office every day?"

Mrs. O'Connor's mouth flattened. "He would have made an excellent doctor."

"He would be good at whatever he wanted to do. He's that kind of man. But don't you want him to be happy?"

His mother sniffed. "Happiness is fleeting. I didn't want him to live like we've had to live with never enough money to do what we wanted to do."

Mallory shook her head. "You've got a nice house, money to get your nails done every week, you dress well. What more did you need? Would you have wanted your husband stuck in a job he hated just so you could have lunch at the country club?"

Mrs. O'Connor's cheeks reddened, and she pressed her lips together again. She wouldn't answer that because the answer would have been yes. Yes, she would rather her husband worked at a job he hated so she could move in the same circles as the ones she'd grown up in.

Kate tried to smile, but tears glittered on her lashes. "Hasn't this family been ripped apart enough, Aunt Candace? Can't all of you bury the hatchet and let Kevin live his life?"

Mrs. O'Connor got to her feet. She shoved her chair in so hard that it banged against the table. "I'm leaving. I want to be alone." Her kitten-heeled slingbacks clicked against the wood floors as she marched toward the door.

Mallory leaped to her feet and caught her before she got to the front door. "Look, Mrs. O'Connor, I don't want to be your enemy. You're taking all of this too seriously. Kevin and I are just friends now. He offered my family and me a place to stay. Don't let this be another wedge between the two of you, between you and Sadie."

The dislike—no, *hatred*—in Mrs. O'Connor's eyes made Mallory yank her hand back. This woman would never forgive, never get over having her plans thwarted.

Mrs. O'Connor's eyes sparked with rage. "I came over today to invite Kevin and Sadie to dinner at the house. It was going to be the first time in fifteen years that he'd come to the house. My husband finally agreed because it was the only thing I really wanted for my birthday, but you've ruined it. Everything you touch turns to ashes. I hope you're happy with what you've done."

Mallory blinked fiercely against the sting in her eyes. "I've done nothing, Mrs. O'Connor. I won't be here long. Please, just go back into the kitchen and invite Kevin to dinner. I'll leave today. I'll be gone when he gets back to the house tonight."

"No, you won't." Kevin stood four feet away. "I won't be

manipulated. Good-bye, Mom. When you decide you're going to let me live my life, give me a call."

Mrs. O'Connor held out her hand toward him, then it fell back to her side. "What about Sadie?"

Did she really even care about her granddaughter? Mallory wanted to believe the little girl meant more to her than just a tool to be used against her father.

Kevin must have had the same thought. He shook his head. "You've made your choice. Until you choose forgiveness rather than bitterness, I don't want to hear from you. Sadie doesn't need to be around that kind of toxic attitude either."

Tears rolled from his mother's eyes, and she jerked open the door and charged through it. Moments later her car engine revved to life.

Mallory swallowed hard. "I'm sorry, Kevin. I'll just get our things and we'll leave."

He stepped closer and his hand, warm and compelling, came down on her arm. "I don't want you to go. I realized I'm acting as badly as my parents. We both were at fault in our breakup, Mal. Let's start fresh and put it behind us as we figure out who killed your dad."

As the heat of his palm soaked into her skin, she stared up at him and tried to read his expression. Even if they still had feelings for each other, what kind of life could they build surrounded by that kind of hostility?

NINETEEN

The conference room was packed for the special meeting, and Kevin had to stand in the back by the door. The last place he wanted to be this afternoon was in a meeting, especially knowing his father would be there too. By now his mother had probably told Dad about Mallory being at the house this morning.

Kevin had stopped by Ruth and Wimpy's on his way, but that hopeful clue had been a dead end. And DNA testing on the tennis bracelet found on Edmund's boat had come back with no matches.

Ned Chesterton, head of Kevin's division, stepped to the large map at the front. He was nearing retirement age, but the wardens were placing bets that he would die in the saddle. He was only five-eight, but years of weight lifting had bulked up his muscles. His hair was mostly white now with only traces of brown remaining.

He laid some papers on the podium. "The rabies problem has escalated. We've had more cases this past year than I've seen in my thirty years as a game warden." He turned and gestured at the red pushpins on the map. "Ten since this time last year, and we've had three more just this month. And it's only May."

Kevin raised his hand. "Do we know what species is driving the outbreak?"

"We've had one cow, three skunks, and seven red foxes."

Mostly foxes, data that matched what Kevin suspected. The two rabid animals he'd taken in for testing had both been foxes. He listened to Chesterton give a rundown on the problem. The majority of the cases had been scattered all over the county. It was going to be hard to control.

Chesterton stacked the papers on the podium. "I've issued an alert to residents that will go out on TV and radio news tonight. We've got to stay on top of this to make sure no one else is hurt. Our unusually warm spring has a lot of children roaming the woods, so be on the alert. Dismissed."

Kevin started for the door, but Chesterton waved him over. "O'Connor, I want to talk to you." Kevin's dad was already standing near their boss, and he stared impassively at Kevin.

Kevin joined them. "Have you heard how the teenager who was bitten last week is doing?"

The fifteen-year-old had been bitten by a red fox while playing baseball with friends. He and his companions had run screaming to the house with the fox on their heels. It was a blessing that none of the other kids had been bitten.

"He's had three rabies shots so far and will get his final one in another week."

Kevin was all too aware of his dad's distance. Dad hadn't so much as glanced at him. He stood a few feet away with his hands in the pockets of his dull-green pants. Looking at his dad was like seeing his own future in about thirty years. They both stood at six-four and had the same broad shoulders and size-fifteen feet. His dad's nose had been broken twice, so Kevin had escaped the bump, but in all other ways, he was the spitting image of the fifty-five-year-old standing behind Chesterton.

Their boss handed him a paper. "Your father is in charge of charting all the incidents we've had so far. I'm assigning you to help him. It's too big a job for one man. I want you both to personally walk the perimeter of where the animals were discovered and see if you find any more rabid ones. I think there are several dens around incubating the disease."

Kevin wanted to suggest that Chesterton assign someone else, but he recognized the aggressively jutting jaw. "Yes, sir."

His father shifted on the balls of his feet. "I can handle this by myself, sir."

Chesterton skewered Dad with a glare from his icy-blue eyes. "This isn't up for discussion. I'm tired of tiptoeing around you two. You can't seem to bury the hatchet, so I'm going to force the issue."

A muscle flexed in Dad's jaw. "This is none of your business, *sir*. Our personal lives have nothing to do with our jobs."

"You carry this feud into your work, O'Connor. Your son has remained professional, but I can't say the same for you. Just last week you were in the break room talking about how Kevin could do better than this job. Every other warden knows you don't hold our work in high esteem, yet you've worked here for thirty years. What kind of message do you think you're sending to young game wardens?"

Kevin's dad glared back. "I didn't mean it that way and you know it."

Kevin rubbed his neck that had begun to warm. He'd known how Dad felt, but Kevin thought he at least had the good sense not to talk about their family. "I appreciate your desire to help, sir, but I'm not sure this is the right way to go about it."

Chesterton stuck his papers in his pocket. "It's a done deal. Get along or I'll be asking for your badge, Pete. You're old enough to retire, and I won't have you disparage the warden service any longer." He walked off and left them standing alone in the room.

Kevin eyed his father's rigid face. "I guess you're stuck with me."

"Your mother says you have *that woman* at your house. Haven't you learned your lesson? She's poison, Kevin. She'll lead you down the garden path and leave you again. Hasn't she done enough to wreck your life? Look at you—raising a blind child all by yourself because of poor choices you've made. You never seem to learn."

The pressure built in Kevin's chest as his father's words penetrated. "I have a great life, Dad. I'm doing a job I love, and my daughter is the world to me. My choice, as you put it, wasn't to see DeAnn leave me. That was her decision, but you seem to have a problem with anyone making decisions other than you."

"It all started with Mallory. I don't know why you can't see that."

"And I don't understand why you can't seem to grasp that any mistakes I've made were *my choices*. Mallory didn't force me to do anything. She's a wonderful woman, and you'd know that if you took the time to get to know her. She has a great heart and cares about other people, which is more than I can say about you."

He turned away from his father's derisive expression and

headed for the door. The next few weeks would be like running a gauntlet.

The ocean was choppy with whitecapped waves slamming into the side of Mallory's boat. This was her first run out to Allegory Rock, and already at ten in the morning the dock teemed with people waiting on their mail. She maneuvered the boat into the harbor and navigated close to the weathered boards until the bumpers of the boat bumped the pilings. A white-headed man in a suit caught the rope she threw and tied off the boat for her.

"Thanks. I've got lots of packages today." She glanced around and saw the buckets many areas put out for outgoing and incoming mail. The outgoing mail bucket was full, and several packages wrapped in brown paper had been set beside the bucket.

The man in the suit nodded. "Ayuh, I wondered if I might catch a ride back to Summer Harbor with you." A stylish leather suitcase was at his feet.

Mail boats commonly ferried passengers so this wasn't Mallory's first request. "Sure, but we won't get there until about three. I have two other stops to make."

He frowned and shuffled his feet. "I thought you went straight back to the mainland from here."

"I usually do, but the sea is rough today, and I wanted to get these packages delivered before they got wet."

"The mail time isn't supposed to be changed at your whim, young lady."

With his gruff voice and the scowl he directed at her, the initial impression she'd had of a kindly older gentleman vanished.

When she looked closer, she realized he was younger than his gray hair indicated too. "The mail itself is my priority, not passengers. This mail boat doesn't typically carry passengers."

"Your dad took me to the mainland several times. My boat is being repaired, and I have an important meeting in Bangor. Listen, I'll give you two hundred dollars if you'll take me to Summer Harbor before you deliver the rest of the mail."

She was tempted to turn him down because it would add two hours to her day, but a hundred dollars an hour was hard to refuse. The really intriguing thing was that he'd mentioned her father. "Okay, I'll do it." She deposited the mail into the bucket and handed out several packages, then scooped up the outgoing mail. When she returned to her boat, she found the man already seated starboard.

She stopped to hold out her hand. "I'm Mallory."

He barely touched it with a single shake before turning his attention back to his iPad. "Len Nevin."

What a scintillating conversationalist. Once she started the engine, there wouldn't be much talking, so whatever she got out of him had to happen now. "So you rode with my dad sometimes?"

"Ayuh." His attention was still on his iPad.

"Did you ever have an argument with him?"

That caught his attention. He turned off the iPad and crossed his legs in a nonchalant motion. "I didn't know him well enough to argue with him."

He's lying. She saw it in the flicker of his lids and the shift of his face. "Did you ever visit his property in your boat? What's the name of your boat, by the way?"

The skin around his mouth and jaw tightened. "I've never even been to Folly Shoals. Is this some kind of inquisition? The paper said your dad died in an accident, but you're grilling me like you think I caused his death in some way."

He still hadn't told her the name of the boat, but she could look that up easily enough. In spite of her dislike for his manner, she forced a smile. "I didn't mean to make you feel you were under suspicion. I'm trying to figure out what happened to my father. I don't believe it was an accident, but I'm not accusing you of killing him."

Her placating words just made him narrow his eyes. "You're hardly an expert on criminology. If there was something fishy about your dad's death, the sheriff will handle it." He leaned against the seat cushion. "But he doesn't believe you, does he?"

His smug tone made her curl her fingers into her palms. "Actually, he does believe me now. Some additional evidence has been uncovered."

He straightened and his sneer vanished. "What evidence?"

She shouldn't have let him goad her into revealing more than she should. She turned her back on him and went to start the engine. "We'd better get on the road. I don't want you to be late for your appointment."

He stood. "What evidence?"

Her pulse pounded and she backed away. "It really has nothing to do with you. Sorry if I upset you."

Ignoring his scowl, she slid into the pilot's seat and started the engine. As the boat chugged away from the dock, she tried to ignore his glower. Maybe Kevin could find out something about this guy.

TWENTY

If she was going to stay here, she needed to earn her keep. Mallory piled dinner ingredients onto the kitchen counter, then plugged in her iPod and turned on Creed. The aroma of cheesecake from the oven was already wafting in the air. She liked Kevin's house. He'd said it was built in 1902, but instead of the usual small, chopped-off rooms, he'd opened up the kitchen to the rest of the house. The white cabinets contrasted with the gray granite counter and set off the marble subway-tile backsplash. Kate had told her he'd done most of the work himself, even laying the travertine tile on the floor.

Had he done it all for his ex-wife? A pang struck her but she pushed it away. She'd married, too, so she hardly had any moral high ground for the jealousy that took up residence in her chest. DeAnn had been a lucky woman, and she'd thrown it all away.

Carol perched on the bar stool at the island. "Anything I can do to help?"

"I'll help too," Kate said.

Mallory took the cheesecake from the oven and set it atop the stove. "Carol, you can chop vegetables for the salad." Mallory rinsed the veggies and handed them to her along with a knife and a cutting board. "And, Kate, do you want to peel sweet potatoes?"

"Sure. What else are you making?"

"Shepherd's pie with a sweet potato topping instead of russet potatoes. It's pretty good."

Carol cut a green pepper in two and chopped it. "Sounds yummy."

"I'm fixing cheesecake for dessert." The TV came on, then the sound of Peppa Pig's voice. Smiling, Mallory washed sweet potatoes and handed them to Kate. It had warmed her heart to see how Haylie catered to Sadie. Too bad she'd never had a sibling for her.

The French door to the back deck opened, and Kevin stepped inside. A strong spring wind carrying the scent of mud and spring flowers gusted through the door with him. He shut the door and looked around. "I haven't heard Creed in years. Is that your famous cheesecake I smell?"

"It is. With wild blueberries I got from Kate."

He took a step toward the counter, and she pointed at him. "Step away from the cheesecake."

He grinned, then shrugged. "You mean I can't have dessert first?" He glanced through the opening to the rest of the house. "Sadie loves *Peppa Pig*. Even though she can't see it, she loves the characters. I took her to a neighbor's a few weeks ago so she could touch some pigs. She wanted to see what Peppa looked like."

Mallory's chest squeezed. "I can't imagine how hard it must be to watch her go through so much."

"She's resilient though and she's super smart. She's going to be okay."

"She has you for a dad. That's a huge advantage." Though Brian had loved Haylie, he'd been a distant dad, more interested in his work than in altering his plans for his daughter.

The doorbell rang, and she watched him walk through the living room to the front entry. A woman's voice carried over the sound of Peppa Pig, and Kevin took a step back. A moment later a blonde dressed in a stylish jacket over khaki slacks moved into Mallory's view. The woman's hair was up in a French twist, and even from here, Mallory could hear her elaborate bracelet tinkling.

Kevin glanced toward the kitchen, and Mallory frowned at the near panic on his face.

"Holy cow, that's DeAnn, Kevin's ex," Kate whispered. "This isn't going to be pretty."

Mallory couldn't tear her gaze away from the woman. She was drop-dead gorgeous, and the jewelry she wore would buy a new car. "When was the last time she was here?"

"She hasn't been back since she left. Sadie doesn't even know her. She hasn't called, hasn't sent a card, nothing."

Kevin's voice was low and urgent, but Mallory couldn't make out any of his words. DeAnn's focus went over his shoulder, and her eyes narrowed when she saw Mallory. He took DeAnn's arm and steered her toward the door. It clicked behind them, and Mallory could see them standing on the porch talking.

What could DeAnn want after all this time?

Kevin stood on the porch and stared at the woman he used to love. She'd always taken care of herself, but she exuded money and status now. Even he could recognize the expensive jewelry and clothing she wore. The shoes were probably a week's salary for him. Since the day she left, he'd only had curt e-mails from her attorney. Once the divorce was over, she'd quickly remarried, and he'd tried not to think about her or the havoc she'd left in her wake.

He shoved his hands in his pockets. "What are you doing here, DeAnn?"

She tucked a lock of gleaming blonde hair behind her ear. "Was that your old flame, Mallory, in the kitchen?"

Her voice had always attracted him with its husky, sexy tones, but now it failed to do more than stir more panic in his chest. Had she come to see Sadie? He would do anything to protect his daughter.

"That was Mallory, wasn't it? What's she doing here all homey in that apron?" She said the last with a curl of her lip.

Stay calm. "I don't think you have any right to ask questions about my life. What do you want?"

She tilted her chin up and looked him over with those smoky-blue eyes that used to entice him. Looking back, all they'd had going for them was chemistry. No wonder she'd left. His gaze fell to her left hand. A huge diamond twinkled on her carefully manicured hand.

She gave him a sultry smile. "Is it so wrong to want to see how you're doing? And to see my little girl?"

His gut gave a sharp twist. He wasn't going to talk about Sadie, not yet. "Where's your husband? Does he know you're here?"

"Of course he knows. While he was strategizing over the next few days for the campaign, I thought it would be a perfect time for me to visit."

"Campaign? What's he running for?"

Her smile held a gleam of excitement. "Senator of Massachusetts."

He could see her taking her place with the rich and powerful in DC. That explained her appearance here. Did she think he was too stupid to see her reasoning? "And you thought it would help your husband's election if you had a poor little blind girl in tow." He didn't bother to hide his disgust.

Her eyes widened. "It's not like that, Kevin. I want to make sure she's all right, that you're all right. It's actually dangerous for me to be here. If it comes out in the media that I abandoned my blind daughter, it would be the end of his campaign. I just want to see Sadie."

"You don't even know her. You left us and never once asked for pictures or updates on how she's doing. You couldn't be bothered to be any kind of mother until now."

Her eyes filled, and she held out her hand toward him. "Don't make me feel any worse about my actions. I know I made a mistake when I left, but I was depressed and unhappy. The two of us never quite connected, did we, Kevin? We wanted to be a couple, but there was always something in our way. You bonded to her right away, but I . . . couldn't somehow. Maybe it was postpartum depression, but I just knew I had to get away, start a new life."

"And did it make you happy?"

She tipped her head to one side. "I'm content, and that's something. But I want to make amends with my daughter. Sadie is mine, too, not just yours. I was wrong to turn my back on her. I want another chance."

Had he misjudged her? There was a note of desperation in her voice, but he was afraid it was all a trick to use Sadie for her own purposes. "I don't really trust you, DeAnn."

"And I can't blame you for that. But give me a chance to prove it to you."

"I'm not sure how you can even do that. Not after eight years of silence."

Her teeth came down on her lower lip, and she looked down at the porch floor. He wished he could tell what she was thinking.

Sadie often asked about her mother, and he struggled to find a way to make her feel loved even though her mother never called or came to see her. What damage might DeAnn do if Sadie grew to look forward to her visits and calls? And what if Sadie wanted to live with DeAnn someday? It would tear his heart out.

But all that mattered was Sadie's happiness. Second chances. He'd told his mother just this morning that she never forgave and gave anyone a second chance. For the first time, he understood her struggle. When you loved someone as much as he loved Sadie, it was hard to forgive someone who had hurt her. Trust was hard to dredge up out of pain.

Gulls squawked overhead, and the wind soughed through the branches of the trees lining the property. The sounds of home soothed him, and he began to tear down the first brick of his resistance to her idea. They could start small to minimize the possible damage to Sadie.

"I'll let you see her, but I don't want you to tell her who you are. Not yet."

When she looked up, a hopeful smile lifted her lips. "I can live with that. You want to evaluate how we interact. I get it. I wouldn't want to hurt her, Kevin. But she *is* my daughter."

You never showed an ounce of motherly love. He bit back the words as they formed on his tongue. "What's brought about this change anyway?"

She turned and looked out over the greening lawn. For a moment, he thought she wasn't going to answer him, or maybe she was trying to think of a good reason he might buy, but then she sighed and stared him in the face.

"My mother has cancer. She's dying. I realized when my time comes, I won't even have had the joy of a relationship with my daughter. Richard would grieve, but I would go to my grave without my daughter ever knowing that I love white chocolate or I like to dance."

"No legacy." It had a nice ring to it, but he still couldn't put his guard down.

She nodded. "Even that sounds a little selfish, like it's all about me. And maybe that's because I'm a selfish person at heart. But knowing Sadie might make me a little less selfish. I want to learn about being a mother and what that means. It will help me understand my own mom more."

"I'm sorry about your mom. I always liked her."

"She always wanted to see Sadie, and I wouldn't let her." DeAnn's voice trembled.

Another brick in the wall of his resistance tumbled. "How long does she have? It might not be too late."

"Six months, if we're lucky."

He turned back to the door and opened it. "When I introduce you, remember you're just a friend of mine. We'll see what happens."

TWENTY-ONE

The credits for *Peppa Pig* were flashing across the TV screen when Kevin stepped into the living room. He'd remodeled the place after DeAnn left, and he glanced at her to see if she noticed how different it looked. Her focus was fixed on Sadie though, and she didn't even look around at the new leather sofas or the nice rug on the hardwood floors.

Maybe he was wrong. Maybe she really was here because of all the reasons she'd stated and none of the reasons he feared. He glanced across the living room and sent a silent plea to Mallory, who stood at the kitchen island. The trepidation on her face matched that in his heart.

"Sadie, this is my friend Mrs. Blake who has come to town for a few days."

Sadie turned sightless eyes toward him and DeAnn. "Hi, Mrs. Blake."

DeAnn knelt on the rug by their daughter. "Hi, Sadie. You have a nice dog. What's her name?"

"Fiona. She's my best friend. Do you have a dog?"

"I do." Her voice trembled. "She's a sweet Yorkie named Scarlet. She's not as smart as your dog though. All she likes to do is play with a ball."

"Fiona likes to play ball too." Sadie scooted closer to DeAnn. "You smell nice."

"Thank you. I like the smell of your shampoo too. Like the perfect little girl." Tears shimmered on her lashes when she glanced up at Kevin and mouthed, *Thank you.*

He forced himself to smile encouragingly and turned toward the kitchen. They could use a little privacy. Maybe their interactions would be more natural without him looming over DeAnn's shoulder.

He joined Mallory, Kate, and Carol in the kitchen. "She says she's sorry." He pitched his voice low in hopes that it wouldn't carry to Sadie. He motioned to the women to follow him to the back deck.

The breeze from the woods behind the house was chilly. He stood so his bulk would block the wind for the women. "I don't quite know what to believe. She says she wants a relationship with Sadie."

Kate rolled her eyes. "Come on, Kevin, you know how selfish and self-centered she is. She's got a reason for being here, and it has nothing to do with being a mother."

"I'm afraid of that too. Her husband is running for the Senate, and I wonder if she intends to use Sadie to help him win."

Kate nodded. "I knew it!"

Mallory shook her head. "I'm not so sure. She was desperate to win Sadie's favor. You could see it in her actions and her tone. I think it's right to give her a second chance, Kevin. I can't even imagine life without Haylie in it. Maybe DeAnn finally figured out what she was missing."

"She said her mom has cancer and is dying. Maybe she also wants her daughter to know her mom before she dies."

Kate hugged herself against the chill in the air. "I'm not buying it. She has an ulterior motive. Be on your guard, Kevin."

"I am. I told her not to tell Sadie who she is yet, and she agreed." He reached for the doorknob. "You ladies are cold. Let's go inside. I didn't want to say the word *mother* where Sadie might hear it. That girl has hearing like a bat."

He opened the door for the women, then followed them inside. The aroma of something savory hung in the air. "Smells good."

"Dinner is ready, but I wasn't sure if we should interrupt," Mallory said.

What must she be thinking about DeAnn's appearance? While nothing had happened between them, they both recognized the undercurrents. He wished he could tell her that seeing DeAnn had made him realize how doomed his marriage had been from the start. And rushing into a relationship with her had left Sadie without a motherly influence. Even DeAnn's parents had stayed out of the picture. They didn't live close, and when their daughter had left him, he hadn't heard a word from them.

"You're my *mom*?" Sadie's voice nearly screamed out the words.

Kevin's gut clenched, and he wheeled toward the living room. His gaze met DeAnn's calm one, and he detected a hint of triumph in her smoky-blue eyes. In ten long strides, he was beside Sadie, who had leaped to her feet. Haylie sat on the sofa with an astonished expression.

"Daddy!" Sadie clutched his hand. "Mrs. Blake is my mom."

He glared at DeAnn. "What did you tell her?"

"We were just talking, and she guessed." DeAnn rose and brushed the dog hair from her slacks.

He scooped Sadie up into his arms. How did he even begin to untangle this?

She cupped her small hands around his face. "Your beard is prickly. Is it true, Daddy? Is she my mommy?"

He'd never lied to his daughter, and he wasn't about to start now. "Yes, Sadie, she is." His heart ached at the joy on her face. What if DeAnn hurt her? How could he protect her?

The answer was he couldn't. There was no real joy in life without experiencing pain too. The best he could do as a father was to prepare Sadie to handle what life threw her way.

He skewered DeAnn with a glare, but she tipped her chin up and stared back at him. He saw no remorse on her face, but maybe that didn't mean anything.

Sadie turned her face toward DeAnn. "Why did you go away, Mommy?"

That made DeAnn flinch. Surely she must have known that would be the first question Sadie asked. And how she answered it would tell him a lot. If she lied to Sadie, this experiment was over.

"I'm sorry I left. I have no good excuse. You're a wonderful little girl, and any mommy would be proud to have you for her little girl. I hope you can forgive me."

Sadie sagged against him, and a tear escaped the eye closest to him. "I forgive you, Mommy. Will you come see me again?"

"I will if you want me to. But only if you want me to."

"I want you to. Can we go for ice cream sometimes?"

His throat tightened, and he wished this day had never happened. He still didn't trust DeAnn.

Gulls swooped over the whitecaps and squawked at Julia for not sharing her lobster roll as she sat at a picnic table on the dock.

The scent of lobster spilled out of the Lobster Hut, a dockside Folly Shoals eatery, and she played with the edge of the red-and-white plastic tablecloth covering the table. The yellow Windbreaker she had on protected her from the worst of the wind, but her feet were cold in the flip-flops she wore. He'd better come by the time she was done with her sandwich or she was out of here.

She felt Frank before she saw him. The bench groaned under his weight as he settled next to her, and she shot him a look. "Took you long enough."

"I got behind a line of motor homes." His voice, deep and gravelly, was the most attractive thing about him. Though his hair was gray, he was anything but old and weak.

"Things have escalated. She didn't go back to Bangor after we set fire to the house. She moved in with the game warden helping her. The sheriff went to see her, too, and I bet he's questioning whether her dad's death was really an accident."

His stare made her squirm a bit. "All you had to do was get her back to Bangor. That doesn't seem all that difficult."

"She's from here, you idiot! She has support here. I don't think she's going to leave."

"Then we'll have to deal with it here."

She stared into his eyes. They were dark and scary. "That's my call, Frank. But yes, we will have to deal with it." She wasn't hungry anymore and threw the rest of her lobster roll to the gulls, who squawked their appreciation. "I'll try something else. It won't come to that."

But who was she kidding? Mallory was showing unexpected tenacity. And Julia still didn't know if the fire had burned up the evidence.

Mallory saw the tension in Kevin begin to ease as soon as the door shut behind DeAnn. They were side by side on the sofa with his laptop. If she tipped her head just right, she could catch a whiff of the spicy scent of his cologne.

Remember this moment. There were way too many obstacles for any kind of relationship to resurrect between them, and a time like this might never come again.

Kevin called up a website. "So, the guy's name was Len Nevin? I don't think I know him."

"He wore a suit and an attitude. Nothing from your private investigator?"

"I got a text from her. She's still looking." He leaned forward. "Found him. He's a loan shark."

She leaned closer to look at the screen. "A loan shark? Could Dad have gotten the money for the boat from him?"

"It's possible. I think we should pay him an official visit and ask him."

"Is there any way to know if he doesn't admit it?"

He shifted a bit on the sofa. "Not with the office fire. We might have found paperwork, but it's all ashes now. Want to go see him tomorrow?" He shook his head. "Wait, I can't go tomorrow until after three. I'm stuck in a car all day with my father."

"I have to deliver mail until about two anyway so we can go after you get off. You and your father are talking?"

He closed the laptop and set it aside. "Only reluctantly on my dad's part. We've been assigned to investigate the rash of rabies attacks. Our boss is getting tired of the strain our relationship is creating among the game wardens. He wants us to bury the hatchet."

"And your dad isn't willing."

"About as willing as a mama bear to give up her cub. He made it clear we would only talk about work issues."

The pathos in his voice hurt her heart. "I'm sorry."

He smiled down at her, then reached around her with one arm and gave her a gentle squeeze. "You have the best heart of anyone I know. Dad's reaction came at a good time, really. After seeing how he and Mom reacted, it made me stop and think about how I was treating DeAnn. I didn't want to give her a second chance, but I get second chances all the time. From my boss, from friends, from Sadie, and from God."

He still had his arm around her, and she didn't want him to move away. "The more we're hurt, the harder it is to get past it. And it's even worse when that person has hurt someone you love."

"Yeah, that's it exactly." He exhaled. "I don't know what I'll do if she hurts Sadie."

Mallory winced at the thought too. "Are you at all worried what will happen if she wants to take Sadie overnight on occasion?"

"I won't allow that until I'm sure this isn't some media stunt."

"How will you know?"

"I think I will need to talk to her husband and see what kind of guy he is. I've never met him. This is the first time I've even spoken to DeAnn since she left."

"How did you feel when you saw her again?" When he stiffened, she wished she hadn't asked, but the words just slipped out. "I mean, you haven't seen her in eight years, right? That had to be hard."

He shrugged. "I was too worried about Sadie to process it. The only thing I felt was panic. I mean, I'm glad she's happy, but she's a stranger now. Maybe she always was. It seemed a lifetime ago that we were married."

"You must have loved her." Why was she pressing him like this? She had to know if DeAnn was the great love of his life.

"I don't think I really did. It was one of those rebound things after you left." His voice had gone a little husky. "And I haven't dated since she left. Sadie and my job have taken all my time."

Rebound things. Her shoulders relaxed and Mallory leaned her head back against his arm. When was the last time they'd cozied up on the sofa this way? She shied away from the memory. Still keeping his arm around her, he flipped on the TV and called up the guide.

"*Shrek* is on. Want to watch it?"

"I haven't seen that in forever. Haylie loved it when she was a kid. She thinks she's too grown up for it now."

"Are you too grown up for it?" He squeezed her shoulders.

"I'll never be too grown up for it."

His eyes were pools of warm caramel she could drown in. "You know what I love about *Shrek*?" His breath whispered across her cheek and stirred her hair.

"What?" She didn't want to move.

"Only Fiona sees Shrek for who he is inside. You were always that person for me, Mallory. You believed in me and saw what I really wanted in life when all anyone else wanted to do was tell me what I *should* be. You loved me for who I was. I realized that when I saw DeAnn today."

Loved. That wasn't even true. The way she felt about him wasn't in the past tense. Every cell in her body vibrated when she was close to him. When she looked into his eyes, she felt she was looking at the other half of her soul. When his palm cupped her cheek, she closed her eyes and lifted her face. It had been too long since her lips had tasted his, but even as he leaned closer, she remembered that last experience vividly and pulled away.

"Do you remember the day I miscarried?"

The emotion in his eyes quickly shuttered. "Like it was yesterday."

Memories flooded her mind: the smell of the sea with the storm coming, the wind whipping her hair.

Gone. Mallory fingered her still-swollen belly. How could their baby be gone, just like that? All their dreams were rubble around them. Her mom and everyone else assured her there would be a baby next time. But she'd wanted this baby.

Kevin's boat roared through the waves toward Folly Shoals with its headlamp probing the darkness. He'd been with her through it all. Holding her hand, wiping her tears, whispering his love.

He reached across the boat and gripped her hand in his. "You okay?"

Hot tears welled again, and she wanted to wail her pain. "I'll be fine. Your parents will be happy." An edge of bitterness laced her words.

The reflection of the light from the dashboard illuminated his set face. "What are you saying? That you don't want to get married now?"

"There's no real reason to get married right away. You could go to med school if you wanted."

Why was she prodding him like this? Hadn't he already proven his love today as they faced this storm together?

He released her hand and turned the boat toward the dock at Breakwater Cottage. Her parents had gone ahead by a few minutes, and they'd be waiting inside. She wanted to run to her room and pull the covers over her face. Maybe when she woke up tomorrow, this would all be a bad dream.

"I could work a little longer, get enough money for a down payment on a house."

She turned her head and stared at him. Was he seriously considering delaying their marriage in two weeks? "I could work too." How did she manage to get it out with a hitch in her voice?

"We could get married next summer, and I could do right by you. I was worried about being gone from you and the baby so much as I get started with the Park Service. I could be past the worst of it by the time we got married."

The dock was fast approaching even as her heart splintered inside her chest. She'd lost the baby, and now she was losing Kevin.

She blinked, and the past vanished in the pain of the present day. "You were all too ready to put off our wedding."

He sat with his arm still along the back of the sofa even though she was a foot away now. "You suggested it, and I just wanted to do what made you happy."

"What I wanted was for you to hold me and tell me you'd never leave me. Instead, you were fine with postponing it once the baby was gone." Her words were tight and low. Until this moment, she hadn't examined what emotions had sent her running from Folly Shoals.

"Mallory, I'm not a mind reader. I was reeling, just like you. From a logical standpoint, we could afford to enter marriage more prepared. I've regretted that night all too often and have wondered what you would have said if I'd taken you straight to the church and had our pastor marry us."

She would have said yes. Clamping her teeth against the admission, she rose from the sofa. "It's too late now, Kevin. Much, much too late."

Twenty-Two

W ell, that was a bust." Carol raised the anchor as Mallory started the boat engine. "Not a single person had any idea who might have wanted to hurt your dad." It had thrilled her to be invited along on Mallory's run today.

"Aren't you hot?" Mallory tugged at the neck of her Windbreaker. "I'm burning up."

Carol pulled her hood up. Mallory probably thought she'd dressed for a visit to the North Pole. "Old people like me get cold easily. These sweats have special insulation, and I haven't felt that stiff breeze even start to penetrate the pants."

"You're not old. You'll never be old."

"Said the thirty-five-year-old hottie. I can't remember what an appreciative look from a man even feels like. I should lose twenty pounds, and I might see one of those lustful glances." Carol had to smile at all she'd seen the past few days. "Don't think I haven't noticed the longing glances you and Kevin exchange. You seem to be keeping him at arm's length. You need to get over all that past stuff."

Mallory steered the bow out onto a calm sea. A gull swooped down to perch on the railing. "Aw, the lovely day has helped keep me from thinking about Kevin. Why did you have to go and bring him up?"

Carol leaned back on her seat. "I want you to be happy. Kevin makes you happy."

"It's not that easy. There is more at stake than guilt over Mom's death. You saw how his mom acted yesterday, and now his ex-wife is back in the picture."

"Not as competition! You're just making excuses."

"Maybe I am."

Mallory kept her gaze on the gentle swells so Carol couldn't see her face. Some people could be so obstinate. Carol had lost so much in her life that she knew every moment was precious, something not to be wasted. How did she get that across to Mallory?

"I've had enough pain lately. I don't think I could handle any more."

"You're assuming loving Kevin would bring you pain. It's so clear that the two of you belong together. That kind of love doesn't come along very often. If you let it pass you by again, I'll shake you."

Mallory waved at a passing ferry, and the pilot tooted his horn in response. "The thought of facing his mom and dad in town makes my knees quake." She slanted a grin toward Carol.

"Nothing makes your knees quake. You're the strongest, bravest person I know. When Brian died, you were like a rock for Haylie. You figured out what you had to do, and then you did it without complaint. I think you could do anything you set your mind to."

"Spoken like a true friend."

Carol noticed another boat that was moving a little too fast and a little too close. "Look at that guy. He doesn't even act like he sees us."

"I'll slow down." Mallory did something with the controls and the boat slowed, then started to veer starboard, but the other craft veered even closer. "What is that guy doing?"

Carol twisted around to take in the fast-moving boat. "It's probably kids out enjoying the day. Give them a blast on your horn. They might not see you."

"I don't see how they could miss me." Mallory leaned over and gave a couple of toots on the horn, but the boat didn't slow.

Carol could make out two figures on the craft, but they both wore hooded sweatshirts and she couldn't make out much about their features except that they were both Caucasian. When she heard the first buzz past her ear, she dazedly thought it was a bee clear out here on the water. Then something pinged on the side of the boat, and she saw the bullet hole.

"He's shooting at us! Get down!" Carol flung herself to the boat deck, then grabbed Mallory's arm and yanked.

Mallory crouched down under the dash, then reached up to steer the boat. The boat sped up, and Carol risked a glance over the side, then ducked as another bullet dug into the plastic by her head. The guy was shooting to kill.

Mallory raised up, then popped back down again. "See if you can get a signal on your cell phone. I'm not sure how to use this new radio."

Carol pulled her cell phone out of her jacket pocket. "I only have one bar. Let me see if a call to 911 will go through." She punched in the number and held the phone to her ear. Nothing. She shook her head. "It's not going through."

She dared a glance over the side of the boat. The attackers

were closing fast. They must have a really big engine. "Try to get the radio to work."

Mallory nodded and sidled along the boat deck, then grabbed the mic and keyed it. "Mayday, mayday, this is Mallory Davis. We're being fired upon by two men in a SuperSport. I couldn't see the boat ID."

A man's voice crackled across the radio. "What's your location, Ms. Davis?"

She gave him their GPS coordinates. "We're a few miles out from Summer Harbor, but the other boat will intercept us before we get there."

"We have a Coast Guard unit nearby. Dispatching now."

Carol risked another peek over the side. The SuperSport had veered around to come at them from the other direction. It appeared they intended to ram their boat. Mallory changed direction to avoid them, but Carol sensed it was useless. The other boat was much faster. If only she had a weapon, but that wouldn't do much good. She had no idea how to shoot one, but Mallory did.

Mallory grabbed her purse. "Check and see if there are any guns in that cabinet. I can use my small gun, but it doesn't have the range I'd like. Keep your head down."

Carol nodded and crawled to the closest cabinet. After searching it, she shook her head. "Nothing."

Mallory peeked up and took a shot at the approaching boat. One of the men ducked.

The engine from the SuperSport grew louder. Carol popped up for another look and saw the big boat bearing down on them. "It's going to hit us!" She made out two guys, one with broad shoulders and gray hair. The other one was a little younger and wore a baseball cap so she couldn't see the color of his hair.

The words were barely out of her mouth when the boats collided. The impact sent her flying through the air, and she hit her head on the side of the boat.

Her vision dimmed, and she shook her head to clear it. She had to find a weapon before the men boarded their craft and hurt Mallory.

Kevin's boat rode the waves that had escalated with the afternoon wind. A storm was coming. He risked a glance at his dad as he steered toward Folly Shoals. The next interview was with the hotel manager, but Kevin wasn't sure he'd be able to hold out much longer with this uncomfortable silence. His father had only answered in monosyllables and only about the work at hand. The deep freeze had only served to strengthen Kevin's determination not to let his parents rule his life.

The radio crackled to life, and he listened to the report of gunshots fired from one boat to another. He turned up the radio to listen. "We're near there, Dad. We should go help."

His father shook his head but didn't look at him. "We have our own duties to attend to. The Coast Guard will handle it."

Kevin started to nod, then he thought he heard Mallory's name. "Wait a minute." He grabbed the radio's mic. "This is Game Warden O'Connor. Say again."

The dispatcher repeated the announcement, and a chill swept over Kevin. "Mallory's boat is being fired upon." He turned the boat back out to sea. "I have to get to her." The wind nearly blew his hat off his head.

His father rose. "Get out of the way and let me steer this thing. You have no head for duty."

"We're only a couple of minutes from her location. I'm going there, and there's nothing you can do about it."

His father harrumphed but sat back down. Kevin could feel his displeased stare, but it rolled off his back. All that mattered was getting to Mallory. Had she been shot? Who would have fired on her?

He grabbed a pair of binoculars and brought them to his eyes. He could see the boat from here, but he couldn't see any movement. No sign of the SuperSport.

His gut clenched and visions of Mallory lying in the boat with a bullet through her head flashed through his mind. He pushed the engine as fast as he dared, and in moments he was at her boat. Maneuvering close, he cut the engine, then reached over to tie the boats together.

Even from here, he could see the bullet holes. "Mallory, are you okay?"

Her head popped up, then he saw Carol rise as well. He'd never seen a more beautiful sight than Mallory's dark hair and big brown eyes. He nearly slipped in his haste to clamber over the side. "Are either of you hurt?"

Mallory shook her head. "We stayed down."

The boat dipped as he stepped down onto the deck. Try as he might, he couldn't stop himself from grabbing her and pulling her to his chest. She didn't resist but nestled against him with her arms around his waist. Her soft hair touched his chin as he held her close and thanked God that she was safe.

When she began to stir, he let her go. "Can you identify the guy who shot at you?"

The wind blew her hair around her face. "I tried to stay down so he didn't have a good target. Their boat rammed us and I thought they would board us, but they moved off. I think they must have seen your boat approaching. The Coast Guard is on its way too."

He became aware of another engine and nodded. "Here they come now. They'll have a ton of questions."

"And I won't have many answers. I couldn't see the boat's ID, and I don't have much of a description of the two men."

He nodded and lifted his hand to wave at the Coast Guard cutter arriving. Luke Rocco boarded them first.

"Hi, Kevin." Luke touched Mallory's shoulder. "Everyone okay here?"

"Just shaken up." Mallory pulled Carol over to stand beside her. "We stayed down."

"You're both lucky." Luke bent over to examine the bullet holes. "These are from a high-powered gun. Those guys meant business. Did they try to board after they rammed you?"

Mallory moved closer to Kevin again, and he put his arm around her waist. "She said they left the scene. I think they saw my boat coming."

"There were two guys." Carol was pale and looked shaken. "One wore a baseball cap, but I'd never be able to pick them out of a lineup though. Everything happened too fast."

"We'll see if we can collect the bullets, and we'll check the damage to the boat. That might tell us something. Too bad you didn't see the boat name. Anything distinctive about it?" Luke asked.

Mallory shook her head. "I just know the make. It looked fairly new and had blue trim."

"We'll see what we can do. Your boat still appears to be seaworthy." Luke glanced at Kevin. "If you want to get the ladies home, I'll deliver the mail boat to Folly Shoals once we get all we need from it."

"I can do that."

Kevin's dad cleared his throat. "We have work to do and already have been delayed. It would be better if you saw to them getting home, Luke."

Luke raised a brow and looked at Kevin. Kevin shook his head. "I'll get them home. Our business can wait. People are more important than our little project."

His dad scowled at him, then turned to Luke. "Can you drop me off at Summer Harbor? I don't want to fool around with this today."

"Sure, but we're going to be out here awhile."

"It's better than my other alternative."

Mallory's eyes flooded with tears, and Kevin took her arm. "Let's get back."

TWENTY-THREE

The storm had moved in by the time Kevin parked in his driveway and got out. Mallory couldn't drum up the energy to even talk on the ride back. Who would want to kill her? The deadly intent had been very obvious. And the reaction from Kevin's father hurt almost more than the attack.

She squinted through the pouring rain at the vehicle parked in front of Kevin's house. "Looks like the sheriff's here." She opened the door and stepped out into the mud, then rushed for the house. Maybe he'd caught the men who shot at them.

Danny Colton was on the sofa in front of a blazing fire. The coffee cup Kate must have given him looked tiny in his massive hands. Kevin and Carol came in with a gust of wind and rain behind her.

Mallory took off her jacket and hung it on one of the wall hooks. "Sheriff, I hope you have some news for me."

"I do, but it's not what you might expect, Mrs. Davis. Have a seat. This will take some time to explain." His gaze narrowed. "I heard you were shot at today. You okay?"

"Fine, just shaken up a bit. What's this about, Sheriff?"

"I'll get the rest of you some coffee," Kate said. "The girls are upstairs watching a movie. I thought it best they didn't hear this. It might give them nightmares."

Mallory frowned and sank onto the armchair by the fireplace. "What's she talking about?"

The sheriff set his coffee cup on the table, then shook out an Altoids mint and popped it into his mouth. "You were probably too shook up with your mom's death to remember all this, so I'm going to take you through the sequence of events back then. It's important to understand what's happening now."

Carol ran her hand through her wet hair and came to sit on the ledge by the fire. Mallory glanced at Kevin, and he came over to perch on the arm of the chair by her. She leaned slightly against his comforting bulk.

Sheriff Colton snapped his Altoids tin closed and opened it again as if he couldn't stand to sit still.

Kevin nodded. "I remember because Dad found the body and talked about what bad shape it was in. There were propeller marks or something on her head and face."

"Right. And Edmund honored Karen's request to donate her body to science. Wasn't sure if you remembered that."

"I had forgotten that, actually." Kate returned with two cups of coffee, and Mallory took one of them. She wrapped her fingers around the hot mug and let the heat warm her cold hands.

He looked back at her steadily. "It's an important detail. We've got a forensic artist here in town doing some training, and she was using your mom's skull."

Mallory's gut clenched at the mental picture. "Okay." Where was he going with this?

"Gwen Marcey is her name. The artist, I mean. Anyway, during her lecture she mentioned the victim had been murdered."

"Murdered? My mom?"

He nodded. "It's a jeezly situation, for sure. So I've pulled the autopsy records, and Gwen is looking them over. We'll have more information soon so come into the wind." He picked up his coffee cup again. "I know this is a shock."

Shock didn't begin to describe how she felt. "There has to be some mistake."

"Ms. Marcey is the best in her field, and I'll let you know what she says." He rose and put on his hat.

Still in a daze, Mallory got up and followed him to the door with Kevin close on her heels. She shut the door behind the sheriff and turned to Kevin. "I can't begin to imagine what this all means."

His mouth in a grim line, he nodded. "Try not to speculate, Mal."

Speculating was all she could do.

The garden behind the hotel held only bees and a rabbit that scampered away when Julia hurried outside to the grape arbor. The vines had sent out fresh sprigs of green, and the scent of spring flowers filled the air. She pulled out her phone and called her stepson's number.

"You took long enough to check in." Ian's gruff voice told her what kind of mood he was in. But then irritated was his usual state these days. "So your warning didn't work."

"Nope." No one was going to stand in the way of the good life nearly in her reach. "She still hasn't stumbled on the truth."

"You can't know that, Julia. Or that she won't. She's poking around everywhere."

She wandered across the grass to sit on an iron bench by the fountain. The sound of running water soothed her worries. A thought struck her, and a slow smile lifted her lips. "I have an idea. Give me two days to figure out how to execute it."

"Two days is all we've got."

"I know. I'll be in touch." She ended the call and exhaled.

The dying fire crackled in the darkened living room. Mallory sat on the sofa and stared at the glowing embers. The rest of the household had gone to bed, and only she and Kevin were still up. She'd never be able to sleep a wink if she went to bed now.

What did Gwen Marcey's comment mean? It could mean nothing or it could mean everything. Kevin came from the kitchen with a plate of summer sausage and cheese in one hand and a sleeve of Ritz crackers in the other.

He held up the crackers. "I always think better when I have food. I brought enough for you too. You didn't eat a bite of dinner."

Her stomach growled, and she reached for a piece of summer sausage. "Venison?"

"Of course."

"I haven't had venison summer sausage since I left here." She stacked a cracker with cheese and sausage and took a bite. "Yum, jalapeño."

They ate in silence for a minute. The warmth of the fire and her full belly began to relax her. She wiped her fingers on the paper towel Kevin handed her, then stood and went to look at the pictures on the mantel. "There are pictures of DeAnn here."

He joined her in front of the fire. "I didn't want Sadie to forget her mom. Even though she can't see them, I tell her what they look like."

She turned to face him. "Everything is a mess, Kevin. I feel like we're being hit from all sides. Maybe I should go back to Bangor."

"Your house was broken into there too. Running back will just leave you alone and defenseless. Carol is great, but she's hardly able to protect you from a killer like I can. And you have lots of friends here."

"It doesn't feel like it. I mean, Kate, sure. She's still my friend, but everyone remembers what we did. What I did. The sidelong glances and pointed stares are hard to deal with."

"I think you're just being sensitive. I can't blame you with the treatment you've gotten from my parents. But I've lived here through all of it. It's over."

Maybe he was right. Her self-consciousness about being back might have contributed to her feelings of being out of place. "What are you going to do about DeAnn? When is she coming again?"

"She's still in town. I told her she could come see Sadie tomorrow. She wanted to take her out for the day, but I'm not ready to trust her that far. She might just up and take her."

A shudder ran up Mallory's spine at the thought of anyone taking Haylie away from her. And Sadie was so little. "She seems sincere, but it's hard to know if there's an ulterior motive behind her appearance."

His brow wrinkled. "I thought you believed she deserved a second chance."

"I do, but I've thought it through a little more. Her husband is in politics. You just don't know for sure why she's here. I hope it's for all the right reasons."

The logs on the fire shifted, and the blaze crackled as new fuel burst into flames. His presence beside her generated more heat than the fire did though, and she shifted just a fraction so her arm brushed his. Lord help her, but the man enticed her nearly more than she could handle. His male scent, all spicy with his aftershave and skin, made her want to bury her nose in his neck.

It would take all Mallory's strength to resist him every day. She really needed to find another place to stay before she made a complete fool of herself.

He reached out and twisted one of her curls around his finger. "No one has hair like yours—so thick and luxurious. It's so fine textured too." He lifted the strand to his lips and kissed it.

His hand in her hair was sending shivers up her back and making her stomach twist. Her knees started to shake a little, and she struggled to get ahold of herself. It had been so long since she'd been with a man. Brian had been dead for two years, and she hadn't so much as gone out to coffee with another man. She wasn't dead though, and every sense flared to life with Kevin's touch.

She swallowed hard and forced herself to laugh and start for the kitchen. "I'd better put away the rest of the food."

He caught her arm as she took a step. With a quick movement he pulled her against him, then his lips were on hers and every bit of resistance she'd summoned evaporated. She tried to recount all the reasons why she shouldn't be with him, but the taste of him and the feel of his arms drove every thought from her head.

His lips demanded a response, and she couldn't stop her arms from creeping up until she was clasping the back of his neck and pouring every bit of the love she'd denied herself into that kiss.

She forgot the guilt that dogged her. She forgot his family's resistance. No matter how much she'd tried to forget how safe and loved she felt in his arms, now that she was here, she didn't want to leave again.

Somehow they found themselves on the sofa and his hand was on the bare skin of her back. Her fingers had unbuttoned his shirt, though she had no memory of doing it. She pulled his head down for another kiss.

He took a ragged breath, then pulled away and straightened her top. "I think I'd better go to my room. You're way too tempting, and I'm not that strong where you're concerned." His hand cupped her cheek, and he looked down into her eyes. "But know this, Mallory. We belong together, and we both know it. I'll do whatever it takes to make sure you never walk away from me again."

Her throat tightened, and she blinked back the moisture in her eyes. "I . . . I'd better get to bed." She fled before the words *I love you* spilled out of her lips.

Twenty-Four

Kevin shoved open the window in his room and let the breeze blow over his heated face. The fresh air cleared his head, and he looked out over the treetops. He wanted nothing more than to go right back to the living room and kiss Mallory again, but he had to resist. He loved her too much, and this time they would do things in the right order. Marriage first. He wanted his ring on her finger before she came to his bed again.

His cell phone chirped, and he glanced at the clock beside his bed. Ten o'clock, not as late as it seemed. Abby's name flashed on his screen, and he quickly answered it before the call went to voice mail. "Abbs, you found something?"

"This was a hard one to track, Kevin. Someone had worked really hard to bury that adoption."

He frowned and sat on the edge of the bed. "So what do we have?"

"Mallory was two weeks old when she was adopted. Her mother had her when she was in jail."

Kevin winced. "Do we know why she went to jail?"

"Not yet. The names are sealed, and I haven't been able to crack them yet. I'm going to figure it out though. It may just take a little time. Tell Mallory to be patient with me. Hopefully I'll have all the details with my next update."

"Thanks, Abby, I owe you." He squinted out the window, then reached over and flipped off his light. Something had moved outside.

"No problem. Sorry for calling so late, but I knew you were eager to hear. I'll talk to you soon."

He put down his phone and crept closer to the window. He saw the movement again. He strapped on his gun and slipped out his door and down the stairs. Light shone from under Mallory's door so he rapped on it with his knuckles.

She held the door partially closed, and he caught just a peek of her red silk pajamas. "Is something wrong?"

"I saw someone outside. I'm going out to check. If I'm not back in five minutes, call 911."

She opened the door wider and caught at his arm. "Let's call the law."

"I *am* the law. I'll be fine. Lock the door behind me. I've got my key so I'll let myself back in. Just pay attention and listen, okay?"

She nodded, and he hurried to the back door so he could circle around and catch the guy. The screen door squealed as he eased it open, and he winced. Maybe the guy wouldn't hear it from out front. He unsnapped his holster and rested his hand on his Sig Sauer as he crept around the corner of the house.

Cold dew soaked into the ankles of his pants, and his shoes squeaked on the wet grass. The moonless night made it hard to see back here, but one streetlight at the end of his lane should illuminate his front yard.

He paused when he reached the front corner and looked

around. The glow from the distant streetlight only slightly improved his vision, but it was enough to spot the figure standing under the oak tree in his yard.

He drew his gun. "Game warden. You there, come out from under the tree."

The person plunged into the brush at the edge of his property, and his blood pumping, Kevin gave chase. The shrubs lashed at his arms and he tripped over a rock in his way, but he quickly gained on the figure trying to escape.

With a final burst of speed, he lunged forward and grabbed at a flutter of shirt. His grip caused the person to jerk and fall, and Kevin tumbled to the ground too.

He slapped a hand on the guy's arm and hauled him up. The figure was too slight and lightweight to be a man. "What are you doing skulking around my house?"

"It's me, Kevin." DeAnn's husky voice spoke out of the darkness. "I didn't mean to scare you."

He dropped his grip and stepped back. "What the heck do you think you're doing? Don't try to tell me you wanted to see Sadie. It's after ten and she's been in bed for hours."

Without waiting for an answer, he hustled her back toward the house. "You can answer my questions in the light where I can see your face. Mallory will be calling the sheriff if I don't stop her." He gritted his teeth and marched her toward the house.

There was no possible reasonable explanation for her appearance here at this hour. All his earlier reservations resurged full force. She wanted something.

She stumbled a little as they went up the porch steps, then she jerked away. "I can walk by myself."

"I'm sure you can, but I don't want you running for your car until you've answered my questions." He dug out his key and put it in the lock. Before he turned it, Mallory opened the door.

"I was just about to call 911." Her eyes widened as her gaze went over his shoulder and landed on DeAnn. "She's the intruder?"

"I'm not an intruder. I have every right to be here." DeAnn pushed past Mallory.

"Not hardly. This is my property. You signed off on everything when you left."

Kevin and Mallory followed her into the living room, where DeAnn plopped onto the sofa and exhaled. Her French roll had come down in her mad run across the yard, and bits of debris clung to her khaki slacks.

She leaned down and slipped off her right shoe and held it up to show the broken heel. "These are Manolo Blahnik, and they cost the earth. You ruined them."

"I didn't tell you to run. You could have come out from under the tree like I told you. Now, what are you doing here?"

Her blue eyes looked him over, then went to linger on Mallory. "She's the reason you never loved me, isn't she?"

He sucked in a harsh breath. "Deflecting the question isn't going to get you anywhere. What do you really want and why are you here?"

She blinked. "You always said Mallory was in your past, but that's a lie." DeAnn slipped her shoe back on and stood, wobbling a little on the broken heel. "I'm leaving and you can't stop me. But you'll be hearing more from my attorney. I'm going to start exercising my right to see Sadie. That's what I came here to tell you."

He blocked her path. "Don't hurt Sadie just because you're angry with me. I won't stand aside and let that happen. You haven't cared a thing about her in all these years, DeAnn. If I have to, I will contact the media and let them know what the aspiring senator's wife is up to."

Her face went white. "You wouldn't do that."

Her familiar perfume turned his stomach, but he stood his ground and stared her down. "I'd do anything for Sadie."

She pressed her lips together and headed for the door without another word. He exhaled. He hadn't heard the last from her.

Mallory put her hand on his arm. "I'm sorry if my presence escalated things. I can find another place to live while you sort all this out. Maybe you need to think about it."

He covered her hand with his. "Like I said, Mallory, I'll do whatever it takes for us to be together."

Mallory's hands shook as she filled the teakettle to prepare some chamomile tea. The owl hooting outside the window added to her sense of impending doom. She set the teakettle on the cooktop in the island and turned on the heat.

No matter how hard she tried, Mallory couldn't get DeAnn's words out of her head. Maybe leaving here would be the best thing. Just pack up Haylie and Carol and get back to Bangor. Let Kevin get on with his life. She hadn't intended to disrupt anything.

She felt Kevin's presence before she heard him. Turning, she slanted a smile up at him. "Sorry if I woke you. I couldn't sleep so I thought I'd try some tea."

"I wasn't asleep either. I got a call about another rabid animal. I have to go out." His dark eyes swept over her. "I can see what you're thinking, but I don't want you to go."

She bit her trembling lower lip. "I feel like I'm messing up your life."

He stepped nearer and put his hands on her shoulders. "I feel more alive than I have in years, since you left. Don't go, Mallory. Promise me you won't."

With his intent gaze on her and the warmth of his hands seeping into her skin, she couldn't think, let alone make any decisions. "Let's talk about it later."

Disappointment twisted his mouth, and he dropped his hands back to his sides. "I didn't get a chance to tell you that Abby called with information. She's still tracking down the names because the records were sealed pretty tightly, but she found a document the birth mother filled out. You were born when your mother was in jail."

A sick feeling swirled in her belly. "Jail? She was some kind of criminal? That bolsters my theory that maybe she killed my dad."

He nodded. "It sure makes it seem possible. Abby didn't know why she was in jail yet, but she's working on it."

The teakettle shrieked, and Mallory lifted it from the heat. She poured hot water over the tea bag. "This is exactly why I never wanted to find my birth mother. You hear all these terrible stories. If it wasn't for bringing justice to my father, I'd forget the whole thing. And even if she's innocent, once I make contact, there's no going back."

"Let's see what Abby finds out. Maybe she's still in prison and had nothing to do with your dad's death. Then you can ignore the information and never make contact."

"I can hope." She followed him through the living room and set her mug on the coffee table. "It's one in the morning. Do you have to go out often in the middle of the night?"

He went to the door and grabbed his jacket. "It happens. At least you're here and I don't have to call Kate to come babysit. I won't be gone long. Keep the door locked."

"I will." When the door shut behind him, she curled up on the sofa with her legs tucked under her. She heard a sound and turned.

Carol descended the stairs dressed in red pajamas. Her bangs went every which way, and her eyes were swollen from sleep. "What are you doing drinking tea in the middle of the night? And did I just hear the door shut?"

"Kevin got called out. Another rabid animal."

Carol yawned and wandered over to sit on the love seat. "At least the kids didn't wake up."

"Kevin got some news about my birth mom. I was born when she was in jail."

Carol hesitated, then brushed her bangs to one side. "Jail? T-that's unexpected. How do you feel about it?"

"Trust my best friend to get to the heart of the matter." Mallory took a sip of her hot tea. "My real mother was a criminal. What does that make me?"

Carol pointed a finger at her. "You put that talk away right now. There's no shame attached to you because of her mistakes. You're still the same caring, wonderful person you were before you heard that news."

"I wonder what she did to land in jail." Pregnant in jail. What must that have been like? Didn't children born of inmates usually get put into the foster-care system? The shame and fear her mother must have felt tugged at her heart. It was the same shame she'd felt herself when she stared at the positive result on the test strip she'd bought at the drugstore. How had her mother heard the news—from a hard-faced guard?

Carol hugged her knees to her chest. "Did you hear anything about your biological dad?"

"No details on him yet, and very little about my birth mom, really. The private investigator hopes to have more information soon."

"Will you try to contact your mother when you find out who she is? Do you want a relationship?"

"Right now I just want to find out if she killed my dad, but based on this little bit I know, I don't think I will show myself if she isn't responsible. She could be homeless or a drug addict by now. Or still in jail. It's hard to know what I'll do until I know more."

Mallory could just imagine the scene. A woman like that would constantly want a handout for drugs or something. Did she want justice enough to face something so upsetting?

Carol pulled an afghan around her. "Suppose you find out she's a good person who is trying to turn her life around?"

"It's unlikely. I just want all this to be over so I can get on with my life." She took another sip of her tea. "Maybe we should just go back to Bangor and let the law figure this out. At least with everything that's happened, the sheriff is looking now. He has more tools than I do anyway."

Carol looked back at her steadily. "This has nothing to do with getting on with life or avoiding what you might find out about your mother. You're scared of getting too close to Kevin, aren't you?"

Mallory's face went hot. "Can you blame me? His ex-wife showed up tonight and told him she's going to see an attorney about officially exercising her right to see Sadie. I think it might be because she's mad I'm here."

Carol stood and yawned. "Running isn't going to fix this, Mallory. You need to look inside and face what you find. You and Kevin have never gotten over one another. This isn't even about his ex. This is still about the guilt you carry. I think it's time you forgave yourself."

Mallory watched her head for the stairs. Forgiving herself was easier said than done.

TWENTY-FIVE

The building where Len Nevin worked was in Summer Harbor, right in the middle of the downtown area. The street was empty except for a few early tourists. If Kevin hadn't known the guy was a sleazebag, he would have thought the brick building with its Victorian accents was a legitimate place. Even the sign in the window was discreet with small letters offering to cash payroll checks at the cheapest rates around. But an offer like that wasn't saying much.

He put his hand on Mallory's elbow and guided her inside, where the marble floors and Victorian detail added to the high-class ambience. The place almost smelled antiseptic with the scent of some kind of cleaning solution hanging in the air.

"How may I help you this morning?" The receptionist, an attractive blonde in her twenties, sent a perky smile their way.

"We'd like to speak with Mr. Nevin, please."

"Of course. Could I have your name?"

"Game Warden O'Connor."

The wattage in her smile dimmed just a bit. "One moment." She rose and walked down the hall to an office with her high heels clicking on the marble. When she returned, her smile had transformed into a stiff mask. "I'm sorry, but Mr. Nevin will be busy all afternoon."

"I think we'll just interrupt him." With his hand still on Mallory's arm, he guided her around the receptionist to the office door. The receptionist tried to stop him, but he ignored her and opened the door.

Phone in hand, Nevin looked up, and his expression went dark. He put the phone down. "I can call the sheriff."

"I'm a game warden. He'll back me up if you'd care to try."

Nevin's pale-blue eyes looked them over before he leaned back in his chair. "I suppose this is about Edmund Blanchard. You've dug into the records."

Kevin disliked him more by the minute. "Smart man."

Nevin shrugged. "No sense in prevaricating. He came to me for a loan, and I turned him down. No big secret about that."

Mallory glanced around at the pictures on the walls. "Did he say what he wanted the money for?"

Kevin admired her cool tone and calm manner. "And did you speak with him face-to-face?"

"He filled out an application. He said he wanted to pay back a loan he'd taken out to get his boat, that he'd regretted getting it."

Mallory swung back around from her perusal of a wall of awards. Her dark eyes were narrowed and focused. "What loan did he want to pay off?"

"I don't remember where he'd gotten the money originally. I could check his application though." Nevin picked up the phone and asked his receptionist to bring in the paperwork. "The amount he wanted was much too high for his income to support. I'm surprised the original loaner gave him that kind of money."

Kevin knew the kind of boat Edmund had purchased was in the two hundred thousand range. "How much?"

The door opened, and the receptionist entered with a file in her hand. She didn't look at Kevin or Mallory, and her mouth was set in a flat line. She handed over the file and rushed out, shutting the door behind her.

Nevin opened the file. "I could have looked it up on the computer, but I assumed you would want the proof in Edmund's own handwriting. Looks like he requested two hundred and twenty-five thousand dollars."

Kevin saw Mallory's quick intake of breath. That was a heck of a lot of money. Who would have given Edmund that kind of cash?

Before he could ask, Nevin looked up with a frown. "I think this was probably another reason why I rejected the request. Edmund said he got the money from a private individual, and he wouldn't reveal the name so I could verify it." He slid the paper across the desk's gleaming surface so they could look at it themselves.

"Who would give my father that kind of money? That's nearly a quarter of a million dollars. He had no way of even earning that much money in the rest of his career."

Nevin steepled his fingers. "That was my thought too. As I recall he seemed almost desperate to get the money, which made no sense. There was no lien on the boat so it's not like the situation should have been so important to him. I suppose the person might have been charging a confiscatory interest rate, but then ours isn't exactly prime."

Mallory picked up the paper and perused it. "What was his reaction when you rejected his application?"

"He asked me to reconsider and asked how he might convince me. I gave him all the reasons I couldn't give him the money. Before rushing out of here and slamming the door behind him, he muttered something about his life being over." Nevin shrugged. "I was sorry to disappoint him because I liked him. But business is business, and it would have been a stupid decision on my part."

The color drained out of Mallory's cheeks, and Kevin knew she was mulling over her father's final comment. Could whoever he'd borrowed the money from have ordered his death?

Mallory stood with Kevin on downtown Main Street. A nearby fudge shop sent an aroma cloud of chocolate their way. She still reeled from hearing about her father's desperation to get that loan. She had a feeling they were missing something important, but what?

Kevin took her arm and turned her toward the street. "The sheriff's truck is parked in front of the coffee shop. Let's go talk to him."

Woodenly, she let him lead her to the coffee shop. They stepped inside onto wide plank boards. The aroma of roasting coffee wafted through the shop as she looked around for the sheriff. He waved them to his table near the plateglass window to their right.

He looked like a long scarecrow trying to fold himself into a child's seat. "I was about to call you." He tipped his head toward a slender woman in her midthirties with short blonde hair.

Her Burberry jacket and slacks were a deep claret that went

well with her skin. She smiled back at them but didn't say anything, as if waiting for the sheriff to introduce her.

"This is Gwen Marcey. She's the forensic artist I told you about."

"Pleased to meet you." Gwen stood and shook their hands before she sat back down. There was a little smear of graphite on her fingers.

"Have a seat," Colton said. "Gwen has the composite done, and we were just talking about it."

Mallory slid into a seat and scooted closer. The sheriff's voice seemed somber, but maybe it was just her state of mind. Nevin's information had left her reeling. "What did you find in the report?"

Gwen reached for her leather case. "I hope this won't upset you, but I drew a picture as well to show the placement of the wound. Plus, I wanted to make sure the identification of the skull hadn't gotten mixed up. I didn't want to upset anyone if this wasn't even your mother." She glanced at the sheriff, and he nodded. She unclasped the brass buckle on the case and pulled out a large, thick piece of paper, then slid it across the table to Mallory.

Mallory looked down at the drawing, and her lips parted. It was amazingly like her mother. The hairstyle wasn't quite right, but the narrow nose and strong bone structure were a perfect match. Her mother had a tiny chip in one tooth, and Mallory saw that same imperfection in the drawing.

Gwen touched the top of the drawing. "The hair might not be quite right. I looked at hairstyles from that era and guessed."

Mallory managed a jerky nod. "She wore her hair parted on the other side, and it was straighter. She fought the curl with a flat iron constantly. I'd always told her to give it up and admit she lived by the sea."

Even though she'd thought it wouldn't bother her, a lump lodged in Mallory's throat. "It's my mom for sure." She touched the mouth. "Look at the chip in the tooth. The nose is perfect too. It's definitely Mom."

The sheriff exhaled and rubbed his forehead. "I don't know quite how to tell you what Gwen found, Mallory." He glanced at the artist. "Want to explain?"

Gwen tucked a strand of hair behind her ear. "I studied the autopsy photos and the coroner's report. He expected to see a drowned woman, and that's what he saw in spite of the evidence."

Mallory's heart pounded. "What evidence?"

"In studying the photos, I found a small hole in the cranium. I suspect the coroner blew it off as damage caused by the propeller, but it's actually a bullet hole. I noticed it in the skull and wanted to see what he made of it in the autopsy. It was just plain missed."

Mallory gripped Kevin's steadying hand and drew in a sharp breath. "That's impossible. My mother drowned during a massive storm. No one shot her. Could it have been damage from the storm?"

Gwen shook her head. "Someone killed her."

"Could she have killed herself?" Kevin asked.

Mallory gasped and jerked her hand out of his. "What a thing to say! My mother was happy. She wouldn't do something like that to her family. She loved us more than anything."

"I know, Mal, but as kids we don't always know our parents' heartaches." He looked back at Gwen. "Any thoughts on that?"

Gwen shook her head. "The bullet went through the back

of her head. She couldn't have reached around and done that to herself. Someone murdered her."

Mallory felt cold, then hot, then cold again. "Who could have done it? That makes no sense."

The sheriff shuffled in his chair. "Were your parents having any trouble? You ever hear them fighting?"

"No, and don't even try to insinuate my father would hurt her. He was out delivering mail that day. I know because I was with him. We got home around three. I started dinner while we waited for her to come home. She never did."

It felt as though something heavy sat on her chest, making it hard to draw a breath. Murdered. Did that mean Mallory hadn't been responsible for her mother's death?

TWENTY-SIX

K evin watched the color come and go in Mallory's face, and he took her hand again. The news had shocked him, so he knew she was reeling. He motioned to one of the baristas behind the bar. "Could we get two of your largest coffees?" She nodded and went to get them as he turned back toward the sheriff.

Mallory's fingers were cold, and she clung to his hand. "I'm glad Dad isn't here to learn about this. I'm not sure he could have handled knowing someone shot her. Back of the head. Isn't that execution style?"

The sheriff took out his Altoids tin and selected a mint. "It might be. Gwen thinks the size of the bullet hole indicates close range."

Imagining the scene made Kevin wince. The barista returned with the coffees, and he paid her and added a generous tip. "Thanks." He rose and retrieved some cream and sugar. "We just talked to Nevin across the street. He says Edmund tried to get a loan for two hundred and twenty-five thousand dollars." He recounted all the loan shark had told them. "What if Edmund got the money from the mob or something?"

The sheriff glanced at Mallory. "I know you won't want to

hear this, but what if your parents were both involved with the mob in some way?"

Spots of color sprang to her cheeks, and her dark eyes flashed. "That's ridiculous, Sheriff. There was never anything in their lives to indicate something like that."

The sheriff snapped his tin shut. "We're just going over all the possibilities. Try not to get offended as we run through this, Mrs. Davis. We have to look at every angle." He popped the mint into his mouth while his gaze took on a faraway cast. "I never knew them to travel much. Do you remember them going to New York or any other big city?"

She shook her head. "I can count on one hand the times in my life we even went as far as Bangor. When we went on vacation, we usually stayed close, just up to the Canadian border where we'd camp and fish for a week. When I was sixteen, Mom took me to New York City to see *The Phantom of the Opera*. We were together every minute though, and she never spoke to anyone other than hotel and waitstaff."

"We need to find out how your dad paid for that boat. The first thing to do is find out who sold it," Kevin said. "There should be some record of the check."

"Did that already." The sheriff shifted his bulk on the chair. "It was sold by a marina in Portland. I've got a call in to the manager to see if I can find out more, but he's on vacation and won't be back until next week. I got a warrant and requested copies of Edmund's bank account. I should have them anytime. I'll have someone track where that money came from before it hit his bank account."

"Someone else at the marina can't help you?" Mallory stirred her coffee. "We can't wait that long."

"Maybe. I'll call back and request more urgent assistance."

Kevin tried to fit all the pieces together from both deaths, but it was like trying to force a puzzle piece into a place where it almost fit but wouldn't quite snap together. An execution-style murder and a murder connected to nearly a quarter of a million dollars had to be linked somehow.

The sheriff's gaze met his. "I think we need to delve into your parents' backgrounds more fully, Mrs. Davis. We're missing something."

She took a sip of her coffee. "I'm sure it's not what it seems." Her eyes held defiance. "My parents were good people, the best."

The sheriff inclined his head. "I always thought highly of your dad. I never really knew your mother well."

Gwen handed the drawing to the sheriff. "This is your property, Sheriff." After putting her case back on the floor, she studied Mallory. "You don't have the same bone structure as your mother. Do you resemble your father more?"

Mallory's hand shook a bit as she set her coffee on the table. "I'm adopted. I'd thought to try to find my birth parents in case my adoption had something to do with my father's death, but it seems to be immaterial now." She leaned back in her chair and exhaled. "I just don't know what to think."

Kevin wanted to comfort Mallory in some way. Every family had secrets, but most of them didn't end up dead because of them. How did they go about uncovering all those secrets, especially after the fire? Everything was ashes there.

Gwen stood and smoothed the lines of her jacket. "If you're finished with me, Sheriff, I really should get going. Feel free to call me if you have any other questions." She smiled down at Mallory, and her expression held sympathy. "I'm sorry this was such a shock. I hope you find out what's going on and can come to some closure."

"Thanks for your help with this," Mallory said.

Kevin looked through the big window out on the water as he mulled it over. "Has the insurance started any kind of cleanup at the cottage?"

She shook her head. "Not as far as I know. The adjuster has left several messages, but I haven't had a chance to call him back."

"Let's dig around in the ashes ourselves and see if we can find anything. The more I think about the fire, the more I believe it was meant to destroy some kind of evidence. It clearly wasn't meant to kill you. There had to be a reason he torched the place."

"It will be a dirty job."

"It won't hurt us." He rose and picked up his coffee. "No time like the present. We'll call Carol on the way and ask her to get the girls from school."

The shock of seeing the blackened rubble after such a stressful day brought tears flooding to Mallory's eyes, but she blinked them back as she picked her way through the ashes. "We should have brought boots. My sneakers are going to be ruined. Your shoes too."

Kevin stooped to pick up a ceramic flower pot. "Mine are old anyway." He dropped the item and looked around. "There's a lot more left here than I imagined. Lots of things just smoke damaged and not destroyed. I'm hopeful we might find something useful."

She wanted to believe him, but observing the destruction

made her feel hopeless. The upstairs over the kitchen had collapsed, but the part with the bedrooms seemed fairly sound. "You think it's safe to go up?"

He frowned. "Let me check it out first." Stepping cautiously, he moved up the stairs and disappeared from sight. It felt like an eternity before he came back to the top of the stairs. "Seems safe, but watch where you put your feet."

She nodded and went up to join him. The walls were still standing, but fallen insulation and pieces of plaster choked what used to be the hallway to the bedrooms. As she passed, she peered into her bedroom and was surprised to find her bed frame and dresser still standing. "I wonder if the contents are unharmed." She detoured into her bedroom and looked around.

Soot blackened everything from the pictures left on the walls to the bedding and the rug. A heavy coating of black covered her fingers when she tugged open a dresser drawer. Her underwear lay in neat rows inside. They weren't even blackened.

For the first time she felt a surge of hope. Maybe Kevin was right. She hadn't been able to bear the thought of coming out here, but there might be more to salvage than she'd thought.

She shut the drawer and turned to her cedar chest at the foot of her bed. "I have some old pictures and other mementos in here."

The latch with its water and soot damage resisted her efforts, and she moved aside to let Kevin force it open.

He lifted the lid, then stood back to let her rummage through the contents. "It's all yours."

She knelt on the soiled rug and began to lift things out—a music box her grandmother had given her, a picture album from her childhood, a scrapbook from high school. All treasures she had nearly forgotten existed. Her heart felt near to bursting with the job of finding them still all right.

Kevin squatted and flipped through the photos. "There might be a clue to something in these pictures."

"I think they're just pictures from my first year. Me with my grandparents and Aunt Blanche." The cedar chest was empty now, and there didn't seem to be anything earth shattering inside. She rubbed her finger on the front, and the soot came off on her finger. "I think this can be salvaged. My mother said it was an important part of my history."

Kevin closed the album. "What did she mean by that?"

Mallory frowned. "You know, I'm not sure. She never said. I assumed it was an antique or that my grandfather had made it." She studied the lines of the cedar chest. It was rectangular with ornate etchings on the front and stood on rounded feet. "I'd guess it was made in the forties."

"Me too." Kevin stood and moved closer. "Let me turn it over and see if there are any identifying marks."

Mallory went to one side and helped him roll it over on its side. "There's a plate back here." She squinted to read it in the dim light. "It was made by Baxter and Son. And there's another plate below that's engraved with the name Hugon."

"Could be the original owner." Kevin jotted it down in his notebook, then rolled the chest back into place.

After checking the rest of the drawers and the closet, they moved to her father's room. It seemed wrong to be poking into her father's personal belongings this way, but she carefully went through every drawer, pushing aside socks and T-shirts, lingering over an old wallet she remembered and his well-worn belts. The bottom drawer held a plethora of cuff links, ties, and old watches, though she'd never seen him dressed up enough to wear cuff links.

Kevin was going through all the boxes in the closet, but all he seemed to be finding were shoes and old slippers. Every bit of her mother's things had been removed from the bedroom.

"Nothing here of your mom's. Where might Edmund have put those things?"

"I remember him sending some things to Goodwill, but surely he would have kept some mementos." Frowning, she tried to remember if she'd seen any jewelry or other items that had belonged to her mom. "You know, Dad had a little chest in the office that he kept in the bottom drawer of the desk."

They moved down the stairs to the first floor. A large pile of debris barred the way to the office, and Kevin helped her over it and into the room. Timbers hung low and charred in the office. The fire had been hottest here, as if that was where the fire started.

"Careful," Kevin warned. "I'm not sure how safe it is in here. Lots of damage. Tell me where to look and you stay where you are."

She nodded and pointed to the front of the desk. The drawers all hung open, and the soot on the handles had been smudged off. "Someone has been searching for something in here. Open that drawer and see if there's a little chest in it."

He squatted in the debris and ran his hand to the back of the drawer where the small chest used to be. "Nothing here. There might be prints though. I'll ask the sheriff to send over a tech to check." He paused and fired off a text message.

She glanced around and tried to decide where to look.

Kevin's back was to her and he bent over. "Is this it?" He turned around with a little brass chest in his hand.

"That's it!" She stepped closer so she could take it in her hands. "The lock has been smashed." She opened it and stared at the empty inside. "It's all missing. I know there were things in here because Dad used to look at them. Mom's watch, her wedding rings, that kind of thing."

He put his arm around her. "It's getting late. We'll come back another day. Let's take the pictures and scrapbook with us."

"And this." She hugged the brass chest to her. It was a little piece of her family, all that was left to her.

TWENTY-SEVEN

The blood rushed to Kevin's head from his upside-down position on the Twister board. The warm glow from the lamp added a cozy feeling to the evening shenanigans. Thanks to Carol and the girls, dinner had been ready when they'd gotten back. After dinner Haylie had wanted to play Twister, a game he hadn't thought of in a thousand years.

His right arm entwined with Mallory's, and his right leg was over her left one. One or both of them were going to go down in a heap any second.

Haylie stooped down and peered into his face. "I could tickle you."

"You would face swift retribution," he warned.

"Your face is all red."

"Yours will be red from tickling if you make me fall."

She wiggled her fingers at him. "I could tickle you now."

He grinned back. "And I could take you outside and dunk you in the water trough. Sadie, hurry up and spin. I'm dying here."

Sadie spun the dial and Carol, their official Twister referee, called out where it landed. "Right hand, red."

"Not going to make it," he gasped as he saw how far he would have to go.

Their girls had thought the game great fun, but the scent of Mallory's sweet perfume kept his head filled with the impossible—like deliberately falling so he could take her with him and kiss her until they were both breathless.

He focused his thoughts and reached with all his might for the closest red square. His sweaty hand slipped on the plastic Twister sheet, and he fell hard onto the floor. He reached out and snagged Mallory as he fell, and they lay breathless in an entwined heap. He was on his left side, with his left arm under her, and their legs were tangled together.

He stared into her mesmerizing dark eyes. He'd always loved her eyes. A line of gray circled the deep chocolate brown, and there were tiny flecks of light in the irises. She was so soft in his arms, and she stared up at him as if she wanted to stay right where she was.

Haylie stood over them. "Hello? Earth to Mom. You won. Kevin made you fall. Can we have hot chocolate and popcorn?"

"Yay, popcorn!" Sadie jumped up. Fiona barked and raced around her with her tail wagging hard enough to leave a mark.

"I guess I should let you up." Kevin made no move to do any such thing. "Or not." He grinned down at her. He'd like to stay right where he was the rest of the night.

"I guess so." She smiled but didn't try to get up either.

Carol stood and clapped twice. "Girls, come with me, and you can help make the popcorn and hot chocolate. I might even be persuaded to get out stuff to make s'mores in the fireplace."

The girls squealed and followed Carol to the kitchen where much clanging and banging ensued. Kevin reached up and wound a long strand of hair around his finger. It was so fine and thick in his fingers. Her eyes drifted shut, and she turned her chin up just a bit.

"Do I dare kiss you? Haylie will see us," he whispered.

Her lids fluttered open, and her eyes were languid and dreamy. "I suppose we'd better go help."

He pressed his lips to the strand of hair he'd commandeered. "I'm surprised you never cut your hair. It's so beautiful."

Her gaze sharpened and her jaw tightened. "Mom talked me into growing it long when I was sixteen. She said it was the most beautiful thing about me. I've started to cut it off to the middle of my back a few times, but every time I think about it, I just can't do it. It's like that one little piece of her left."

He rolled onto his side and propped his head up on his left hand as he stared down at her. "Your mom wouldn't want you so bound up with guilt that you're paralyzed, Mal. You're beautiful with long hair or short. With makeup or without. You're beautiful inside and out."

Her cheeks heated. "Maybe someday I can believe that." She looked away. "What did you think of what Gwen Marcey said? Someone shot my mom. I still can't quite believe she's right."

"I've seen her credentials. She's one of the best in her field. I think she knows what she's talking about."

"All these years I thought I killed her. And maybe I still contributed to her death. What if she ran out of gas and was left unable to get away when drug runners approached? That's the only people I can think of who might have shot her."

Her theory held validity, but he still shook his head. "I think we're missing something. It can't be a coincidence that both your parents were murdered. I think the office held the answer, but with the fire, it'll take a lot of digging to ferret it out."

"We have to figure it out. Whoever is behind this doesn't seem to be giving up. I'll be next, or Haylie."

"Over my dead body. I promise you that I'll find this guy and stop him."

"I hope we can." She sat up and ran her fingers through her long hair. "Here comes our hot chocolate."

Mallory ran the window of Kevin's SUV back up as he parked in front of her aunt's house. "Thanks for coming with me on your day off. Seeing Aunt Blanche is not exactly the most fun way to spend this gorgeous day."

"Aw, our movie isn't done yet," Haylie said from the backseat. "Can we stay in the car and watch it?"

"You can finish it on the way home. Aunt Blanche is looking forward to seeing you."

"She barely knows me," Haylie grumbled as she got out. She held the door open for the dog to jump out and for Sadie to scoot across the seat and stand too.

Mallory shielded her eyes from the sun's glare and looked at the house. She hadn't been here in years, but the small story-and-a-half cottage hadn't changed. The dingy white paint was still peeling, and the shutters had faded so much they barely held a tinge of green.

Her aunt opened the screen door and beckoned to them. The wind caught her long white hair and blew it around her angular face.

Mallory took Haylie's hand, and for once, her daughter didn't pull away. Aunt Blanche could be intimidating with her beanpole height and extravagant hair.

"I made cookies," Aunt Blanche said in her gravelly voice. "I remembered you liked gingersnaps, Mallory."

"I still do." Mallory led the small troupe inside.

The house smelled of cookies and lemon furniture polish. The wood floors, though scratched, gleamed from a recent cleaning. And her aunt had painted the walls at some point. Mallory liked the welcoming pale-lemon color.

"I've got milk poured for the girls at the kitchen table." Aunt Blanche pointed through the door, and the girls went that way with the dog. "I've got some cookies and tea for us in the living room. I don't get company very often."

Mallory perched on the old sofa, the same brown tweed from when she'd been a girl. The cookies were irresistible, and she didn't even try to resist. She bit into a still-warm cookie. "These are just as wonderful as I remember, Aunt Blanche."

Kevin settled beside her and grabbed a cookie too.

"You said you wanted to talk to me about your mother." Aunt Blanche had never been one to beat around the bush. "That seems a rather odd thing to talk about after all this time."

Mallory swallowed the last of her cookie, then took a sip of tea. "We had some news yesterday about Mom's death."

"Well, that's certainly remarkable. What is it?"

Mallory launched into the story of the forensic artist and what she'd discovered.

Aunt Blanche put down her tea. "Shot? That's seems unlikely."

"The sheriff is investigating, but it appears both my parents were murdered. There has to be some connection."

"I wouldn't know what it was."

Kevin leaned forward with his small plate of cookies balanced on his knees. "I think whoever set fire to the cottage was trying to burn up evidence in the office. Any idea what that might be?"

"None at all."

Mallory searched her aunt's face. Maybe she really didn't know much about the murders, but she must know something that could help them. "I found some old letters before the house burned down. They were from my birth mother." She told her aunt what her father had said that indicated her mother might have been responsible. "What do you remember from my adoption?"

Her aunt pushed her long white hair out of her face and frowned. "I hardly see where this is relevant now, Mallory. That all happened a long time ago. Edmund and Karen were good to you. Are you going to go digging up all that birth parent nonsense?"

"I've never really wanted to know about them, but I want to know now. We need to follow every rabbit trail to find out who is behind this. He's targeting me and Haylie now."

Aunt Blanche pursed her lips and didn't speak for a long moment. "I'll tell you what I know, but it's giving me the williwaws."

"That's all I ask. I need to follow every lead."

"You were just a newborn when they got you. Your mom's best friend when they were teenagers called her one day and told her he needed her help."

Kevin put down his cup of tea. "Her friend was a man?"

"Indeed." Aunt Blanche's eyes narrowed and her mouth grew pinched. "I never trusted that relationship, but Edmund pooh-poohed my concerns."

"So what kind of trouble was he in?" Mallory couldn't quite figure out what this had to do with her.

"From what I understood, he came from a very well-to-do family and was well known in society circles. He was married, but he also had a floozy on the side, and she was pregnant. He needed a place for the baby."

Mallory put her hand to her throat and stared at her aunt. "That's not what I was expecting. My biological father probably wouldn't want an illegitimate daughter crawling out of the woodwork." Her mind spun with possibilities. "The boat! Did Dad ever tell you how he got the money for the boat he bought last summer?"

Her aunt shook her head. "I assumed he'd borrowed it."

Maybe he did. But what if it was more than that? What if he'd been blackmailing her biological father? He might have gotten fed up with it and had Dad killed. Blackmail. What was she thinking? That wasn't something the straitlaced father she knew would do.

"What about my birth mother? What do you know of her?"

"Not much. Your mother took one look at you and didn't want to hear anything about another mother. As far as she was concerned, you were hers now and forevermore."

Kevin snagged another cookie. "What were their names?"

"I never heard them say. I think Edmund and Karen wanted to forget where you'd come from."

Mallory thought it over. "From a connected family. Boston maybe? Or New York?"

"I think Boston. Lots of old family money there."

"Did my biological father ever try to see me? Or my birth mom?"

Aunt Blanche's faded blue eyes narrowed. "Not that I know of. Your mother wouldn't have allowed it. She was like a mama bear where you were concerned."

Mallory swallowed past the lump that formed. Mom had

been an amazing mother, and she still missed her. "I'm glad we're finally getting to the truth. It's been a long time coming."

Her aunt put her hand to her flat bosom. "Edmund is with her in heaven."

"That he is." Mallory liked to think about them walking hand in hand in a meadow.

Her aunt smiled and pushed the plate toward Kevin. "Eat up. If there's one thing I like, it's a man enjoying his food."

TWENTY-EIGHT

The sun warmed Kevin's arms as he sat in his shirtsleeves by the water. He'd brought the girls to the lake to fish, and their squeals of delight made him smile. And watching Mallory's slim figure flitting back and forth between them as she baited their hooks wasn't a bad way to spend the afternoon either. Carol sat on a large rock with her face turned up to the sun.

Kevin's phone rang, and he looked at it. "Hey, Abby. I hope you have some news for me."

"Okay, got a pen? I'm going to be rattling off some names."

He fished a pen and small pad from his pocket. "Go."

"It took some doing. Someone really didn't want this to be found. Mallory's birth mother, Olivia Nelson, was in prison for embezzlement. She worked for the birth father, Thad Hugon, as an accountant. Olivia claimed someone set her up to make sure Thad didn't break up his marriage over her, but I wasn't able to prove it. Thad took custody of Mallory when she were born and brought her to the Blanchards. The Hugons are really wealthy. Ultra rich. Thad is nearly sixty and dying though. Brain cancer. He and his wife had no children. The wife died of a heart aneurysm about five years ago."

Kevin thought through the chain of events. "So Mallory might be able to inherit."

"Only if he dies without a will or he actually leaves her something. A man with that kind of power and wealth would have attended to his succession."

"I think Mallory and I should pay him a visit and see what we can find out. You have contact info?" He jotted down the address and phone numbers Abby gave him.

The line crackled a bit, then cleared. "You may have trouble reaching him. I tried to call him and didn't get anywhere. His secretary said he was too ill to take calls and would no longer be in the office. I tried his house, and his nurse told me the same thing."

"Did you tell them what you wanted?"

"No, no. I just said I needed to talk to him about an investigation I was involved in."

"Mallory can be frank, and maybe we can get to him. It's worth a try. Thanks, Abby. Any idea of the mother's whereabouts?"

"Nope. I'm looking though, and I'll keep you posted if I hear anything else. Talk to you soon."

Kevin put his phone away and turned toward the water as Mallory approached. "There's another avenue we can check out." He told her about Abby's call. "The cedar chest at your house had Hugon inscribed on the bottom of it. It came from your father's family."

She gasped. "But if he's sick, he wouldn't have anything to do with Dad's death."

"Your birth mother is still out there though."

"Abby doesn't know where she is?"

He shook his head and released her shoulders. "Not yet, but

she's working on it. We can go see your biological father however." He told her about Abby's failure to talk to him. "But if you show up at the door claiming to be his daughter, I bet we'll get into the house. You game?"

"Of course. When do you want to go?"

"How about tomorrow? Claire can fly us there and back. We might have to stay overnight. Maybe Carol won't mind watching the girls." He frowned. "I'm not sure it's safe to leave them alone. I'll ask Luke to watch out for them while we're away. He'll want something to do with Claire gone."

Mallory's face went pensive. "It will be so odd to actually see one of my birth parents. I wonder if I look like him."

"We'll soon find out." He rose as Haylie shrieked that she'd caught a fish. "Hang on. You can land him."

As he helped Haylie reel the fish to shore, he hoped he wasn't leading Mallory into more heartbreak.

The flight to Boston had been quick and easy, and Mallory sat with Kevin in front of her biological father's mansion in the convertible he'd rented at the airport. Mallory craned her neck and tried to peer through the bars surrounding the estate. There had to be acres and acres here, all locked up as tight as a tick. From what she could see of the big stone edifice beyond the gates, the place was as big as a palace. Monied wasn't quite as lavish a term as this estate implied. More like Bill Gates rich.

"We can't get in. Did Abby say anything about how to proceed past the gates? We can't even reach the front door."

"Let's see." Kevin put the car in Drive and pulled up to the gate.

A man came out from a brick guardhouse. He wasn't smiling. "May I help you, sir?"

"Would you inform the house that Mr. Hugon's daughter is here to see him?"

Indecision flickered across the guard's face. "To my knowledge he doesn't have a daughter."

"He does, and she has paperwork to prove it. Please inform whoever is in charge inside."

"Names?"

"Game Warden O'Connor and Mallory Blanchard Davis."

The guard backtracked to his building, picked up the phone, and called the house. It seemed like a long time before he hung up and returned to their car. "Mr. Hugon's nurse has a call in to his attorney about this matter. She says Mr. Hugon has no children." His bright blue eyes held suspicion.

"Fine. We'll go to the media instead." Kevin shot her a glance.

Alarm registered in the guard's face. "One moment, please."

This time on his call, his hands moved with animation, and Mallory heard his voice. Though she couldn't make out any words, it was clear he was pleading their case.

He turned and pushed a button, and the gate opened. Kevin drove through and turned into the stone-paved drive that circled the front of the mansion. The double doors at the entrance were made of some exotic wood and looked hand carved. The stone mansion was three stories high, and the windows were mullioned like some castle from Ireland. The dormers in the roof made it appear even taller.

Kevin turned off the engine and pulled out the key. "Ready?"

Her chest felt tight but she nodded. "Let's do it." She shoved open her door, then stepped onto the stone drive. The paving matched the mansion, and the drive alone had to have cost the earth. What kind of people would give away a baby when they could obviously afford to keep it?

Shoulders squared, she marched to the door with Kevin at her side and pressed the doorbell. Her heart fluttered in her chest as she waited. Would she even be allowed to see her biological father? And the bigger question was, did she even want to?

After what seemed an eternity, one of the massive doors opened, and a woman in her midforties stood in the opening. Her slim body seemed lost in her nurse's scrubs, and her blonde hair grazed her jaw in a short, stylish bob. Her cold eyes skimmed them and dismissed them just as quickly. She held out her hand. "I'd like to see your proof, please."

Mallory's fingers tightened on the folder she carried. "I'll show it to my birth father only."

"Mr. Hugon is too ill to be disturbed with something unless I can verify it's true."

"Fine. I'm sure the media will be happy to talk with me." Mallory stared her down. If the woman wanted to play chicken, she was game.

Uncertainty flickered in the depths of her blue eyes. "You wouldn't."

"Try me. I insist on seeing my father."

The woman appraised her again. "You do have a certain Hugon look." She stepped aside. "Come into the reception room. I'll see what Mr. Hugon says. He's likely to turn you away."

"You haven't told him we're here yet?"

"No. I wanted to take your measure for myself. It's my duty to protect him."

Mallory and Kevin followed her into an expansive entry tiled with marble. A double curving staircase seemed to be suspended in the air as it rose to the second floor. Craning her neck, Mallory saw that it continued on up to the third floor. The reception room the nurse led them to was grand as well, easily twenty by forty feet with understated white leather furniture and nickel lighting. A thick Persian carpet covered gleaming walnut floors, and the crown molding and baseboard were wide and lavish. In spite of its obvious cost, the room felt welcoming and warm.

"Please be seated. I'll be back." The nurse turned on her comfortable shoes and left the room. Her rubber soles squeaked up the marble stairs.

"I can't believe she let us in," Kevin whispered. "You were a tiger."

"I just kept thinking about Haylie. She deserves to know if she has grandparents. We both need to know where we came from. And maybe there will be an answer to Dad's death."

"Since your birth father is so sick, I doubt he had anything to do with the attacks. But maybe we can set that question to rest for sure." Kevin stepped to the massive white-plaster fireplace. "Look here."

The marble mantel held pictures in brass frames, and Mallory picked up one of a distinguished man with dark hair and eyes. He stood beside a beautiful redhead who looked to be in her fifties. He appeared to be a little older and had wings of gray in his dark-brown hair.

"It might be your father. Same coloring and shape of face," Kevin said.

Mallory stared at it a long minute before setting the frame back on the mantel. She turned toward the doorway as the nurse's shoes squeaked toward the reception room.

"Mr. Hugon will see you. Follow me."

TWENTY-NINE

The staircase was four feet wide, and the banister appeared to be made of the same exotic wood as the front door. Mallory licked suddenly dry lips as they climbed to the second floor and went down a wide hallway with twelve-foot-high ceilings. Beautiful paintings graced the walls, and she paused a moment to admire what appeared to be a Monet. It was like being in a museum.

The nurse paused in front of a wide bedroom door. "He's having a good day right now, but be on the lookout for his strength to give out. He has brain cancer, but I suspect you already know that. Glioblastoma. He's had all the treatments possible, and the cancer returned last month."

Mallory's eyes flooded with tears. She didn't even know the man, but she grieved for what he must be going through. "Thank you for telling me."

The nurse's gaze searched hers, then softened. "Go on in. I'll be right outside the door. He wished to speak to you without my presence."

"How did he seem when you told him I was here? Was he surprised, dismayed?"

"Not surprised. Somewhat eager, I would say. Which of

course reassured me since I'd allowed you inside." She inclined her head toward the door. "Hurry before he gets too weak to speak with you."

Mallory nodded and looked to Kevin for reassurance. They had to do this. He gave a slight nod, and her hand went to the doorknob. She turned it gently, and it swung open silently to reveal a huge bedroom filled with sunlight from large floor-to-ceiling windows around the room. The blue and gold bedding added a cheery splash of color against the padded white-leather headboard of the king bed in the middle of the room.

A gaunt man propped up with pillows sat on the left side of the bed. His gray hair was thinning, and though he beckoned her with a shaky hand, the resemblance to the man in the photo was unmistakable.

She approached him and managed a tremulous smile. "Hello, Mr. Hugon. I'm sorry to disturb you."

"I'm glad you're here."

His voice was a thing of pure beauty. Deep and rumbling, with a note of authority that made her stand up straighter. With a voice like that he could have wooed any woman when he was younger. And even with the disease ravaging his body, he held some of the good looks she'd seen in the photo.

"Please, be seated." He regarded Kevin. "You're looking after my daughter?"

My daughter. The confirmation made Mallory's knees go weak, and she sank onto one of the chairs beside his bed. He wasn't trying to deny anything.

"I'm trying to, sir. I'm Kevin O'Connor. I've known Mallory since we were kids."

"That's good, that's good." He struggled to sit up a bit in bed. "It's a sorry situation when I have to hold court in my bedroom, but such is life. God's been good to me in my later years, though I thumbed my nose at him when I was young. I don't have long to make things right." He turned and scrutinized Mallory, snaring her with the compelling intensity of his gaze. "You look like me."

"You admit I'm your daughter?"

"Of course. I'm surprised it took you so long to come see me. I told my attorney to contact you six months ago and ask you to visit. I feared you didn't want to see the man who gave you away."

"I never heard from an attorney."

"No matter. You're here now." He gestured to the water pitcher on the bed stand. "Could I trouble you for some water?"

"Of course." She poured ice water into the glass and held it so he could drink through the straw.

"Thank you, my dear." He waved the glass away. "I suppose you want to know what happened and why."

She set the glass back on the silver tray. "Yes, I would."

"I often vacationed in Maine, and I met Karen there one summer. She and I struck up a friendship when I was sixteen. We stayed best friends in spite of the distance. I helped her get into college when it was time, and she was always there to listen to my woes." He smiled slightly. "My father was a dictator of the worst kind, and I never knew how to deal with it."

"I didn't think Mom went to college."

"She dropped out after a year and returned home to marry your father. I didn't blame her. To tell you the truth, I envied her. She always knew what she wanted. I only knew what I didn't want—the life my father wanted for me. But I didn't know how to break free. I never did figure that out, and here I am still chained to what he created for me." His chuckle was deep and rich.

"You were never romantically involved with Mom?"

He shook his head, then winced and put his hand to his temple. "We were just friends. I married the woman my father picked out for me, the daughter of his best friend. I was as happy as I could be with someone else in charge of my life. Then I met Olivia. Hired her as my secretary, actually. How banal, eh?"

"Olivia was my mother's name?"

His eyes brightened. "Oh, she was a lovely sight. All lightness and laughter. She blew off any restraints on her. A free spirit. I admired that."

"You were already married?"

"Yes. I'd been married about five years when I met Olivia. I was going to leave my wife and marry her, but my father discovered she'd been embezzling money from the company. I was devastated. I'd thought I could trust her implicitly."

"She went to jail?"

"She did. After she was convicted, she sent me a message and told me she was pregnant. I'm ashamed to say that I couldn't tell my wife. The shame would have destroyed our social standing. Karen and Edmund had just found out that Edmund was sterile, and I asked if they would want to take you. They were thrilled at the thought. I had my attorney pay support, of course. I didn't want to shirk my duties totally."

Support? There had never been extra money when she was growing up, but she hesitated to bring it up now. "Thank you for telling me. They were good parents."

"I knew they would be. I'm sorry you lost your mother so young."

Did he know her father had died? "Dad died three weeks ago. We believe it was murder."

His lips parted and shock darkened his eyes. "I hadn't heard. Oh, my dear, I'm so sorry." He reached an age-mottled hand across the covers to grasp hers.

Her fingers closed around his cold hand. "We also just found out that Mom didn't die in the storm as we'd thought. She was shot in the head, execution style."

He pressed against the side of his head, and his color drained even more. A slight moan escaped him as his eyes went glassy. She looked over at Kevin, who rose and went to the door.

In moments the nurse was there with an injection in her hand. "I need to alleviate his pain. Can you come back later?"

"Of course." Kevin took Mallory's arm and escorted her to the hall where he closed the door behind them.

"Kevin, I don't think we ever got any support."

"There are a lot of questions his story generates. Maybe we can find out more when he can talk again." He took her arm. "Let's go grab some lunch."

Servers hurried past with plates of steaming lobster and crab bisque. Kevin's stomach rumbled at the rich, buttery aroma and the platter of desserts that went past. They'd both ordered oysters as well as crab bisque, and he sipped his coffee and watched Mallory over the top of his cup.

She set down her water glass. "Quit staring at me. I'm not going to freak out."

"Lot to take in today. I liked your dad. He didn't pull any punches."

"I wish I'd known him longer. I don't think he'll make it more than a few weeks at best. Maybe not even that."

"At least we know he's a Christian." He glanced out the window at the boats sailing by. The day with Mallory stretched in front of him, and he wanted to milk every moment. "His story made me doubly grateful for your influence on my life, you know."

Her eyes widened. "What do you mean?"

"He had a controlling father, too, but he didn't break free like I did. You gave me the courage to stand up for what I wanted. Thank you."

Color flooded her cheeks. "You would have done it anyway. You always knew your own mind."

Kevin wasn't so sure, but he let it go. "Maybe."

"I've been thinking about what he said about telling his attorney to pay child support. Maybe we should talk to the attorney."

"What good would that do? It's not like it matters now."

She ran her finger around the rim of her glass. "No, but what if Dad got the money for the boat from him?"

Kevin leaned back in his chair and thought about it. "I guess it's possible, but why would your dad be so desperate to pay it back? Especially if he felt it was due him from years of no support?"

"Maybe he didn't want to be beholden to him or something. It's hard to say. I just have a feeling we should talk to him. Or at least ask my father about it."

"It's worth a try."

The server brought their lunch, and they fell silent and tucked into their food. Kevin thought about what Mr. Hugon had told them. The one thing he hadn't mentioned was Mallory's birth mother's present status. Was she dead or in the area? Maybe he didn't know.

Mallory's cell phone rang, and she pulled it from her pocket, frowning at the screen. "Mallory Davis. Oh yes, thank you. We're just finishing lunch. We'll be over in a few minutes." She ended the call. "My father is alert and wants to see us again."

"I had a feeling he had more to say." Kevin scooped up an oyster and swallowed it down. "We should probably check in on the girls and Carol. Maybe your father will give us the contact information for his attorney." He held her gaze. "I wouldn't be surprised if Thad intends to leave you his estate."

She inhaled and sat back. "Heavens, I hope not. I wouldn't know what to do with a house that big. And I know nothing about his business or anything. Surely by now he's drawn up his will and everything is settled. I don't want to cause trouble."

"He has no other children."

"Maybe he has a brother or a sister. A cousin. Anyone but me. I don't want it."

He believed her. The Mallory he knew wouldn't be comfortable here in Boston. She belonged on the beach with bare feet and wind-blown hair. She was his free spirit. He knew what Mr. Hugon had meant about his lover, Olivia. Mallory lit up a room when she came in too.

They finished eating and drove back over to the Hugon house. This time the guard automatically opened the gate for them without even coming out, and the nurse met them at the door.

"He's been fretting since you left," she said when they stopped outside his bedroom door. "Every minute is a gift right now, and he has some other things to tell you. His pain should be all right for at least an hour, and I fed him some soup. Go on in."

Kevin pushed open the door and gestured for Mallory to precede him. He shut the door behind them, then stood back while she approached the bed.

Mr. Hugon's color was better, and he smiled when he saw Mallory. "Ah, my dear girl, I hope you enjoyed your lunch. You should have stayed here. My cook makes a mean lobster stew you would have enjoyed."

"Another time." She stood at the side of the bed, then leaned down and brushed her lips across his cheek.

His eyes went wet almost immediately, and he turned his head away as she sat on the chair. Kevin was touched that he seemed to really care about Mallory. Why hadn't Hugon sought her out before? He'd only begun looking six months ago. Maybe he hadn't wanted to interfere with her life. That would make sense.

Mallory leaned forward and put her hand on his. "Is my birth mother still alive? What's happened to her?"

Mr. Hugon's smile faltered. "She got out of prison about ten years ago, and I haven't been able to track her down. I'll admit I didn't try very hard. Time flew by as it often does, then I was diagnosed with cancer, and life got rather disjointed. I've instructed my attorney to find her, but so far he's come up empty."

Disappointment flickered in Mallory's eyes. "Can you think of anyone who might have wanted to harm my parents? Someone burned down their cottage recently. I think they were trying to destroy evidence of some kind."

Mr. Hugon's brow furrowed, and he said nothing for a long

moment. "If my father were still alive, I might suspect him, though he should have been nothing but grateful to Karen and Edmund. But with my father one never knew how he might try to protect his all-important interests. However, he's been dead a year now."

Kevin approached the bed and stood at the foot. "Who runs your company now?"

"My attorneys are at the helm. The two of them have helped me for many years and know the business inside and out. I have many companies in my conglomerate, and my team is excellent."

"No brothers or sisters, uncles or cousins?" Kevin asked.

Mr. Hugon shook his head, then turned to his daughter. "Only you, Mallory. You're the last of the Hugon line, and I wouldn't saddle you with the burden of this business I never wanted, though my lawyers are drawing up a codicil to my will to ensure you have enough money for the future. It should be ready for me to sign in a day or two."

"That's not why I came. I just wanted to know more about my background."

"Dear girl, I know that. But it's the right thing to do." He glanced at Kevin. "Do you have a place to stay tonight?"

"Not yet. I was going to call and get a hotel."

"Please, stay here. As you can see, there is plenty of room and I would enjoy the company."

Kevin glanced at Mallory to see what she wanted and saw a shy smile lifting her lips. "Thank you, sir. I'll bring in our suitcases."

THIRTY

Claire sat on the balcony of her mother's house overlooking the Atlantic. Boats dotted the harbor, and she sighed with contentment as she sipped a cup of tea and nibbled on the still-warm ginger cookies. "I've missed this view, Mom."

Her mother, dressed in a subdued blue dress and heels, smiled at her. "It was such a surprise to see you. What brought you to town?"

Claire told her about Mallory's search, and her mother pursed her lips at the name Thad Hugon. "I can't say I'm surprised he wasn't faithful to his wife. They seemed a strange couple. Your father and I have traveled in those same circles for years, and they were always off talking to other people. When it was time to leave, they were as stiff and formal as strangers."

She shifted her attention toward the sea, and Claire could see the wheels turning. Her mother had lived here a long time. Might she know something important about this situation? "Have you ever heard the name Olivia Nelson?"

Her mother blinked and straightened. "Olivia? Why, of course. It caused a huge scandal when she was caught embezzling funds and sent off to prison. I met her several times. Why do you ask about her?"

"She's Mallory's birth mother. Mallory was born when Olivia was in prison."

Her mother gasped and put her hand to her throat. "Oh, good heavens! I never dreamed it would be someone I know. She's out of prison now, you know."

"When was the last time you saw her? Would you have any idea where she went when she got out?"

"She applied for a job at Cramer Aviation and told your father she hadn't taken any money. Harry felt sorry for her, but he couldn't hire her, not with his close connection to Thad. He believed her enough to give her a letter of recommendation though. He got a call from a potential employer about five years ago. It was in Bangor, I think. Or maybe Augusta. I can't remember."

"So she's in Maine." Claire made a mental note to tell Mallory this piece of news. "Do you remember the name of the company or anything about it?"

Her mother twisted her heavy rings around on her finger. "I think it was the IT department of some company. I don't know if she got the job or not. I'm sorry I can't remember more about it." Her lips parted and she gasped. "Oh, I almost forgot. She changed her name after she got out of prison. She started using her middle name, but I can't remember what it was."

"I bet the private investigator can figure it out." She reached for her tea and took another sip. "H-how's Dad doing?" It was a touchy subject because of everything he'd done, but it was impossible to turn off the spigot of a lifetime of love.

Her mother shrugged her slim shoulders. "He says the food is terrible, and his cell is cold. It's only three years though, and he'll be out."

"And the business?"

"Thanks to you, the merger went through, and I've been leaving the running of things to the Goughs. You are welcome to take over if you want, however."

Claire wasn't even tempted. "I'm happy up in Folly Shoals. The house you bought us is perfect, Mom. Thanks again for being so thoughtful. It's truly lovely, and it's going to be spectacular when the remodel is done. Luke and I bought a bigger boat too. I'm having a website done to start running charters and tours. We'll take tourists out to see whales, birds, and other marine life."

Her mother's mouth held a pinched line. "I just wish you were closer, Claire. I hardly get to see you."

"You could move closer, maybe get a summer cottage." Her mother would never leave the hustle and bustle of Boston for long, but short stints in Maine would keep them connected.

"That's a thought. I'll consider it." Her mother held up the plate of cookies. "You're too thin. Have another cookie."

Claire smiled and took another ginger cookie. "Once a mother, always a mother."

The dining room was the biggest Kevin had ever seen, easily thirty feet long and twenty feet wide. The gleaming wooden table had to have been handmade because he counted forty chairs tucked around it. Four chandeliers hung above it, and the coffered ceiling had gold accents. The dark, scrolling wallpaper added to the opulent atmosphere.

The staff had set the table for five at the closest end of the table, and only that chandelier was on, which brought a sense of coziness to the cavernous space. Kevin led Mallory to the two place settings on her father's left.

Mr. Hugon sat at the head of the table in a gold silk robe. "I hope you'll forgive me for not dressing for the occasion. I knew my strength would be gone if I changed my clothes."

"You look very nice." Mallory slid into the chair closest to her father that Kevin pulled out for her.

He sat beside her and looked across the table at the empty place settings. "Who else is joining us?"

"My attorney, Richard Blake, and his wife. They should arrive shortly."

Richard Blake. Where had Kevin heard that name? Then it hit him. DeAnn's husband was a Richard Blake. Could it be the same man? Though he was running for the Senate, he was an attorney, wasn't he? Kevin hadn't been interested enough to pay much attention to the facts Kate had told him.

The doorbell pealed a sonorous tone, and a few moments later footsteps clattered on the marble floors. Kevin looked toward the doorway and saw DeAnn approaching on the arm of a distinguished gentleman in a suit. Kevin guessed his age at sixty. She wore a black sheath dress that showed off her figure, and Richard's suit was impeccable. She hadn't seen him yet as her attention was focused on her host. She advanced about five feet into the room before her gaze connected with Kevin's.

The dazzling smile on her face faltered. "K-Kevin, what are you doing here?"

Her husband's deep-set blue eyes were congenial, and he had the kind of magnetism that would serve him well in politics. He glanced at Kevin with a friendly smile before moving on to

Mallory. "You must be Thad's daughter. He was quite excited to meet you."

"Richard, I can see you haven't made the connection yet. This is Kevin O'Connor."

The brilliance of Richard's smile only blinked. "You're right, I hadn't realized. Forgive me." Hand extended, he advanced to Kevin, who rose and shook hands with him.

Kevin sat back down and watched DeAnn give Hugon a gentle hug. "I had no idea you knew Mr. Hugon."

DeAnn tinkled out a fake laugh. "I've eaten here many times since I married Richard."

Hugon leaned back in his chair and rested on the armrests. "How do the two of you know each other? I'm quite lost."

"DeAnn was married to Kevin years ago for about half a minute," Richard said.

"It was actually three years, but we divorced eight years ago." Kevin reached over and took Mallory's hand. He could use the moral support right now. No wonder DeAnn had left him if she had this lifestyle in her sights. The guy seemed nice enough, though obviously a lot older. She would be a rich widow one of these days.

"Oh my." Hugon blinked and made an obvious effort to mask his surprise. "I hope it's not too uncomfortable for you all."

"Of course not," DeAnn said quickly. "I saw Kevin just the other day when I was visiting our daughter." She shot Kevin a warning glance. "We're on friendly terms."

Mallory's fingers squeezed his and he squeezed back. This wasn't the time or place to get into DeAnn's shortcomings as a mother. He respected Hugon too much to add any stress to the evening. "You've been his attorney long?"

Richard joined his wife on the other side of the table and sat in the chair nearest Hugon. "I was a young whippersnapper lawyer fresh out of college. Thad and I were roommates, and he asked his father to give me a chance. Luckily Mr. Hugon took a liking to me and asked that I be added to the firm he used. Two of us have taken care of Thad's legal matters all these years, but my partner is semiretired now."

DeAnn slanted a smile up at him. "You're a likable guy."

Richard's dimple flashed when he smiled back. "I think you're a little prejudiced, sweetheart."

Kevin warmed toward him with that show of affection. He didn't hold any grudges against DeAnn, and he would have hated for her to have ended up in a bad place. "Looks like you're ahead in the latest polls."

"Thad has been a great help. His belief in me gave me the confidence to even try for the Senate."

A young woman in a voluminous white apron over a red dress appeared in the doorway. "Are you ready for dinner to be served, sir?"

"Yes, please," Hugon said.

Mallory touched her father's arm. "Are you all right? Should I call the nurse? You look a little pale."

His other hand came down on hers. "I'm as fine as I'm going to be, my dear. I'm so glad I got a chance to meet you before I died. You've made me very happy."

She looked down at her hands and blinked back tears. This was harder on her than Kevin had thought it would be. Even though she hadn't known him long, Hugon was the sort of father anyone would want. Powerful but compassionate. Rich but gentle. Or so he seemed. Unless everything he'd told them so far was a lie, Mallory's life would have been safe with him. But Hugon wouldn't be around for long.

Kevin glanced across the table at the Blakes. Richard probably didn't care if a long-lost daughter showed up, but had it upset DeAnn? Her color was high, and she seemed a little flustered by their sudden appearance here.

THIRTY-ONE

The bedroom Mallory had been given held a massive four-poster bed that barely took up any of the impressive square footage. The pink-and-cream frothy concoction that covered the mattress felt like real silk. The paintings displayed on the cream walls looked like they should have been in a museum, and the attached bathroom housed a huge claw-foot tub as well as a glass-enclosed shower with two showerheads. The counter over the double sink cabinets looked like real marble, and the gold fixtures were spotless.

She bounced on the edge of the mattress. It would be like sleeping on a cloud, and she couldn't stifle the little giggle that escaped her. So this was what it felt like to be unbelievably wealthy. What would her life have been like if she'd never been given up for adoption? She doubted she would be the same person. Perhaps she would have been so spoiled that no one would have liked her for herself—only for what she could give them.

She gave a little shake of her head and got up. Hugon was a man with his feet firmly planted on the ground. He would have made sure she didn't get too full of herself. An entire wall of closets caught her attention, and she crossed the large room and pulled open one of the doors. It opened into a space larger than her bedroom in Bangor. Hatboxes and other types of boxes were stacked on shelves at the back. She thought this closet would have been empty. Whose bedroom was this?

She'd just started for the back of the closet when she heard a peck at the door. Her heart leaped into her throat. Had her father taken a turn for the worse? And when had she started to think of him as her father and not as her biological father?

She hurried to the door and yanked it open, then sagged with relief. "Kevin, thank goodness. I was afraid something had happened to my father." Motioning him to come in, she turned back to the closet. "Come see what I found. I was just about to investigate. And what are you doing wandering the halls so late?"

"I was lonely in that huge room. Wow, this place is something." He shut the door behind him and followed her. "I've never seen a closet this big."

"Me neither. And look at these old hatboxes. People haven't worn hats since the sixties. I wonder if maybe they belonged to my grandmother." She went back to the shelves and lifted down a box, then set it on the carpet and opened the lid.

The scent of lilac wafted to her nose as she pushed aside tissue paper to reveal a pillbox hat, à la Jackie Kennedy. She nearly squealed with delight. "I wonder if the owner wore it to the White House or just emulated Mrs. Kennedy? It's beautiful." The lovely blue hat looked unworn and pristine. She pulled down another box and another until hats of all shapes were heaped around her.

Grinning, Kevin leaned against the doorway and watched her. "You're like a kid at Christmas. What delights you so much about the hats?"

"I've seen all the pictures from the fifties and sixties in

history books. The ladies were so classy and elegant. It's almost like stepping back into an episode of *Leave It to Beaver*. It makes me wonder if my birth parents were like that, all calm reason and smiling."

"Your own mom and dad were pretty great."

"Of course they were. I didn't mean that. But I'm faced with the fact that my life could have taken another path if things had been different. Not that I wanted that path, but it's intriguing to consider, don't you think?" She tried on the blue hat and stared at herself in the full-length floor mirror. A different woman looked back. One with style and flair—if she only squinted right and didn't look at her jeans and T-shirt.

He straightened and his grin vanished. In a couple of steps he was in front of her. He plucked the hat from her head, then dropped it to a chair before pulling her into his arms. "If you'd lived here all your life, we never would have met. I would have been poorer for it. Knowing you has made me a better person."

She leaned her head against his chest and listened to his steady heartbeat under her ear. "I doubt that."

"I used to watch you even before we were old enough to date. You were the kid who stuck up for the fat boy being bullied. You always helped the kid who was struggling with his homework, and you never let what people thought about you change how you behaved. And after we started dating and I got to see you at home, I loved the way your family was so close. You'd walk in the door and tell your mother every detail of your day. And what's more, she was interested. I didn't have that at home. It made me resolve to be that kind of parent when I was grown up. Your example made me quit the football team even though it made my dad mad. It made me start trying to talk more to my mom."

"How is it that I never knew all this?"

He pressed his lips against her hair. "A guy doesn't like to admit he has areas he needs to change, especially a perceived jock like me. Your parents raised you well, Mal."

"I know." She looked down at all the hats. "I wonder if my father would let me have some of them. Or if he would at least tell me who they belonged to. Maybe I can bring hats back in fashion."

He tipped her face up, and his lips came close enough she could feel the whisper of his breath. "I think he'd do anything for you right now. Just like I would."

Almost without realizing it, she closed her eyes and lifted her face to meet his kiss. His embrace was like a haven, a place she wished she could stay in forever.

The commotion in the halls took awhile to penetrate Mallory's sleep. She lay on her side snuggled in a down comforter as soft as a baby's breath, and she didn't want to wake up. Then the pounding at her door made her eyes snap open, and she sat up in bed.

Her pajamas fully covered her, so she ran to the door and threw it open to see her father's nurse standing in the doorway in her nightgown. "What's wrong?"

"It's Mr. Hugon. He's dead." The woman's voice wobbled, and a tear tracked down her face. She ran her hand through her hair, making it stand up on end in a way that emphasized the tragedy.

Mallory's throat tightened, and she couldn't speak for a long moment. Her eyes burned, and she bit her wobbling lip. "I'm so sorry. He seemed a good man."

"He was the best. D-do you want to see him before the funeral home comes? You know, to say good-bye?"

Mallory took a step back and nearly shook her head, then she inhaled and nodded. "Thank you. I'd like to pay my respects. He made sure I had a good life, and I'm thankful for that."

Following the nurse down the wide halls left her confused. She'd never find her way back without a guide. The door to her father's room stood open, and Richard stood on the right side of the bed. He wore jeans and a loose-collared shirt. His hair looked uncombed as if he'd rushed here right out of bed.

She slanted a glance at the bedside clock. Three in the morning. No wonder she felt fuzzy and disoriented. "Could you wake Kevin, please?"

The nurse nodded and rushed away. Mallory advanced into the room and went to the left side of the bed. Tears flooded her eyes as she stared at her father's peaceful face. "I wish I'd gotten to know him better."

"There was no one like him," Richard said softly. "I'm going to miss him."

She turned at the sound of footsteps rushing down the hall. Dressed in pajama bottoms and a T-shirt, Kevin came into the room. He stopped when he saw her father lying in the bed, then stepped to her side and slipped his arm around her waist.

She leaned against him, taking strength from his presence. "He's gone."

"I'm sorry, Mal."

"Me too." She said a silent good-bye to Thad Hugon, the man who had given her life.

Richard cleared his throat. "This might not be the time to bring this up, but your father drew up a will leaving you quite a lot of money. I brought it with me for him to sign, but he was too weak last night after dinner and I'd planned to bring it over this morning. Because it's unsigned, there isn't a lot I can do."

"I never wanted his money. I'm just glad I got a chance to meet him before it was too late. It nearly was. It would have been if Kevin hadn't found out who he was."

"Good luck indeed." Richard nodded. "I know it made his last hours much happier. He was able to die in peace."

"He doesn't appear to have died in pain," Kevin said.

"The nurse told me she'd given him a shot for pain about an hour before she found him dead."

Mallory's throat tightened, and she suddenly didn't want to be here any longer. The meeting with her father had gone better than she'd ever dared dream, but they were no closer to figuring out who had targeted her mom and dad or finding out who had burned down Mermaid Cottage. And she'd given away a little piece of her heart to the man in the bed.

She moved out of Kevin's grip. "I could use some coffee. There's no going back to sleep now. How about the rest of you?"

"I wouldn't say no." Kevin took her hand and walked with her toward the door.

"I should get back to tell DeAnn what has happened, but I could delay long enough for coffee." Richard followed them and shut the door behind him. They walked in silence downstairs, and Richard pointed to the door past the staircases. "The kitchen is this way."

Mallory followed his erect figure through the maze of rooms until they stood in the biggest kitchen she'd ever seen. There were marble counters on two islands, and a wooden one on two more. A length of quartz covered the cabinets against the wall, and she counted eight ovens and six cooktops. She spied a coffeepot in one corner and quickly found the grinder and coffee.

"There's coffee cake here too." Kevin lifted the glass cover off the cake on one of the marble-topped islands and carried it to the big wooden table by the window. Richard wandered after him and sank wearily into a chair.

"Is your work with my father's companies over now?"

Richard shrugged. "Not quite. I'll take care of executing his will. His partner is buying out Thad's share of the companies. Thad has donated most of his money to others. He left your daughter a quarter of a million dollars for college. She should be able to go anywhere she chooses."

The grandeur of her father's gift made her catch her breath. "So much. I had no idea." She poured the coffee into mugs and went to join the men.

"He was worth nearly one billion dollars." Richard accepted the coffee cup she offered.

She couldn't even wrap her head around that much money. And he'd given it all away. Her vision blurred with tears, and she swallowed hard. He'd been a good man, the best.

"What will happen to the family's personal belongings?" she asked.

Richard took a sip of his coffee. "Sold at auction. Is there anything in particular you'd like? I'm sure your father would want you to have it."

"In my bedroom closet there are tons of women's hats stored. I'd love to have some of them. I assume they belonged to my grandmother?"

He nodded. "Most likely they were. Help yourself to anything of a personal nature like that. Thad would have been pleased that you cared."

She smiled back at him. At least she'd have a few mementos of this side of her genealogy.

THIRTY-TWO

Mallory hadn't had much to say as they took off from Boston in Claire's small plane. The entire trip had saddened her, and Kevin almost wished he hadn't suggested coming down here. Her shoulders rubbed his in the second-row seat, and she sat with four hatboxes heaped in her lap. Richard had urged her to take her father's watch and class ring from college. She'd also come away with several picture albums.

Richard had been more than accommodating, but Kevin had been relieved to get out of his presence. The guy was a paragon, and DeAnn was lucky to have him.

Claire, her blonde hair tied back in a ponytail, glanced over at them as she banked the plane over Boston Harbor, then headed north. "Mom told me your birth mother changed her name and was looking for a job in Maine five years ago."

The engine made it hard to hear, so Kevin leaned forward. "Did she remember the name?"

Claire shook her head and raised her voice. "She said she was using her middle name so that's a place where your investigator can look. And she works in IT."

"That's a big help, Claire, thanks." Mallory's voice was subdued.

He shot her a glance, then stared down as Boston Harbor vanished from sight. "Penny for your thoughts."

Mallory pulled a long swath of dark hair over her shoulder and settled more comfortably in her seat. "I was about to ask you the same thing."

"They're not worth that much." Shuffling on the uncomfortable seat, he shifted until he could get his arm around her. "I was just thinking how nice it was that you got some of your father's mementos."

She hugged a hatbox to her chest. "I know it seems silly that I wanted these. I could see the amusement in Richard's eyes, but I don't care. They're a tiny piece of my history, and I'll treasure them."

"I wish your father had had some idea of who killed your mom and dad."

She tucked a strand of hair behind her ear. "I'd hoped he might have an idea about the money for the boat. I never got a chance to ask him about that. With his generosity, I can see where he would have happily bought them a boat."

"Richard might be able to tell us. He handled all his legal affairs."

She nodded and turned to look at the blue ocean. "He gave me his card. I'll give him a call when we get home."

He plucked her hand from its resting place atop a hatbox. "I like hearing you call my house home." Her hand was so soft yet capable. He laced his fingers with hers.

"I can never thank you enough for giving us a place to stay. We would be back in Bangor now if not for you."

Something about the formality of her words raised an alarm. It almost sounded like good-bye, but they had a lot of work ahead of them. They weren't anywhere close to finding out who killed her parents. He bit his tongue and let her talk.

She turned away from the window and faced him. "I've been thinking that I may never know who killed them, and maybe it's time to give up looking. I could spend my entire life searching for answers and find none. Just like Mom's death. I thought it was because I distracted her when we argued and her boat ran out of fuel, but all along she'd died another way. Even if I pursue it, there's no guarantee we will ever find the truth."

"Someone burned down your house. I don't think you'll be safe until we find that person."

"He knew we weren't in there. I think he accomplished what he set out to do and destroyed whatever evidence he was after. There hasn't been another attack on me at all."

"Dixie out on Walker's Roost was attacked because someone thought she'd implicated him in some way."

She caught her lower lip between her teeth. "That's true. But there have been no prowlers around your house. If I quit poking around, whoever it is will relax. Haylie and I will be safe."

"You don't know that, Mal. Maybe he's just biding his time, hoping you go back to Bangor where he can get to you. He might be afraid to show his hand while you're at my house."

Her dark eyes were troubled. "But how long can I put our lives on hold while we chase after an old mystery? Mom died fifteen years ago. That's a long time, and I don't think we'll ever find out what really happened. And even Sheriff Colton wasn't sure Dad was murdered. He only went along with our theory after the cottage burned down. But maybe the two things aren't connected. Maybe the fire was all about burning up evidence."

She'd put a lot of thought into this. "What kind of evidence, if not about your dad's death?"

"Maybe about where he got the money for the boat. It could be anything. I'm just trying to think outside the box. We thought the two incidents had to be related, but maybe they aren't." She stared into his eyes. "I'm not the same girl I used to be. I don't really belong here anymore. I see the whispers and glances when we go to town. Everyone remembers what happened to Mom. I'm as bad as a flatlander in their eyes."

"You never used to care what people thought."

"I know. I'm just not sure I can find that carefree girl you spoke of last night in the closet. I'm not sure she exists anymore. Guilt can change anyone."

"But now you know it wasn't your fault. Your mother was shot."

"You're forgetting my theory that she was stuck high and dry in the path of a drug runner. I still think that's likely what happened." She leaned her head back against his arm and closed her eyes. "I'm so tired."

His gaze wandered over the planes and angles of her face. Her skin was smooth and unblemished, pale from lack of sleep but still beautiful. He wouldn't let her walk out of his life again. Somehow he'd find a way to help rid her of the guilt she carried.

Ever since they'd gotten back from Boston two days ago, Mallory had been quietly contemplating her options. She remained paralyzed, unsure what to do. Her heart wouldn't let her walk away from Kevin without a fight, but she couldn't quite embrace the idea of staying here forever, especially in the face of his family's opposition.

May had come in with an abundance of spring flowers, and the gorgeous blue of the sky was echoed in the ocean. Saturday morning she packed a picnic lunch and told the girls they would visit Aunt Blanche, then head out for a day of canoeing. Kevin was going to meet them after a call to pick up a moose hit by a car. Carol had cried off, saying she had a new client's social-media campaign to plan.

Fiona stuck her head out the front passenger-side window and barked at the birds as they passed. The girls talked in the backseat, and Mallory let her thoughts wander as she drove to her aunt's. She had to make a decision soon. Haylie would be out of school in another few weeks, and if they were going back to Bangor, that would be the time to make a move.

What was the right thing to do? She'd prayed for wisdom, but she had no clear sense of direction yet.

After parking in front of her aunt's house, she opened the door for the dog, then told the girls they could stay in the yard and play with her while she checked on Aunt Blanche. She didn't intend to stay long, but she felt guilty that she didn't look in on her more often.

She knocked at the door, then pushed it open when her aunt told her to come on in. She found Aunt Blanche in the kitchen taking a batch of cookies out of the oven. The sight and aroma of the chocolate chip cookies made her mouth water. "Can I have one?"

"It'll burn your mouth." But Aunt Blanche shoveled one off the spatula and onto a paper plate for her.

Mallory leaned on the surface of the Formica countertop

that covered the island. It held the scars from many years of cookie making and pie dough rolling. She and her mother had come here every year to make goodies for Christmas, and by the time they left, the counter was piled high with cookies, pies, and candy. She missed those days.

She popped a hot piece of cookie into her mouth, then sucked in air to cool it. "Ooh, it's hot."

Aunt Blanche finished sliding the cookies onto a plate and smiled. "You always did need to figure things out for yourself."

"I went to Boston a couple of days ago." She blew on her plate a moment. "I . . . I met my biological father."

Aunt Blanche's movements froze, then she put down the spatula and looked up. Her careful expression revealed little of her thoughts. "You found him."

"Found him and lost him all in the same day." She told her aunt what had happened. "He's left Haylie some money for college."

Aunt Blanche sniffed. "As well he should. Did you learn anything of interest?"

"He was a nice guy. Wealthier than you can imagine, but nice in spite of it. I didn't get a chance to ask him if he gave Dad the money for the boat."

"With that kind of money, you would have thought he might have paid support for you."

"He said he did."

"That's a lie. Your parents never saw a penny of support from anyone." Aunt Blanche hesitated, then her gaze shifted and her lips flattened. "I told your mom she should ask for money for your college. I don't know that she ever did."

"When was this?"

"The week before she died." Her aunt chose two cookies for herself and put them on a small paper plate.

"I still can't believe someone shot her. I wish I could accept I had nothing to do with it."

Her aunt's brows winged up. "Why, child, why on earth would you blame yourself? A storm is an act of God. God decided your mama had endured enough on this mean earth and took her home to glory. Nothing you could have done to cause it or stop it."

"You know. She didn't fill up the boat after our fight. Maybe she got stuck out there and couldn't get back, then got in the way of some drug runners and they killed her. But I got her stuck out there."

Aunt Blanche shook her finger in her face. "Mallory Blanchard, you stop that right now. Do you think any of this took God by surprise? Do you think you have the power to change what he's ordained and set in motion? We all do things we wish we hadn't, but God doesn't strike us dead for it. Nor does he exact a dreadful retribution. Have you been walking around all these years thinking this was all your fault?"

Mallory licked her dry lips and managed to push one word past her tight throat. "Yes."

"Don't do what I did and ruin your life because you think that's all you deserve. I fought with the man I loved, and it pushed him to go to war. He died in Vietnam, and I buried myself here in this house as punishment. But I didn't tell him to go. I didn't put him in front of that bullet. Your mama always checked her fuel before she left. If she got distracted and failed to do it that morning, that's not your fault. All we can do is learn from our mistakes. We can't go back and change them.

God isn't holding it over your head, you know. You're the only one doing that."

Was it that easy? The pressure began to lift in her chest. She'd have to think about it.

THIRTY-THREE

Spring flowers carpeted the roadsides. The balmy May temperatures lifted Kevin's spirits and reminded him that renewal came in cycles. He only hoped and prayed the spring would bring a renewal between Mallory and him. He'd made it clear to her how he felt, but she continued to hold him at arm's length. This place had worked its magic on them when they were younger. Could it do it again?

His muscles flexed as he rowed the canoe with the four of them across the river to his favorite picnic area. He hadn't been here since Mallory left town fifteen years ago, and he glanced at her back at the stern as she used an oar to steer toward the island.

She'd caught her long hair back in a braid that reached to her waist, and her toned arms were bare in a red sleeveless top. She looked toward the island with a smile curving her pink lips, and her face was pensive as if she was lost in thought. Their gazes locked, and he knew she remembered this place as well as he did.

The canoe bumped the sand, and he kicked off his flip-flops and jumped over the side to haul it onto the shore. Shrubs and small trees started at the edge of the sand, but picnickers had cleared the highest point. The last time they were here, there was a grill, a table, and a fire pit.

He helped the girls out of the canoe, then pulled it well out of the water and picked up the picnic basket and grilling supplies. Mallory grabbed the old blanket and the cooler of water bottles. Brambles along the rocky path scratched at his bare legs, so he held them out of the way so the girls didn't encounter any thorns. The dog nimbly guided Sadie up the slope, and she only stumbled on the rough ground a couple of times. Different terrains like this were good for her to experience.

They reached the wildflower meadow at the top, and he set the picnic basket down on the table. "Doesn't look like anyone has been here yet this year." Dead leaves had collected around the grill and the table, and debris choked the fire pit.

He got busy cleaning things out with the old broom someone had left here long ago, then took the girls to his favorite fishing spot and got them started. "You need to catch us some lunch."

Haylie wrinkled her nose. "How can we eat it with heads and scales?"

"I brought my fillet knife. Your job is to catch it. Mine is to make sure it's ready to eat."

"What's Mom's job?"

"To look beautiful." He slanted a grin Mallory's way and chuckled when her face went pink.

"Gross," Haylie said.

"You look just like her so I'd be careful about saying something like that."

"I do?" Haylie tucked a strand of dark-brown hair behind her ear, and her bracelet tinkled on her arm.

"Yep."

"You like my mom, don't you? Did you use to date or something?"

Mallory tossed a worm at her. "Don't say it like me dating was the most distasteful thing you can imagine."

"Ew!" Haylie stared at the squirming worm. "I don't have to bait the hook myself, do I?"

Kevin chuckled. "A real fisherman knows how to bait the hook."

"Then I'll only be a pretend fisherman. You bait it." Haylie thrust her pole at him.

"I can put the worm on the hook myself. Look." Sadie gently felt along the line and hook, then tested the point a bit. Then she wound the worm onto it as if she could see every movement.

"Good job." Kevin tossed the line into the water for her. "Whoever catches a fish first gets to pick what we do the rest of the day."

"No fair. Sadie is the only one with a line in the water. Can you put the worm on for me? Please?"

"I'll do it, you little chicken." He baited the hook, then threw the line in.

Mallory retreated a few feet away to a rock where she stretched out her long legs. Kevin watched her a few moments as she closed her eyes and lifted her face to the sun. She opened her eyes again as he approached.

"You look like a sleek black cat sunning itself." He squatted beside her and picked up a handful of sand to let it run through his clenched fist.

She smiled. "You always did like to do that. What's so fun about letting the sand run out?"

"I used to do it just because it felt good, kind of mind-numbingly rhythmic. As I've gotten older I watch the sand and imagine that they're seconds of time. Every single one might be all we have. I look at Sadie and want to make sure I do right by her. I think about my job and sometimes wonder if I'm making a difference at all. The sand is a reminder that this day is the only one we might have to do something that will change someone's life."

"How philosophical you sound. Most days I'm just trying to make it through in one piece and don't think about the bigger picture." Her gaze wandered over to the girls. "Life is moving by like a fast-flowing river. I want to build a dam to slow it down, but it just keeps churning along. Most of the time I can barely hold my head above water."

He let the rest of the sand run out through his fingers, then brushed off his palm on his shorts before plucking her hand up. "You've been pensive ever since you saw your aunt this morning. Is everything all right?"

Her fingers tightened around his. "Aunt Blanche kind of yelled at me for blaming myself for Mom's death. She asked me what made me think I could control the situation when God decided a person's time was up. I hadn't thought about it like that, I guess. I realized that being in control is just an illusion. I really have no control at all." Her chuckle was halfhearted. "I'm not sure I like that realization."

He picked up more sand and turned her hand over so her palm was up, then trickled some sand into it. "We just do the best we can today with the time we're given."

Her full lips curved up, and she leaned over to brush a kiss across his cheek. "You're the best man I know."

He grinned. "You smell like gunpowder. Been practicing with my gun?"

"Gotta stay accurate."

He reached over to cup her cheek. Before he could kiss her properly, Haylie shrieked that she caught a fish.

"Later," he whispered to Mallory.

Kevin stared out the window of the SUV as they passed budding trees along a long dirt driveway. He'd spent the morning beside his father in a silent ride echoing with recriminations. His dad's cold shoulder had done nothing but reinforce Kevin's determination never to be like that. When he was growing up, he'd thought his dad put the stars in place. Back then, there had been lots of smiles, throwing around a football, and fishing trips with Kevin and his brother.

What had changed Dad into such a bitter, unforgiving man? Kevin had never stopped to think about what might have caused him to change over the years. He'd been so different when Kevin was a kid. Maybe his parents' marriage had been unhappy under the surface, and that knowledge had fueled his father's desire to make sure Kevin didn't make a mistake.

What Dad didn't know was that while Mom's pregnancy might have ruined his life, Mallory's pregnancy had set Kevin free.

His dad stopped the SUV at a ramshackle house. Kevin looked around for the woman he'd talked to last night. "I was called out here the other night and captured a rabid fox."

His dad didn't answer but shoved open his door and stepped out as the vehicle dinged a warning. Kevin reached over and snatched the keys from the ignition. One of these days someone was going to steal his dad's SUV. Kevin got out and jogged after his dad, who marched up to the door and pounded on it.

"Game warden," his dad called out.

While they waited, Kevin glanced around the scruffy yard. An old '57 pickup on blocks sat under a dead tree. Tin cans, beer bottles, and an old radiator littered the side yard. A rusting baby swing was upended under another tree. The place hardly looked lived in, but he'd been out here recently so he knew the owner had to be around somewhere.

"I'll check the barn." He pointed to the wooden structure behind the house. Barn was too nice of a word for the graying building with half the roof falling in.

The lock was broken, so he opened the latch and struggled with the screeching hinges to open the door. "Hello? Mr. Kennedy?"

He stepped inside the dusty-smelling building. A rustling sound made him wheel to the right, and he saw a man crouching in the dirty straw. "Mr. Kennedy?"

The man made a strange sound, a choked garble. He scrabbled back into the corner when Kevin took a step that direction, and his change of position put the man into a shaft of light streaming through a large hole in the side of the structure. Abraham Kennedy.

Kevin held out his hand. "It's okay. I'm not going to hurt you. It's Game Warden O'Connor, Mr. Kennedy."

The door behind him scraped, and his father stepped inside behind him. "What's going on?"

His dad's gruff voice galvanized Kennedy into action. He leaped to his feet, and howling incomprehensible syllables, he rushed at them both. Kevin stepped aside, but his dad didn't move as fast, and Kennedy barreled into him. Spittle flew from his mouth, and he grabbed the older man's throat with his hands.

The guy has rabies.

It took a second for the reality to jolt Kevin into a response. He grabbed the man by the collar and tried to haul him off his father, but Kennedy screamed harder and gnashed his teeth at his victim.

His father's face was ashen as he struggled to avoid being bitten by the enraged man.

Kevin put Kennedy in a choke hold and finally managed to drag him off his father, but he ducked his head and bit at Kevin's arm. His teeth snagged Kevin's sleeve, and Kevin struggled to gain control of him.

"Dad, cuff him!" He wrestled Kennedy to the ground again, but the man was getting harder and harder to control.

His father whipped out handcuffs and leaped atop the other man. Finally wresting Kennedy's hands behind his head, Kevin's father managed to slap the cuffs on him, but Kennedy continued to moan and lunge at Kevin.

Without thinking, Kevin reached out to grab the man's shoulder. "Calm down, Mr. Kennedy."

In an instant the man sank his teeth into the exposed skin on Kevin's wrist. The pain barely registered before Kevin yanked his hand away.

His father grabbed the man's collar and yanked him back, tied him to the wall with a length of rope he found, then stepped away.

Kennedy continued to lunge toward them. "No, don't! Red eyes!"

The dismay in his dad's eyes made the gravity of what had just happened sink in.

Kevin stared at the bite on his arm. The man's teeth had broken the skin, and blood oozed from the wound. A series of rabies shots was in his future for sure.

His father grabbed his arm. "We have to wash that."

He half dragged Kevin to the house and kicked in the door. The house reeked of something rotten, and Kevin stumbled over garbage on the floor as his dad shoved him to the sink and turned on the hot water. His father rolled up his shirtsleeve, then lathered the wound with dish soap and warm water. The sting of the soap finally penetrated the fog surrounding Kevin.

"At least you've had some rabies vaccines. You won't need immune globulin, just two more vaccines."

Kevin grabbed a piece of paper towel from a holder on the wall, then patted his arm dry. "We'd better call for an ambulance for Kennedy."

"And for you."

"I'll be fine." His gaze met his dad's, and for the first time in years he saw a hint of the father he remembered.

Thirty-Four

The sting of antiseptic hit Mallory's nose as she rushed through the ER doors and approached the registration desk. "A game warden was just brought in with a rabies bite. Kevin O'Connor."

The receptionist, a pudgy brunette in her midforties, looked at her over the top of her glasses. "I didn't think he was married. Who are you?"

"A-a good friend. He called me." He'd actually texted her and told her not to worry, that he'd be home as soon as he could. But she'd asked Carol and Kate to stay with Sadie and had rushed here.

The woman pursed her lips, then pointed to Mallory's right. "Through those doors. I'll open them for you. He's in room three."

Mallory went toward them and they opened. She hurried down the hall, her feet slipping a little on the highly polished vinyl tile floors. She skirted an aide pushing an old man in a wheelchair and found room three. A doctor and nurse turned at her entrance, but her gaze went straight to Kevin, who was sitting on the edge of the examining table.

The nurse, a pretty blonde in her twenties, stepped aside to allow Mallory to go to Kevin's side. His welcoming smile lifted her anxiety a notch.

She looked at his wound. It wasn't as bad as she'd feared. "A man bit you, really?"

On the way here she'd had visions of skin torn and bloodied, but from what she could see, it was a simple bite.

His smile dimmed. "Poor guy has rabies. I checked on him six weeks ago when he reported a rabid fox, and he assured me he hadn't been bitten. But I think he was just afraid of the rabies shots. Lots of people think they're painful, but they aren't that bad anymore."

"Rabies?" The blood rushed from her head. "Will the vaccine fix it for sure?"

He nodded. "I had two vaccines already since I'm in a high-risk group with my job. The painful part of the treatment is the immune globulin, which has to be packed around the wound to prevent the virus from spreading, but I don't have to have that done."

"No stomach shots?"

He took her hand. "See, that's what most people think. But it's just an intramuscular shot into the arm now. I already had it, and I'll get another one in three days." He squeezed her fingers. "I'll be fine. I can't say the same for Kennedy. It's fatal."

The doctor turned toward the door. "I think we're about done here, Warden. You can go home as soon as the nurse puts on an antibiotic and dressing."

"I'll step out to the waiting room and call Carol and Kate. They were both at the house when you texted me, and they're waiting for news. I can run you home. You don't have a vehicle here, do you?"

He released her hand and shook his head. "Dad brought me over. I told him to go on home. So I'll just ride with you."

She left him with the nurse and hurried to the waiting room. When she was digging in her purse for her phone, she saw his dad sitting in the corner by the vending machine. Her stomach plunged, but she approached him anyway.

His head was down as he perused a magazine, and he didn't look up until she cleared her throat. "Mr. O'Connor, I saw you sitting here and thought maybe you were waiting for news of Kevin."

His face was a forbidding mask of frowning disapproval, and she felt about as welcome as a flea. "The nurse is bandaging his arm now. They washed it and he got a shot."

"Of course. I was just waiting to take him home, but now that you're here, I see I can go."

"I'm sure he'd want to see you."

"Not likely." He rose and brushed past her so closely that she nearly lost her balance.

He took only a couple of steps before he wheeled around and skewered her with a glance so filled with dislike that she took a step back. For a moment she almost thought he would hit her.

"Why don't you just crawl back into whatever hole you came from and leave my son alone?" His voice was a hiss filled with venom. "We don't want you here."

Her throat closed, and she fumbled for something to say. How did she even combat that kind of hatred? "You don't really know me, Mr. O'Connor. You were always working when we were in high school, and I only saw you a handful of times. How can you even profess to know what I'm like or label me?"

"All I have to do is look at your actions. You ruined Kevin's life. If not for you he would have been a doctor by now. Now he's stuck in this same podunk place as me without hope of ever having a better life. You tried to trap him."

"He's happy, Mr. O'Connor. He didn't want to be a doctor. Being outdoors and making a difference for Maine wildlife is what he wanted to do all along. You should take that as a compliment. He saw what you did and envied it."

The older man's lip curled and he snorted. "Ridiculous. Tell me, were you ever really pregnant, or did you just say that so he would drop out of school to marry you?"

The strength went out of her at his accusation. "If that was all I'd wanted, wouldn't I have kept up the lie until we were married? Instead, I lost the baby and told Kevin. He still wanted to marry me, b-but Mom died right after that."

None of her words made an impact. He had his own view of the events, and nothing she said would change his opinion of her. She turned and rushed for the women's room, and once the door swished shut behind her, she went to splash cold water in her face.

She didn't belong here. Not anymore. She glanced at her watch. Now she was going to be late getting Haylie from swim practice.

Julia parked down the street from the indoor pool in Summer Harbor. Dusk was on the horizon, and the sky glimmered with color. Today was the day she'd snatch the kid. She'd watched enough to know the girl often sneaked away from the other kids after practice. She was always alone, so it was a great time to grab her as long as her mother didn't arrive early. Julia had dyed her hair black, and she used darker makeup to disguise herself. It should be good enough in the dark that the kid wouldn't be able to identify her later.

The kids left one by one, and Julia watched the clock. Mallory could get here anytime. She had to get the kid as quickly as possible. She'd already left the note on the steps back at the game warden's house.

Finally Haylie came out and walked off down the street a bit. Julia jumped out of the car, popped the trunk, then walked toward the girl. "Hello, have you seen a puppy come this way? He's a Yorkie, about so big." Julia used her hands to measure out the size of a small puppy. "I need to find him before dark. The owls will be out and he'll be dinner."

The kid possessed a worried expression. "No, I haven't. I love Yorkies. Where have you looked?"

"Up and down the road. He ran off when I opened the door, and I couldn't grab him. Little rascal. His name is Chance. How about you go that way and call him, and I'll go this way?" She pointed toward the car.

"Okay. I'll have to get back in a few minutes though. My mom will be here." Haylie went down the street. "Here, puppy. Come here, Chance."

Julia took a quick look around. No one seemed to have heard her. Circling around on the other side of the road, Julia crept along the tree line, then darted across the street to crouch by the open trunk. She took out the strips of duct tape she'd prepared and waited, her pulse throbbing in her throat.

"Here, puppy." Haylie's coaxing voice was near.

Julia saw the white flash of Haylie's sneakers, and she reached out and grabbed her, slapping a strip of duct tape over her mouth before she could scream. She quickly trussed up her wrists with duct tape, then tipped the struggling girl into the trunk.

Haylie tried to kick her, but Julia grabbed her legs and duct taped them together. She slammed the trunk lid down, then hurried to slide under the wheel and get away before anyone noticed. Luckily, no neighbors were around.

The girl's terrified eyes bothered her, but Julia put what she'd done out of her mind and drove the speed limit out to the remote cabin she'd found. Brush scraped along the side of her car, but it was a good sign that no one had been out here since she'd discovered this abandoned place on a walk. She hoped not to have to use it for long. Surely Mallory would walk into the trap when she read the note Julia had left on the front porch.

She let the car roll to a stop outside the cabin. It was a big place, but no one had lived in it for a long time. Tonight in the dark it appeared positively forbidding, and she wished she'd thought this through a little more.

Julia got out and left her door ajar so the light would spill out. She'd left a full kerosene lamp on the big porch along with matches, and she lit it. Ignoring the thump of Haylie's feet hitting the trunk's lid, Julia carried the lamp inside and looked around. No one here. She'd cleaned the place up as best as she could, but it was far from the comfort of a Hyatt.

It would have to do. Holding the light high, she went back outside and popped the trunk. Haylie's terrified eyes haunted Julia again, and she looked away. She set the lantern in the trunk and undid the duct tape from the girl's ankles, then jerked her out of the trunk.

Haylie wobbled a little, then found her balance. Tears trailed down her cheeks, and a muffled cry came from behind the duct tape, though she'd worked on loosening it during the ride.

"I'm going to take the tape off your mouth, but no one can hear you scream so don't even bother, okay?" Julia waited for the girl to nod, then took hold of one edge of the tape and jerked it off.

Fresh tears ran down Haylie's face, and she gasped at the pain. "Please, let me go," she whimpered.

Julia hardened her heart at the kid's terror. Sometimes you had to hurt other people to get what you wanted.

THIRTY-FIVE

Where was she? Mallory's heart pounded as she pulled to a stop in front of the pool. Darkness shrouded the tree-lined street, and the steps were empty. "Do you see her?"

Kevin looked around, then shook his head. "We're a few minutes late. Maybe she stepped inside."

"Or maybe Carol picked her up and forgot to tell me. She knew I'd gone to the hospital. I'll call." She punched in the number, and Carol answered on the second ring. "Did you get Haylie?"

"Haylie? No. I thought you would on your way home. By the time I could have gotten across the water to Summer Harbor, it would have been seven. Isn't she there?" Panic simmered in Carol's voice.

"I'll go inside. I'm sure it's fine." But dread tightened Mallory's gut as she ended the call.

"I'll go with you." Kevin opened the door and got out. They both went up the steps to the door. He pulled on it, but it didn't budge. "It's locked. Could she have caught a ride with someone?"

"Not without calling me first." Her mouth went dry, and she cupped her hands to her mouth. "Haylie!" No answer.

Her cell phone rang and she grabbed it, exhaling with relief when she saw Carol's name on the screen. "You found her?"

"Mallory, someone has her! I found a note on the steps outside." Carol's voice was shaking. "Let me read it to you. 'If you want to see your daughter again, go to your house at Bangor and wait for my call. Don't tell the police or anyone else.'"

Her knees went weak and her vision blurred. "Kevin is with me. We'll find her. We have to find her." She grabbed his arm and he steadied her. "Someone has Haylie! How can that be? People were right here." She heard the edge of hysteria in her voice and struggled to dampen it as she told him about Carol's call. She needed every bit of wisdom she possessed to figure out what to do.

"I'll call 911, then look around. Stay calm." He pulled out his phone.

She grabbed his hand. "What if he kills her because we called the police? He said not to call them."

"I'll at least talk to the sheriff. We can't do this alone. Stay here."

"I'm coming with you!" Without waiting for more of an argument, she rushed down the steps, calling for her daughter. Maybe it was a practical joke meant to scare her. She'd surely find Haylie sitting somewhere waiting for her.

Staring into the shadows on either side, she rushed down the street. Kevin called to her, but she just picked up speed. She wasn't going inside. Haylie was out here somewhere, needing her. About a hundred feet from the pool building, she caught sight of something gleaming in the moonlight.

Mallory sank to her knees in the gravel beside it. The pieces of stone bit into her knees through the jeans she wore, but she welcomed the pain.

"He has her," she said as Kevin knelt beside her. "That's her bracelet. She wears it nearly every day." She couldn't summon the courage to pick it up.

"I've seen it." Kevin pulled out his cell phone. "Don't touch it. I'm calling Danny. He'll want to run it for prints."

Of course. As Kevin explained what had happened to the sheriff, she stared at the silver bracelet winking back at her from the wash of moonlight. She'd made it for Haylie after Brian died, and her daughter only took it off long enough to shower.

He hung up and slipped his arm around her. "Danny will be here in about half an hour."

"Where could he have taken her? You know every inch of this countryside."

He gestured out at the darkness. "There's a lot of area up here to cover. I can't even count the many places he could have her stashed. Unless we have some kind of lead, it'll be hard to find him. I think we have to see what he says when he calls." He cupped her face in his hands. "We'll get her back, Mal. Hold on to your faith."

Her eyes burned, and she forced a swallow past the constriction in her throat. "I'll try."

Kevin's house swarmed with sheriff's deputies inside and out. Floodlights turned the night into day as men and women searched for clues about Haylie's captor. The voices of the searchers carried on the cold wind of night. Kevin stood with the sheriff on the porch as he finished telling Danny what he knew about the abduction, which wasn't much.

Danny popped a mint, then put the Altoids tin back in his shirt pocket. "This has to be related to her father's death and the arson at the house. We still don't know what the kidnapper wants."

Kevin watched a deputy with a metal detector sweep the front yard. He told the sheriff about Len Nevin. "I think the boat is the key. How did Edmund get that kind of money?"

"I'll make finding out a priority." He clamped his big hand on Kevin's shoulder. "Going to go check on progress." He was so tall Danny had to duck a bit to avoid the porch ceiling light as he went toward the steps.

The boat, always the boat. Kevin thought again of Mallory's suspicion that Edmund had gotten the money from her biological father. Where had that money come from?

Kevin rubbed his head and turned toward the door as it opened. Mallory looked out over the hectic scene and stopped. "Did they find anything?"

He stepped aside. "I don't know yet. They're bagging anything of interest, but the forensic lab will have to go through it all to see if there's anything that might direct us. How are you doing?"

"How do you think?" Her voice wobbled. "I want to be out there in the thick of things looking for her."

Carol twisted her hands together. "I'm a little worried about going back to Bangor. Someone broke into her house looking for her. How do I keep her safe?"

"Take her to your house, not hers. The sheriff will call the Bangor police and ask them to stake out the house for protection. If they won't, I'll figure out something. The main thing is for the perp to see you leaving, that she's obeying orders."

Mallory looked up at him, her dark eyes haunted. "He *will* release her, won't he? If I do everything he says?"

What did he say to that? There were no assurances. "I think he will."

She turned and clutched his shirt with both hands. "What if he doesn't? I have to get her back, Kevin. I have to!"

He gently settled both hands on her shoulders and pulled her against his chest. Her body trembled like a frightened rabbit. "We'll find her, Mal. Stay strong."

"I'm trying," she said in a choked whisper. "But what if . . . ?"

"Don't think about the what-ifs."

"Maybe I should let Richard Blake know. He might be able to call in some detectives. Maybe the FBI. He has connections."

"That's not a bad idea. Want me to do it?" He pressed a kiss against the top of her head.

"I'll do it on the way to Bangor. I just want to find her, Kevin."

"There's an Amber Alert out, and the entire state is looking for her. We'll find her." He held her tightly against his chest and prayed his comforting words were the truth.

THIRTY-SIX

The clock on the mantel chimed three times, and Carol felt a rising sense of panic as she paced Kevin's living room. They had to find Haylie, they just had to. Everyone wanted to rush Mallory to Bangor as ordered, but it was wrong to leave now. Carol just knew it.

Sheriff Colton stepped closer to her. "How you doing, Miss Carol?"

"How could someone snatch her like this? And without a trace!"

The sheriff hiked up his belt a bit, then sighed. "These guys have to be professionals. The man waited for the right opportunity, then darted in and grabbed her."

"But why Haylie? She's just a kid. She's not a danger." Carol's voice wobbled, and she fought hard to hold her composure.

"That's the million-dollar question."

Carol thought through everything she knew. Karen had been shot fifteen years ago, and Edmund had been murdered recently. The house had been torched to destroy evidence, but only one kind of evidence tied everything together. It was knowledge she'd been trying to push away for a month, but she had to face up to it now and admit the truth.

She looked into the living room where Mallory sat with Kevin. The pallor on her dear face tore at Carol's heart. "I need to talk to Mallory."

The blood roared in her ears as she went to kneel in front of Mallory and Kevin. How did she even begin? Mallory would think it a betrayal, and maybe it was. Carol hadn't thought it through when she first embarked on this plan, though she'd often thought of this moment. "I think I know what it might be all about." The constriction in her throat grew, and she swallowed it down. "I think it might be related to your adoption, Mallory."

Mallory's lips trembled. "My adoption? I don't understand. Why take Haylie?"

Carol's eyes burned, and try as she might, she couldn't keep the tears from falling down her face. "There are things I . . . I have to tell you. Important things that might help us find her."

Mallory tucked a long strand of hair behind one ear. "What could you know about this, Carol?"

"More than you imagine. I'm your mother, Mallory."

Her daughter's mouth went slack, and those beautiful brown eyes widened. She went even whiter than she'd been as she gave her head a slight shake. Her hands came up as if to ward off an attack. "You're Olivia Nelson?"

Carol nodded. "I started using my middle name after I got out of prison."

"Why didn't you tell me?" Mallory's voice was hoarse.

Kevin's arm curved around Mallory's shoulders, and he pulled her into a protective embrace. "This is a crazy time to admit it, Carol."

Carol ignored him. This was between her and her daughter.

"I tracked you down several years ago, then moved to Bangor to keep an eye on you, get to know you. I knew I didn't deserve to be part of your life, not after everything I've done. But I thought maybe I could make it up to you a little without you even knowing."

Mallory continued to stare at her as if she expected her to morph into someone else any moment. "You should have told me."

Carol lowered her eyes. "Yes, yes, I suppose I should have."

"What do you know about all this? Do you know who has Haylie?"

"Who got Thad's money? I think that's where you need to start looking." Carol could see the lightbulb go off in Kevin when his jaw dropped, and she nodded. "Someone is afraid Mallory has a claim to more of his estate than she thinks she's getting. That person wants to make sure she never collects. That Haylie doesn't collect either. With both of them out of the way, the money is safe."

Hope dawned in Kevin's face. "Richard Blake, his attorney."

"Maybe. Richard is a nice guy though and has always been devoted to Thad. Did a lot of the money go to him on Thad's death?"

"He never said. He's campaigning in Bangor though. A little convenient, don't you think?" Kevin looked at the sheriff. "Can you go with me to pay Richard a visit?"

The sheriff rose. "There's nowhere else I'd rather be."

"Should I go with you? He'll recognize me and know the truth is out."

"That might be helpful," the sheriff said. "You are Mallory's mother so you have the right to be there too."

Carol looked back at her daughter, who still hadn't moved. "Mallory?"

She leaned forward to embrace her, but Mallory drew back and shook her head. "I . . . I have to process this, Carol. Just go with the sheriff. I don't know how to feel about this. Not yet."

Not exactly the warmth Carol had hoped and prayed for when she'd thought about this moment. But then, what right did she have to expect anything but loathing?

The darkness outside was nothing compared to the darkness threatening to swallow Mallory whole. A black pit yawned in front of her, and its name was *terror*. Sheer terror at the thought of what Haylie might be going through right now.

And on the heels of that terror, she heard Carol's voice in her head confessing who she was. Mallory pressed her hand to her throbbing head. That revelation was the last thing she wanted to deal with right now. How could Carol have just given her away like that? The woman she thought she knew wouldn't have done it. Did she even know her?

Kate had insisted on driving the car to Bangor, and she glanced over at her. "I can see the tension in your shoulders. Hang on, Mallory. We're following the kidnapper's instructions. Kevin will find her."

"I shouldn't have been late." Her warm breath fogged the window. "What kind of mother allows her daughter to be snatched from under her nose?"

"The guy would have just snatched her from her bed or something. A determined criminal is going to find a way." Kate's face was pale and set in shadows in the dim light of the instrument panel. "The other kids said she walks off by herself. Haylie is fourteen, old enough to know better with all the warnings you've given her. You did everything you could to make her aware of the danger, but she didn't listen. This is on her, not you. You're a good mother, the best."

Was any of that true? Mallory groaned. She'd tried and tried to pray, but every time she thought she could move on from her past, something slammed her face-first into the mud again. Her face felt hot and her eyes burned.

"Mallory, are you listening?"

"I'm trying to." She lifted her head and stared at the lights twinkling on the outskirts of Bangor. "I'd take her place if I could."

"I know you would. So would her grandmother."

"Don't talk about her! I can't even think about that now. She admitted that moving next to us may have brought this danger into our lives. I wish I'd never started looking for her. It's all such a mess. What if I never see Haylie again?" It was hard to even force the horror in her brain past her lips.

It happened all the time. The news was full of children who died, of mothers who never came home, of fathers who died in car accidents. Why should she be special?

"Whoever took Haylie is the one to blame. Not Carol, not yourself. Not anyone else."

"What if I'm being punished?"

"Oh, Mallory. God forgave you long ago. I don't know why you can't forgive yourself. Let it go. Let's deal with this problem. It has nothing to do with punishment."

Before she could answer, her phone rang and she grabbed it

from her purse. The screen read *Unknown*. "Hello?" Her voice was shaky.

"Glad to see you've left town as I instructed." The words were garbled by some kind of electronic device. "I'm going to let your daughter out down the street from your house just after noon tomorrow. Be waiting there to get her. Don't come back to Folly Shoals, and stop any investigation into your father's death. Do you understand?"

She licked her dry lips. "I do. Please, let me talk to Haylie. I have to know she's all right."

Kate steered the car to the shoulder and turned off the engine. She pulled out her phone and began to type something. The sound of a sent text message whooshed out.

"Remember what I said. If I hear you're still poking around, I'll kill her next time. There will be no call, no warning."

Even through the distortion of the voice, the menace and intent were clear. Mallory gripped the phone tighter. "You have my word. Please, just let me hear her voice."

"She's sleeping, and I don't want to wake her. If I hear her crying one more time, I might have to shut her up for good. Just do what you're told and things will be fine. Tell the sheriff you don't believe your father was murdered. Rein in the boyfriend too."

Her gut clenched in a sudden spasm as she remembered the men and women searching Kevin's yard. This had gone way beyond any amateur investigation she was doing. "I don't know if I can. The sheriff isn't in my control."

"Do what I tell you or she'll die."

The cold words made her want to vomit. "How do I know Haylie is even still alive? You won't let me talk to her."

"If you do what you're told, you'll see for yourself tomorrow afternoon."

The phone clicked, and Mallory held it out to look at it. The call had ended. A scream built in her chest and throat. What he wanted was more than she could do, more than she could control. How did she live under the constant threat of Haylie being killed?

Kate touched her arm. "Mallory? What did he say? I texted the sheriff to let him know he'd called, but I don't think you were on long enough for him to trace it."

"H-he wants me to get the sheriff to quit investigating."

Kate's eyes widened as Mallory told her what the kidnapper said. "They have to find him. We can't live with a constant threat like that."

Mallory's phone dinged with a text message. It was a video. She pressed the Play button, and the screen showed a run-down house with a metal cot in one corner. Haylie was on the cot with her eyes closed, but as Mallory watched, her daughter rolled to one side. She was alive!

The sunlight glared in her face, and Julia groaned as she rolled over with her arm over her eyes. The kid had sobbed and cried for her mother last night until Julia was ready to scream. The musty smell of the old house had filled her chest with phlegm, and she couldn't wait to get out of here.

She got up and glanced at the sleeping kid. It had to have been three before she finally shut up. Peeking at her watch, she saw it was after eight. No wonder the sun was so bright, even through the trees. She opened the cooler and took out a tub of strawberry yogurt, then dug in the bag she'd brought for a plastic spoon. This would all be over in a few hours. She'd be able to get out of this wilderness. The thought of Washington beckoned and eased her grumpiness. Soon.

The sound of a motor came through the windows. She grabbed the gun on the table and peered outside, then relaxed when she saw Frank get out of the black four-wheel-drive truck. He'd come after her demand last night. She glanced at Haylie and saw she was still sleeping. Stuffing the gun in the waistband of her jeans, she slipped out the door to meet him in weeds along the overgrown track.

Frank's gray hair stood on end as if he hadn't slept all night. He waved away the swarm of insects that dive-bombed him. "What was so important you had to drag me to this mud hole?" His voice was loud enough to cause a flock of birds to take flight.

"Let's sit in the truck and get away from these bugs. I'll tell you what we have to do. I can't do it alone, and I need help."

"Let's get it over with." He got in the truck.

She slid in the passenger side and shut the door. The truck's new smell was overlaid with his overpowering cologne. "We have to eliminate the kid and Mallory."

His sleepy black eyes looked her over. "I thought you didn't want to hurt the kid."

"Things have heated up and there's no other choice."

"I thought that might be the case so I came prepared. I brought an injection that will put her to sleep. Permanently. No pain, no fuss." He pulled out a syringe and laid it on the console between them. "One little stick and our problems are over. And there's a pond deeper into the woods. I brought you rope and an anvil to sink the body. No one will ever know. I assume you want me to grab the woman?"

She always wondered what he was thinking, but it was impossible to tell. Those black eyes were fathomless, like looking into a gravel pit at night. His evil was just as bottomless as a pit too. They made a good pair. Until the last few weeks, she hadn't realized what she was capable of herself.

Her fingers closed around the syringe. How hard could this be? She could inject the kid and just leave her in the house. By the time she was found, the body would be decomposed, and the authorities might not even know who it was. By then she'd be in Washington living the high life. She could do this.

THIRTY-SEVEN

Claire angled the dashboard vents to blow heat on her feet and turned to look at the budding trees crowding the narrow road. "It's so chilly this morning. We'll have to get that driveway done first thing. It's nearly impossible for a truck big enough for building supplies to get down that muddy track."

Luke, looking impossibly handsome in his red shirt and jeans, cranked the heat up a bit warmer. "I've already got that ordered." He reached over and squeezed her hand. "Nine months and you're all mine."

She returned his squeeze. "I'm already all yours."

"I can make sure of it." His smile faded and he slowed the truck. "Looks like that truck is turning into our lane."

Claire squinted through the glare of the windshield at the big black pickup. "It's got out-of-state plates so I don't think it's a hunter. Plus, we have warnings posted."

Luke slowed his SUV even more. "Everyone in the county is looking for Haylie. I'm sure it's nothing, but I think I should have a little peek at what's happening at the house." He shoved the SUV into Park, then killed the engine and opened his door. "Stay here."

"Not on your life." She opened her door and got out. "We're probably overreacting."

"Not many know this place is even out here so how'd that truck know where it was? It's not the contractor's truck either. My Spidey sense is shooting fireworks."

She tucked her hand into the crook of his elbow. "Let's indulge it then, just in case."

The truck had long since escaped their view, so they hurried up the muddy track. She stopped and clutched his arm tighter. "I hear voices, like maybe an argument."

He nodded and pulled her with him to the turn in the drive where it angled toward the house. Car doors slammed as they neared, and she saw two heads inside the pickup, but the tinted rear window didn't leave much detail. The door to the house stood open.

"They're using the house for something," she whispered. "I think we'd better call the sheriff and Kevin." She tugged on his arm.

"I can handle this myself."

"Luke, this isn't your jurisdiction. We can go back to the road and wait for Kevin or the sheriff. If these are the kidnappers, they have to come back out this way." She saw the reluctance on his face. "You know I'm right. Come on, we have to get out of the trees so I can get a signal."

Luke finally began to move back the way they'd come. "What if Haylie is in danger? I don't like this, Claire."

"If help will be awhile, we'll go back in. But let's make sure of what's going on first." She pulled out her cell phone and saw two bars. "I'm calling Kevin."

Mallory had forwarded the video two hours ago, but no matter how many times he watched it, Kevin couldn't quite place why the room looked familiar. He'd seen it somewhere, but where? The vast forest along Downeast Maine held many abandoned buildings and cabins. This place could be anywhere.

He dropped his phone in his pocket and got up from the chair in his office. The place was a mess. He didn't spend much time here, and the rabies case files were stacked high since he'd had so little time to work on them. He'd combed through his files looking for a clue to where Haylie might have been taken, and nothing was coming up. Maybe his boss would have an idea. He went down the hall to Chesterton's office and rapped on the door.

"Come."

He opened the door and stepped inside, taken aback to see his father slouched in a chair on the other side of Chesterton's desk. "Sorry, I didn't know you were busy."

Entering his boss's office was always like stepping inside the office of a taxidermist. The mounted heads and fish lining the walls always made him feel like he was being watched. Chesterton was an avid hunter, and his prize was the large moose head over his bookcase. The thing dominated the room, and Kevin had always wondered why his boss hadn't taken it home to a place where the scale would be more in keeping with it than this boxy, gray room.

"Have a seat." Chesterton looked alert in spite of the early hour. He indicated the chair beside Kevin's dad. "Any news on the search for the little girl?"

"That's why I'm here. The kidnapper sent this." Kevin handed over his phone. "Could you look at this video and see if you recognize the house? Something about it is familiar to me, but I can't place it."

Chesterton leaned back in his chair while he watched the video. Kevin sank onto the chair beside his father but didn't look at him. He'd hoped his parents would join the townspeople in looking for Haylie, but he hadn't seen either of them at the organized search that spread out from Summer Harbor.

Chesterton handed it back. "Looks like a thousand other run-down houses in the area. At least she's alive."

"For now." He recounted what the kidnapper had demanded of Mallory. "I need to drive to Bangor. I want to be there when Haylie is released."

"If she's released," Dad said. "You and I both know it's a crapshoot with these guys."

Kevin pressed his lips together and refused to let his father bait him. None of them knew how this would end, but he was determined to hold on to hope.

His father held out his hand. "I'll take a look."

Kevin handed over the phone. His dad had been in these woods more than he and Chesterton combined. If Chesterton was an avid hunter, his father would be called a professional. They'd grown up on game meat.

"She's supposed to be turned loose a little after twelve."

His dad grunted and glanced at the clock on the wall next to the twelve-point buck head. "Best to catch them in the act if you can."

"Exactly. We've called in the Bangor police to help us nab him when he lets her out, but I have a feeling it won't all go down as planned. Why telegraph his intentions that early? He'd have to know we'd be waiting to arrest him. I think he has something else planned."

His father straightened and frowned. "I know this place."

Kevin tried to hide his excitement. It might be just like his dad to dangle some hope, then yank it away. "Where is it?"

"You and your brother used to like to play at an old hunting house while I checked my traps. It was down the old Paschal fire lane. I can't remember the last time I was out that way. It's mostly overgrown now, and I don't think anyone really goes there."

Kevin had a vague memory of it, but he couldn't quite think how to get there. "On Folly Shoals?"

His father nodded. "There's a big forest out behind Hotel Tourmaline. You go past the hotel on the way on the way to Mermaid Point. There used to be a sign for honey at the turnoff, but I think it fell down a few years back. There's a break in the fence, and that's about the only way to tell where it is."

"I know where you're talking about. Claire's mother bought it for her and Luke. I'll go there now." Kevin took his phone from his father. "Thanks, Dad. Appreciate it."

His dad cleared his throat. "I'll go along with you if you like. Show you where to turn."

Kevin was tempted to turn down his offer, but it felt almost like a peace offering. And he could use some backup. Most everyone was out combing the woods for Haylie. "Thanks. Let's take my truck."

His father fell in step with him as they hurried to Kevin's truck. Clouds scudded across the sky in an ominous swirl that pointed to a coming storm. The wind tried to tug Kevin's hat from his head, and he had to keep a hand on it. The crossing to Folly Shoals was going to be rough. He glanced at his watch. Nine o'clock. Only three hours before Haylie was supposed to be released. Was she still at the house, or had the kidnapper moved her?

Carol's small house felt alien after being gone. Mallory peered out the living room window before resuming her pacing across the tan carpet. Carol had given her the house keys so they could wait here, and Mallory wanted to poke into every crevice and distract herself by learning more about the woman who had lied to her all this time.

Kate handed her a mug. "You need coffee." She'd showered and changed into navy sweats this morning, and her dark-blonde hair was still damp.

Mallory wrapped her cold hands around the warm mug and inhaled the aroma. "Smells good."

"I put some omelet muffins in the oven. I know you don't feel like eating, but you should. It's going to be a stressful day. They'll be ready in a few minutes." She set down her coffee and went to throw another log on the fire.

Mallory glanced at her phone again. Nothing. "Do you think he will really release her?" The question was the same one she'd asked ten minutes ago.

Kate put the poker back and turned to face her. "He said he would. We just have to hang on to hope. Why don't you go take a shower while breakfast cooks? You'll feel better."

"He might call while I'm in the shower."

"It's only nine. Take the phone into the bathroom with you

just in case. Besides, pacing the floor will just make the time go by even more slowly."

Mallory forced a smile. "And you're just worried I'll wear a path in Carol's carpet."

"Guilty as charged. Take a bath instead of a shower and sip your coffee. Sometimes taking a bath gives me inspiration. You might think of something you've forgotten."

Mallory turned toward the bathroom, but her phone rang. The screen revealed an unfamiliar number from Summer Harbor, and she caught her breath as she answered it. "Hello?"

"It's Sheriff Colton, Mrs. Davis. I wanted to let you know the policemen are already in position around your house. You're not there right now, correct?"

"I'm at Carol's." She mouthed, *Sheriff* to Kate, who was listening with wide blue eyes. "You think he might release Haylie sooner than noon?"

"I think it's wise to be prepared. Also, Kevin and his father are on their way to a house Pete recognized from the video you forwarded to Kevin."

Her pulse leaped. "I knew I shouldn't have left! I need to be there."

"The men are right outside, busy as bees. We have all the bases covered. They could have already left the house, so you stay where you are. I'd like you to go to your house as soon as possible. It's safe now since we have the place staked out. The kidnapper may even try calling your home phone. We've got a tap on it."

"Okay, I'll go there right now."

"Text me when you arrive. Then look around and see if anything is out of place."

Mallory ended the call and told Kate what was happening. "I don't understand why Kevin didn't let me know he might find her at that house. Haylie is *my* daughter, no one else's."

"I'm sure he didn't want to get your hopes up in case the place was empty or it's the wrong house." Kate gave her a small push toward the door. "Go on over, and I'll bring the muffins when they're done."

Mallory pulled on a jacket and grabbed her purse. Carrying her coffee, she walked across the yard to her house next door. From the outside, the cottage looked just the way she'd left it. The swing still swayed gently in the breeze, and Haylie's bicycle leaned against the wall on the other side of the porch. The outside light was on though. Had she left it on? So many things had happened in the past week that she couldn't remember.

She mounted the steps and tried the door. The knob turned easily in her hand, and she pushed open the door. Had the police been here and unlocked it? Maybe she hadn't locked up when she and Kevin checked the house after the break-in. The house had a musty, unlived-in smell even after just a couple of weeks.

She checked her phone. What was happening with Haylie?

THIRTY-EIGHT

Brambles crowded in along the narrow road back to the lane to Claire's house but not as badly as Kevin had expected. He'd had to drive slowly to keep from getting stuck in the mud, which was as sticky as quicksand. "And there's Claire and Luke, just where they said they'd be."

Their call had convinced him they'd find Haylie any minute. He'd been tempted to call Mallory, but he didn't want to get her hopes up in case they were wrong.

"Fresh tire tracks. Three sets." His father grunted from the passenger seat. "Good thing it's mud season."

No one could track better than his dad. Mom used to quote *The Princess Bride* and say Dad could track a falcon on a cloudy day. That might be a stretch, but Kevin had seen his father look at a blade of grass and tell the weight of the animal that had just passed that way. Kevin gripped the steering wheel and prayed they'd find Haylie alive and unharmed.

"Park there behind Rocco's SUV." His dad pointed out a break in the brambles where he could pull his truck off the road a bit. "Let's go in on foot so we take them by surprise. It's only around the next curve, just past the big clump of birch trees."

Kevin slowed the truck and pulled it into the bit of clearing. "Can you get out on your side?"

His dad didn't answer and just shoved open his door and stepped out into the brush. Kevin shrugged and got out too. His boots sank into the mud and made a sucking sound as he walked. Claire and Luke hurried to meet them.

Luke drew his gun. "No one has come back out."

"Is there a path or do we follow the drive?"

"There's a path that goes in the back way. This way." His father went to the right of the truck and stepped over a fallen log covered with moss.

Kevin followed him with Claire and Luke on his heels. The trail was a little easier going since fallen leaves and vines covered some of the mud. The air held a hint of wood smoke, and he hoped it came from the house.

His dad pointed out a patch of morel mushrooms to him. "Gonna come back and get them later."

Marking his territory. Typical.

They climbed toward the stand of birch trees and paused to take stock of the house below in the clearing. A tiny curl of smoke came from the chimney. A car was parked to the side of the house. "I don't see the truck you mentioned. I thought there was only one way in and out."

His dad shook his head. "There's a fire trail he could have taken." He unsnapped his holster. "I'm going to circle around back. You go to the front. Make a big noise, call out your name, and say you're checking on the place. Don't say anything about Haylie. Luke, you circle around to the right. Claire, you stay out of harm's way."

She scowled but nodded and stepped behind a big oak tree.

Kevin let his dad take the lead. There was no room for egos today when all he wanted was to get Haylie back safe and sound. Hand on his still-holstered gun, he advanced down the hill. Quaker-ladies, wood sorrel, and trilliums carpeted the overgrown yard around the house.

Once his dad disappeared behind the house, Kevin walked toward the front. "Game Warden O'Connor. I'm here to check on a report of a disturbance. Is anyone inside?"

In spite of the smoke curling above the roof, the house felt deserted. He walked up the stairs and across the porch boards. The door hung partially open, and he knocked on it with firm authority. "Hello? Anyone here?"

Only silence answered him, so he pushed open the door with one hand and kept the other on his gun. The door squeaked a bit as it swung open, and he looked into the interior. It was mostly dark with a few sunbeams streaming in through the dirt-covered windows. He advanced inside, stopped in the middle of the room, and looked around. An old cot was in one corner, and the blanket and sheets on it seemed new.

He stepped over and picked up the blanket. Moving it brought the smell of new fabric to his nose. A sweater he recognized was under the blanket. His dad had been right. Haylie had been here.

He went to the back door and opened it. "Dad! There's no one here."

Luke's head popped up from behind a bush. "Have they been here?"

"Yeah. Come see." He retreated back to the house to look for more clues.

Kevin had been sure they'd find Haylie, that he'd be able to return her to her mother by the end of the day. But what if the kidnapper reneged on his promise to let her go? What if he'd taken her out to the woods to kill her?

His gut clenched at the thought of finding her body out here somewhere, and he pushed away the mental image to examine everything in the house. He couldn't afford to miss anything. He looked through the trash.

His father's heavy tread came across the wooden floor behind him. Kevin pointed out the bedding. "And there are candy wrappers in the trash as well as a partial sandwich. The bread isn't that hard either."

His father went to the old stove. "Still has some wood in it. I'd guess the kidnapper added these logs about two hours ago." He turned and went toward the front door. "I want to see the tracks."

Kevin followed him outside and down the steps where they both knelt and examined the tire tracks. "These tracks look like a car, not a truck or SUV. I'm surprised it got back here with the mud."

"Two vehicles though." His father pointed at the set by his feet. "These look like truck tires."

"We saw a big black truck here half an hour ago." Luke motioned to Claire, who ran to join them.

"What do you think of these tracks?" He estimated them at about an hour old, but his dad was the real expert.

His father touched the impression in the mud. "About fifteen minutes ago."

"That was my guess too." Kevin rose and looked at the trail. "The tires went out a different way. Where does this trail lead?"

"It's a pretty bad one, but it eventually leads out to a fire trail and over to the highway. A car would have a rough time of it. We might be able to intercept them."

"Luke, you go guard the main exit just in case they've found a way to circle back. I'll get the truck." Kevin rushed down the trail toward his vehicle. He didn't want to call Mallory until he'd found Haylie.

Julia stopped her car and stared at the pond. It looked murky and deep, the perfect place to hide a body. Her hands tied behind her back, the kid lay curled on the backseat with her eyes closed and breathing heavy. She'd cried and screamed the entire way here, and thankfully, had finally fallen asleep.

She fingered the syringe in the pocket of her jacket. One stick and the kid would never wake up. Clean and efficient. The girl wouldn't suffer. All Julia wanted to do was finish this and leave. Go somewhere far away where she could forget what she was about to do. Swaying palm trees, tropical drinks, and cabana boys would push the guilt away.

She opened her car door and got out. First, she needed to figure out the best place to dump the body. She had rope and an anvil in the trunk. The last thing she wanted was for the corpse to surface.

Flies and gnats swarmed the perimeter of the pond, and she waved her way through a cloud of the pesky insects to the wider edge of the water. She picked up a pebble and launched it into the water. It looked deep enough here. All she had to do was inject the girl while she was sleeping, then carry her here and dump the body.

After retracing her steps, she opened the back door and pulled out the syringe. The fetal position the girl was in took her aback. It was so childlike. Julia could inject her here, then drive around to the other side of the lake where it was even more deserted.

The kid blinked and opened her eyes, then sat up. Her throat worked, and her wide, terrified eyes stared past Julia's shoulder at the water. "W-why are we here? I want my mom."

Julia's golden window of opportunity had vanished. She should have moved faster. "Never mind." Julia slammed the door shut and got back under the wheel. She started the car and drove forward.

Haylie's shoulders shook with the weight of her cries. "You're going to kill me, aren't you? Listen, my mom has money now. She can pay a ransom. My mom was adopted, and she just found out her real dad is rich, super rich. I'm sure you've heard of him. Thad Hugon. H-he lives in Boston. Please, call my mom. She'll get whatever money you need."

Julia heard little of what Haylie said. Just a few more minutes, and it would all be over.

Mallory paced from her living room window to the front door and back. The kidnapper had said Haylie would be released at noon, and it was nearly that now. She'd seen no sign of her daughter though, and staying inside the house as ordered was driving her crazy.

Where was Haylie? And why hadn't Kevin called? He should have gotten to the house over two hours ago.

When she heard a sound from the kitchen, she thought her friend had finally come over. "That you, Kate?"

Starting to turn, she caught a glimpse of a figure dressed in camouflage rushing at her, too fast to form more than just an impression of broad shoulders and a tanned face. He hit her and she went down before she could even scream.

The breath left her lungs as his weight slammed her onto the wooden floor. Her head bounced on the floor, and she heard his gruff voice but couldn't make out any words as her consciousness wavered.

Stay awake.

Her inner command did little to hold back the darkness pressing in on her, but she strove to hang on to the last bit of light she could see. She was barely awake as he slapped a piece of duct tape over her mouth, then wound another length around her wrists.

He yanked her to her feet, and she struggled to focus on his face, to imprint his appearance into her fuzzy brain. She had to remember every bit of this, from his gray hair to his scary eyes. It might be important.

Wincing at the grip on her arm, she marched with him to the kitchen and out the back door. The sunlight struck her in the face and helped her manage to come out of her stupor. She struggled as he rushed her to the trees at the back of her yard.

He shook her and hissed in her ear, "If your friend comes over here, I'll shoot her, so shut up unless you want to see her blood spattered all over the grass."

She immediately quieted and let him shove her into the shadows of the trees. Why weren't the police here? Surely they'd been watching the back of the house too. Or maybe that was the one who had gone in to use the restroom at Carol's.

Mallory cast her gaze back and forth, trying to see if any help was likely to come her way or if she'd have to get out of this on her own. Nothing but grass moved in the shadows.

Was he taking her to Haylie? The thought made her stop struggling. She could endure anything if she could get Haylie free.

A gate at the back of the privacy fence opened into a heavily wooded park, and he pushed her through it, then shut the gate behind him. On the other side of the park, a black truck idled at the curb with the passenger door open. She strained to see if Haylie was inside, but the interior was too dim to make out any details.

Hope began to throb in her chest. Maybe the kidnapper had chosen this way to give her daughter back to her. Mallory picked up her speed, eager to get to the truck and see if Haylie was waiting for her.

The air was cooler here in the copse of trees, and gooseflesh rose on her arms. They reached the truck and he pushed her inside. She fell to the hard floor, and he slammed the door shut. She couldn't call her daughter's name with the tape on her mouth, so she looked around frantically. The rear seat of the truck was empty except for some tools and an old tarp.

Her abductor climbed into the driver's seat. His dark eyes met hers in the rearview mirror, and she saw no mercy, no compassion in his hard gaze. He gunned the truck away from the curb.

THIRTY-NINE

The car had been through here not long ago. Kevin's dad pointed out crushed vegetation just springing to life and the fresh tire tracks in the mud. Then Kevin and his dad got back in the truck and made the same turn as the kidnappers. They had to proceed slowly since the track was so narrow, but even so, brambles scraped at the sides of the vehicle.

He glanced across the seat at his father who was puffing on a cigar with his window down about two inches. Kevin didn't mind the odor because it somehow reminded him of better times when his dad would take him and his brother out fishing. He'd have the cigar clenched in his teeth, and the smoke would curl around them as if tying them together.

"Thanks for coming with me, Dad. I don't think I could have gotten here ahead of them without your shortcut."

"No problem." His dad took another puff of his cigar, then pointed ahead. "I just got a glimpse of blue. I think they're just ahead of us. Turn at the next fire road, and we can cut them off."

Kevin whipped the truck into the narrow dirt track. After the freezing and thawing of the hard winter, the potholes were big enough to swallow a moose. The truck bottomed out a couple of times, but he made it through to the main road again.

"Park sideways in the road here. They won't be able to get past us."

Kevin nodded and stopped in the middle of the narrow road, ripe with the scent of mud and decaying vegetation. He opened his door and stepped down into the muck. A swarm of gnats enveloped his head, and he swatted at them. At least they weren't black flies.

His father exited the truck with his gun in hand. Kevin drew his as well. His father motioned for him to take a spot by a large oak tree while his father stepped to the other side of the road and took up position behind a boulder.

They didn't have long to wait. The whine of a car engine mingled with the buzz of the gnats, and a blue Ford Focus eased around the curve in the road. Kevin peered through the gloom of the forest and saw a figure in the front seat. The passenger side was closest to him, and he closed his eyes for a brief moment, then opened them again. Where was Haylie? What had the kidnapper done with her?

The car slowed as it neared the truck. The driver's head swung from side to side as if looking for a way around the truck. The driver had no choice but to stop.

As soon as the car quit rolling forward, Kevin leaped from his hiding place and stepped in front of the car. "Out of the car!" His gaze met that of the driver. A woman? She looked vaguely familiar too.

"Kevin!" The passenger door flew open, and Haylie nearly fell out in her haste to get to him. "You found me." Barefooted, she sprinted through the mud toward him.

Relief as sweet as ripe blueberries rushed into his chest. He hugged her tight against his chest with his left arm, keeping his

Sig trained on the driver. "Are you all right? I didn't see you in the car."

She nodded. "I was scared and lying down. Where's Mom?"

"Trying to get you back by doing what she was told. I'll call her." He waved the gun toward the car. "You there. Out of the car."

His father stepped to the driver's side and yanked on the door. "It's locked." He rapped on the door and waved his gun. "Out. Now."

The woman's face was a stiff mask. She opened the door and stepped out into the mud. Slim and dressed in stylish jeans and a blue sweater, she was in her fifties. Then Kevin placed her. She was staying at Hotel Tourmaline. Why would she have taken Haylie?

He motioned her toward him. "You're Julia Carver."

"Yes." Her lip trembled as his father seized her arm and marched her over to Kevin. "I was supposed to kill the kid, but I couldn't do it." Her voice sounded incredulous, as though her reluctance to take a life surprised her. "See for yourself. I untied her. I was taking her back."

"Why'd you kidnap her? What's going on?" He kept his arm around Haylie who still trembled.

Julia met his gaze boldly. "It's complicated."

He read Julia her rights in a monotone. "Tell me," he said through clenched teeth.

"What will I get if I tell you how to save the Davis woman?"

Her cool voice ramped up his rage. "Where is she?" Mallory had to be all right.

His father tossed the butt of his cigar into the mud. "Let's get her to the sheriff. Maybe he can make her talk."

Fear flashed across her face. "Look, I'll tell you what I know if you'll let me go. You might be fast enough to save her if you hurry."

He curled his hands into fists. "Save her from who?"

"I . . . I was supposed to kill Haylie, and Frank is getting rid of Mallory. I couldn't hurt her though, so I threw away the syringe and was taking her to find her mother like I'd promised." She gestured to Haylie. "Ask her. She'll tell you I was taking her to her mom."

Haylie nodded against his chest. "She was, Kevin."

His gut twisted, and he pulled out his phone. "Mallory has protection so Frank won't get anywhere either." He called Mallory's number and waited as it rang several times. No answer. That didn't mean anything. She was fine with the police covering her place. She had to be.

He glanced at his father. "I'll call the sheriff." Before he could punch in the number, his phone rang and Sheriff Colton's name flashed on the screen. "O'Connor here. We've got Haylie. She's fine. I couldn't get Mallory, so can you let her know?"

"She's missing, Kevin." The sheriff's grim tone vibrated with worry. "A policeman left his post just long enough to run to the restroom, and the guy struck. Hauled her out through the back. We've lost them."

Kevin inhaled and stared at his father, who took a step closer to him. "We'll be there as soon as we can." He hung up, then swallowed hard to keep his voice from trembling. He pierced Julia Carver with his glare. "Mallory's been taken. And you're going to tell me exactly what is going on." He looked at his dad. "Call Luke and have Claire meet us at the airfield."

Mallory struggled at the bonds, but they were too tight to budge. She was in the basement of a house, and the sound of dripping water came from somewhere. A miasma of mold, decaying metal, and earthen walls seeped into her nose and pores.

Her captor had chained her up here at least an hour ago, then left. She had no idea if he was still upstairs or what he planned to do to her. She'd tried to talk to him, but he hadn't responded. Hadn't even looked her in the eye. She'd never met someone with the mob, but he fit her view to a T.

She tugged at the chains again. "Help! Somebody help me!" Though she screamed the words so loudly that her throat hurt, she didn't have much hope. She'd seen how remote this place was on the drive in. Surrounded by trees, the house was set back a good quarter of a mile off a dirt road. She hadn't seen another house or a car for miles on the way here.

"Help!" Testing its strength, she tried to pull the chain off the stone wall, but it held fast. The ring attached to the stone looked new, like this place had been prepared just for her. The thought nearly paralyzed her with terror, and she sank to the cold dirt floor.

Her captor's pronouncement about Haylie had devastated her, but maybe he'd lied to subdue her. She had to pray and hold on to hope. What was this all about anyway? She didn't understand. She knew nothing that would warrant death.

Footsteps thumped across the floor over her head, then a heavy tread came down the steps. A man's camouflage pant legs came into view, then he stepped into the light.

She backed into the corner when she saw his leer. "What are you going to do with me?"

He shrugged massive shoulders. "I already told you. You're going to join your daughter in the grave, though it might take a little while. You won't get out of your chains."

Only then did she see he carried a gun and a pitcher of water as well as some sandwiches in plastic wrap. "I like to keep things sporting." He set the pitcher and sandwiches within reach of her chain. "I'm leaving you a little sustenance. I'm also leaving this gun and one bullet for you to load it with. Once you've well and truly given up, you can end it yourself with one shot. Otherwise, you'll stay here and slowly starve to death."

"You're a monster," she whispered.

"I've been called that before. But a quick, clean kill gets boring after a while. I'll check back in a week. You'll be dead one way or another. Sounds fun, don't you think?"

"How many people have you killed?"

"I've lost count. It's my job, and I'm good at it. But I like to liven things up a bit. Makes my life more interesting." He laid the gun on the floor, then the single bullet beside it.

His smile made her skin crawl. She wouldn't go down without a fight. Dropping to her knees, she grabbed the gun and the bullet and started to jam it into the chamber.

He grinned and sauntered away. His cruel laugh echoed off the stone walls. "I'll say this, girlie, you've got gumption. You would have shot me dead if I'd stayed. But it wouldn't have done you any good. I don't have the key on me."

The basement door slammed, a lock clicked into place. Sobbing, Mallory covered her face with her hands. There had to be another way. She had to save Haylie.

FORTY

Mallory sat on the cold dirt floor with her back against the stone wall. The gun lay on the floor in front of her, right beside the food and water. Every muscle in her body ached from her struggle to free herself, but her wrists remained shackled to the wall. The *drip, drip* of a faucet somewhere in the basement was driving her crazy, but it was all part of the frustration she felt from her helpless situation. Her captor had been gone about half an hour.

She licked dry lips. It had been forever since she'd had water, hours before she'd even been kidnapped. For all she knew, the water and food were poisoned, so she hadn't dared taste any of it.

Drip . . . drip.

She knuckled her eyes and inhaled through her nose and exhaled through her mouth. Crying wouldn't do anything but give her a headache. Giving up would only get her dead. There had to be a way out of this situation.

Listening to the water, she had a thought. Where was that faucet? Maybe she could get some clean water from it.

She rose and tested the length of her chain. Only about six feet. She couldn't see well from the dingy bare bulb swaying overhead, but she shuffled along in the murky light and encountered a small shelf about chest high. It held some boxes of something that might be rat poison and something else she thought might be laundry soap. No help there.

She moved forward another foot until the chain yanked her back, then turned to her left and walked in the dark until she could go no farther because of the chain. There was no wall to touch so she must be in the middle of the room.

She picked up the chain and made her way back to the gun. It beckoned her, invited her to give in, to get out of this situation the only way she had open to her.

No!

She snatched up the gun and took it with her to the wall. One bullet. That's all she had to get out of here. Her fingers trailed up the stone wall and touched the stainless steel eyebolt that held the chain. She'd tested it often enough to know it was secure in the stone.

If she failed, she'd be stuck here until she slowly died of dehydration and starvation. Not an enticing thought.

And what if Haylie needed her? She wasn't ready to believe her daughter was dead. Her soul and heart would know the truth, and right now she didn't sense that Haylie was gone from this earth. And Kevin. Now that she faced the thought of never seeing him again, she knew she still loved him and always had. And her mother. She couldn't die when so many important things remained unresolved.

Fear compressed her chest, and her gaze swiveled back to the murky shadows. Wait, maybe there was something. She scurried back to the shelf and ran her fingers under it to see how it was supported.

She swept the shelf's contents to the ground, then lifted the wooden board off the metal brackets. Though she couldn't see well, the brackets didn't feel securely attached to the wall when she jiggled them. She wound her fingers through the ends of the bracket closest to her and gave it a jerk. It budged a little, so she yanked on it from the other direction and was elated to discover it was even looser. Mallory continued to wiggle it, then finally gave it a last hard pull, and it came away in her hands.

She took it back to the little light she had and examined it. The metal was old but solid, and the edge that attached to the wall was small enough to stick inside the link. Maybe she could use it as a pry bar to open the link in one of the chains. She examined each link to see if one seemed weaker than any other, but the chain was new. The eyebolt was an even stronger gauge than the chain, and there didn't seem to be an easy way to pry it open.

She selected a link in the chain and set to work with the bracket. She twisted and pried, maneuvered and chipped at it, but half an hour later it looked much the same as it had before. The link edges still touched securely.

Her mouth was so dry. She swallowed and looked at the water. Just one sip. Surely she could taste any poison in it. Cautiously, she uncapped the bottle and took a tentative sip. The wetness slipped down her throat, and she wanted to gulp the whole thing, but she forced herself to put the cap on and set it back down. While she waited, she worked on the link some more, but it was no use. She'd never get free this way.

She felt no effects from the water other than slightly refreshed so she took another drink, then put the bottle back down. The gun mocked her, teased her. What if that one bullet was all she needed to get free?

A faint odor came to her nose, and she lifted her head and

sniffed. Was that smoke? She didn't feel any heat, but the scent made panic beat against her ribs like the wings of a frightened bird. Maybe her attacker had set fire to the house in spite of the choices he'd given her. The acrid odor intensified, and she thought she heard the crackle of flames.

She picked up the gun and looked at it again. She could put the muzzle right at the crack in the links. It might drive the two edges apart, and she'd be free.

It also might ricochet off the stone and hit her. She embedded the link into the dirt floor as best as she could, then put the gun barrel against the weakest part. She closed her eyes and prayed, then pulled the trigger.

The sheriff parked his SUV in front of a palatial mansion in Bangor's historic district. He'd met Kevin and Carol at the airport. Stephen King's stately brick home was just down the street. "The Blakes are staying with some supporters this week rather than in a hotel."

Kevin opened his door and got out. "I guess the Best Western wasn't good enough for them."

Carol exited the backseat and looked up at the house. She was pale. "It was good of Pete to take Haylie."

"Yeah." His dad had surprised him by offering to take Haylie and pick up Sadie as well. At least Kevin wouldn't have to worry about anyone getting past his dad's defenses.

Kevin rehearsed what he planned to say. He'd choke Mallory's whereabouts out of Richard if he had to. "Stay behind us," he told Carol.

He let the sheriff take the lead since he had more authority to demand some answers than a game warden. Sheriff Colton approached the big Victorian home and pressed the doorbell next to the massive double doors. Moments later a woman around forty opened the door. She wore a black dress and heels that showed off her slim figure. Pearls that looked real hung around her neck.

Her welcoming smile showed off perfect teeth. "May I help you?"

"Sheriff Colton and Game Warden O'Connor, ma'am. We'd like to speak to Richard Blake."

Her smile faltered, and she looked from the sheriff to Kevin, then back again. "He's in the living room. Please follow me." Her heels clicked on the glossy walnut floors as she led them to a large open living room.

The fireplace was massive and ornate, overlaid with antique tile, and the rug in the middle of the floor looked expensive. Richard and DeAnn sat on a tan leather sectional that ran the length of one wall, turned, and continued on to another wall. Another man sat on the other side of the sofa, and Kevin assumed it was the woman's husband.

Richard stood. "Kevin, is something wrong?" His attention moved to the sheriff, and his frown deepened.

The sheriff glanced at the woman who had escorted them in. "Could we speak to the Blakes in private, please?"

"Of course." She signaled her husband, and the two of them left the room.

DeAnn stood as well, and Richard took her hand and looked at the sheriff. "What's this all about?"

Kevin stared at him, trying to read more about his character.

"Mallory is missing, kidnapped. The perp says she'll be dead by week's end. Since this is Wednesday, that doesn't give us much time to find her."

Richard took a step back. "What can I do? I'll help in any way I can." He looked down at DeAnn. "This is terrible."

She put her hand to her mouth. "I'm so sorry. That poor woman." She shot a wary look at her husband.

Kevin took in her stance, the way she twisted a lock of hair in one hand and clung to her husband's hand with the other. Did she know something?

"Julia Carver is in custody and is being questioned. She's singing about everything she knows. She indicated some connection to a man named Ian Jenkins and is blaming him for what's been happening."

"She's his stepmother," Richard said. "I'm still confused. Are you saying Julia had some part in this kidnapping?"

DeAnn swayed, and he thought she might faint. She sank back onto the sofa and put her face in her hands. "Julia is my friend. Richard promised her a job as head of his personal staff if he's elected. I'm not sure what she's done, but you say she's in custody?"

Sheriff Colton pulled out his notepad. "What can you tell me about Ian Jenkins?"

Richard put his hands in his pockets. "Ian was Thad's partner and CFO of the corporation. He's buying out all the businesses, and then the money is being dispersed to Thad's beneficiaries, mostly charities. Ian has been one of my biggest supporters in my run for the Senate."

Kevin thought through the convoluted story Julia had told him. "According to Julia, she's been working behind the scenes to make sure Ian got what he wanted so he'd support you in the election, then she could get what she wanted. Ian told her he'd shot Karen Blanchard fifteen years ago when Karen asked for support money for Mallory to go to college. Ian had been embezzling funds from Hugon, mostly hiding it as child support for Mallory. He intercepted that request and went to make sure Karen didn't tell Thad that he hadn't been sending the support. Things got out of hand, and he shot her."

"That's not all he did," Carol said. "He framed me for the missing funds, and I went to prison for it. No one believed me when I said I didn't do it. He's got a lot to answer for."

Kevin shot her a glance. Mallory would want to hear all about this.

"Ian killed this woman?" Richard took a step back and shook his head. "It seems incomprehensible."

"Julia found out about it all when Edmund asked Thad for money for a boat. He thought it only fair since he'd never gotten any support money for Mallory. By that time Thad was dying, and Julia feared all the money Ian hoped to gain from Thad's death would be diverted to Mallory and Haylie. He had no guarantee Mallory would let him stay in control, and she'd be unlikely to sell to him without having financials run. His embezzlement would come to light, and he'd go to prison. Edmund had cold feet and tried to get a loan to pay Thad back. When Julia got wind of it, she came here to assure him everything was fine and to leave things as they were."

"And things 'got out of hand' again, I assume?" Richard's lips twisted, and he shook his head.

Kevin nodded. "Julia came to Folly Shoals to make sure Mallory stayed ignorant. At first she hoped to eliminate any evidence of Mallory's parentage. She didn't seem to know who her biological father was so that seemed doable. Things escalated until Julia felt she had to eliminate Mallory and Haylie."

DeAnn twisted her hands together. "She killed Haylie?"

"No, we found her in time. But Mallory is still missing and we're running out of time. Julia's hired gun has Mallory. Do you have *any* idea where she might be?"

DeAnn nodded. "I . . . I gave Julia the keys to the Hugon vacation house. It's near Alligator Lake. I can give you directions." She grabbed a pad of paper and a pen and scribbled them out. "I hope you find her, Kevin. Hurry."

He snatched the paper from her fingers and ran for the door.

FORTY-ONE

Wisps of smoke from the gunshot had curled around the basement. She waved it away and peered at the link, then let out a yell when she saw the chain had fallen apart. She was free from the wall, though a two-foot chain still hung between the metal cuffs on her wrists.

Her ears still ringing, she stumbled to her feet and rushed for the stairs. The rough wooden treads were lopsided. She had to hang on to the handrail as she climbed them. The heat and smoke intensified as she drew near the basement entrance. She touched the door. Warm. Her fingers closed around the knob, then released it quickly. Too hot to handle. The fire had to be right on the other side.

Think!

She retreated back to the basement. There were likely small windows down here somewhere. Her tiny light suddenly went out, plunging the basement into total darkness. She froze, her heart pounding. She couldn't even see her hand in front of her face. The fire must have taken out the electrical. Disoriented, she swayed with her bare feet on the dirt floor and tried to figure out which direction to go.

Breathe. In and out, in and out.

She got control of the panic, then remembered the water. Holding her hands in front of her, she went back toward the chains and found the bottle. She doused water all over her clothes, then turned back toward the basement door. Fire was eating through the top of it. That way held certain death, so she went the other direction until her hands touched cool stone. Her foot touched something hard and she realized it was the other bracket, so she grabbed it. She might need it.

She felt her way along the wall, following a dim glow just down the room, until her fingers touched glass. She shuddered when her fingers encountered spiderwebs, but the crackling fire drove her on. She had to escape.

Raising the metal bracket in her right hand and shielding her eyes with her left arm, she smashed through the window. The dirt floor muffled the sound of falling glass, but nothing could mask the intensified roar of the fire as it continued to consume the door.

She cast a terrified look behind her, able to see a bit now that the fire was illuminating the stairwell. There, a chair to stand on. She moved it under the window and hopped up on it. It was hotter higher up, harder to breathe, and her lungs burned as she hoisted herself up and through the window.

The smoke swirled around her, choking off all thought, all reason. Panic flared again as she got partway through the window. The ground outside rolled uphill, and she couldn't get any purchase to pull herself the rest of the way through the opening. Her strength was fading, hunger, thirst, and stress having taken their toll.

Breaking the window had fed the fire, and it roared louder behind her, like something out of a nightmare. It was coming.

She had to get free. The smoke rolled her way, enveloping her head. Her vision wavered, winking out as the smoke smothered her.

She laid her cheek on the cool grass outside and closed her eyes.

Lights flashing on his SUV, Sheriff Colton had broken all speed limits on the way to Alligator Lake. Shouting at him to go faster, Kevin rode shotgun and pointed out every turn. He caught a glimpse of Carol's strained white face in the back. Her lips were moving, and he knew she was praying. They were on the final track back to the house. As they got closer, a strange glow lit the horizon, and he squinted at it. Wrong time of year and wrong direction for northern lights.

Then it hit him. "The house is on fire! Go-go-go!"

If he could have gotten there faster, he would have jumped out of the speeding SUV and ran the rest of the way, but it was all he could do to sit there gripping the armrest. He pulled out his cell phone and called for an ambulance and fire trucks.

"Please, God, please," he whispered as the SUV pulled to a stop in front of a fire that appeared to have fully engulfed the two-story house. He leaped out of the SUV and ran toward the house with Carol on his heels. "Go around the other side!" he yelled to the sheriff.

The intense heat drove him back as the front of the house collapsed, shooting flames high into the night air. Smoke billowed out, choking his lungs. "Mallory!" He screamed her name over and over as loudly as he could. How could anyone live through such an inferno? He had to find a way in.

He ran toward the side of the house. Maybe the fire was less intense at the back, but the flames were high here too. As he neared the back, he heard a moan and saw a figure lying half in and half out of a window. Flames flickered in the basement, and he rushed to touch the inert figure. He recognized the dark-brown hair in a braid.

"Mallory!" He grabbed her under the arms and dragged her the rest of the way out of the basement. Sparks flared on her jeans, and he smothered them with his hands, then carried her farther away from the intense fire.

The fire's roar was deafening as more of the house fell into the consuming cauldron of flames. He put her down on the cool grass, then pulled up the jeans on her legs to inspect her skin where the denim had been singed. There was some redness and blisters, but no third-degree burns.

He knelt by her head and lifted her onto his lap. She smelled strongly of smoke and was covered in soot—her face, her arms, her clothing. "Wake up, baby." The skin on her face looked tight and shiny, and he knew she'd be feeling first-degree burns there too. She needed a hospital and oxygen.

Tears streaming down her face, Carol knelt on the other side. She patted Mallory's face. "Wake up, honey."

He looked toward the front of what remained of the house. "Sheriff, over here!"

Colton came running from the back of the house toward Kevin and Mallory. "Is she alive?"

"Yeah. I think she's suffering from smoke inhalation, and she has some first- and second-degree burns, but I think she'll be okay. We need to get her to the hospital."

The sheriff nodded. "I'll help you carry her. Taking her

ourselves will be faster than waiting for the ambulance to arrive. We can call them and arrange to meet them to begin treatment." He whipped out his phone and spoke into it.

Kevin didn't need any help carrying Mallory's slim frame. He lifted her in his arms and held her close, thanking God she'd survived as he headed toward the vehicle. What had happened in there? He suspected the ordeal had been hideous, but his girl was a fighter.

Carol opened the back door of the SUV, and he got Mallory into the backseat, then climbed in with her while the sheriff went around to the driver's side. The overhead light revealed her bloody wrists.

He curled his hands into fists. She must have been chained down there. If he got his hands on Frank Richards, there wouldn't need to be a trial.

"The ambulance is on its way. I'm keeping them on the line so we can coordinate when we are approaching each other," the sheriff said.

As Colton drove away, Kevin heard the scream of fire trucks, but it was too late for this house. The second floor had collapsed, and soon there would be nothing left but ashes.

He pulled Mallory closer and willed her to stay asleep a little longer. The burns would be painful.

Her lids fluttered and her dry, cracked lips parted. "Haylie?" Her voice was a hoarse croak.

He touched her reddened face. "She's fine, sweetheart, just fine. She's waiting for you at my dad's house. She wasn't hurt."

Her dark eyes peered up at him from her dazed face, then softened with a tenderness he'd been yearning to see. He gathered her closer. "It's me, baby. You're safe."

Panic flared in her eyes and she struggled to sit up. "The fire! It's coming!"

"You're out of the fire, safe in the sheriff's car. The house is gone, but you're fine. A few burns are going to hurt some, but you'll live. Thank the good Lord." His voice broke, and he swallowed hard.

She relaxed back against his chest with a sigh. "You're sure Haylie is all right?"

He pulled out his cell phone. "I'll call her right now. She's waiting to hear that you're all right. Carol's right here too."

Mallory turned her head and reached a hand toward her mother. "Stay with me."

Tears rolled down Carol's face. "Always, honey, always."

Kevin called his father's phone and it rang only once. "Did you find her, Kevin?"

"I got her, Dad. She's all right. We're on our way to the hospital. Mallory's got a few burns, but she's okay. I'll tell you all about it later. She needs to hear Haylie's voice."

"Of course. Girlie, here. Your mom is on the phone."

"Mom!" Haylie's voice was full of tears.

Kevin handed the phone to Mallory and watched the tears slide down her cheeks as she spoke with her daughter. Up ahead a siren screamed toward them and the ambulance would take her away any minute.

But they had all the time in the world now.

FORTY-TWO

The hospital hallway hummed with activity, and Mallory heard the distant rattle of food trays and the squeak of nurses' shoes as she lay in her room with her hand in Kevin's. Haylie was on her way, but right now Mallory was content to rest. The pain medication had numbed her burns some, but the relief of knowing Haylie was all right did far more to bring her peace.

Kevin lifted her hand to his lips and kissed her palm. "There's so much to tell you. Some of it needs to wait until Carol gets back with coffee and Haylie arrives."

Any idea of sleep vanished, and she raised the head of her bed. "Tell me."

Kevin ran through what he knew of Julia's actions and Ian's involvement.

"Oh my word." Mallory couldn't quite take it all in. It was too much. So much evil in one person. "So she killed Dad, then burned down our house and hired someone to kill me while she took care of Haylie."

"Yep. She abducted Haylie, then couldn't kill her as she'd planned." He leaned over her bed and smoothed her hair back from her forehead. "I couldn't have endured losing you again." He buried his face in her neck.

She clung to him, even though his five-o'clock scruff rasped against the tender burned flesh on her face and neck. It was a delicious pain that proved she was still alive. Her fingers found the thick brown hair at the nape of his neck and squeezed. She never should have left, but they had a second chance to do this right.

"Mom!"

Kevin released Mallory at the sound of Haylie's voice, and Mallory turned her head toward the door, then held out her arms. Haylie flung herself on top of her. Sobs shook her body, and Mallory held her close and kissed her forehead. She hadn't been sure she would ever have the opportunity to hold Haylie again. The despair had been hard to hold at bay in the basement.

Haylie finally got up, wiping tears from her eyes. "I was sure you were dead. I'm sorry, Mom. Sorry I've been such a jerk to you."

"I know." Mallory patted her hand.

Haylie smiled and beckoned to Carol, who had stepped inside with a tray of coffees. "I knew Grandma would take care of me."

Grandma. Mallory's gaze found Carol's face. There hadn't been time to talk about their new relationship.

As Carol came toward her, Mallory reached for her hand. "Whatever led you to me, I'm grateful. I . . . I don't quite know how we'll find our way through this, but we'll figure it out as we go. That's what families do."

Carol's fingertips brushed the hair back from Mallory's face with a tender touch. "That's right, Mallory. That's what families do. I'm content with whatever role you can give me."

Mallory reached out with her other hand and took Kevin's

hand. With his strong fingers encasing hers, she just might find the strength to get through this maze.

From the cliff Mallory could see the lights of Hotel Tourmaline. Kevin had taken Sadie there to stay with her mother and grandmother for the weekend. The ocean waves rolled to the shore in the golden glow of the pinkish haze over the moon. A mermaid moon was the perfect time for what she intended to do. A new life and existence awaited her.

Scissors in hand, she stood on the seawall staring out at the waves. Her mom's spirit felt close right now. Was she looking at her from heaven? Mallory pulled one lock of hair over her shoulder.

The spicy scent of Kevin's cologne alerted her to his presence before he touched her arm, and she turned to smile up at him. "You must have sensed I wanted you here. How did it feel to drop Sadie off for the weekend? Are you surviving it?"

"It was easier than I thought it would be. DeAnn's mom was so eager to see her, and Sadie was so excited that it made up for my reluctance." He cupped her face in his palm. "You sure you want to do this?"

"You don't want me to?"

"I've never been a guy who cared about hairstyles. Far be it from me to dictate how you wear your hair, or anything else. You'd be gorgeous, sweet, and kind even if you were bald." His smile flashed in the moonlight.

"Spoken carefully like a man who doesn't want to get in trouble." That was one of the many things she loved about him. He gave her the freedom to be herself, to choose.

His grin widened. "I'm telling you the truth though. Short hair might suit you. I could see that long neck of yours. And kiss it to my heart's content. That might take awhile."

"You can have all the time you want to do that." She shivered as he lifted the heavy hair from her neck and nuzzled it. The delicious sensation of his warm lips on her skin about derailed every other thought as she snuggled into his embrace. "I don't have to do this now." She pulled his head down for another kiss.

"Yeah, you do." He lifted his head and stepped back. "I want to watch."

"Crazy man." She stepped closer to the edge of the cliff and lifted a long lock of hair, then brought up the scissors.

For a long moment, she wasn't sure she could do this. Mom's voice sounded in her head, telling her never to cut her hair, that it was her one true beauty. What if she hated it after she did it? She'd had long hair for nearly twenty years.

She could grow it long again if she hated it. The guilt she'd hugged around herself like a cocoon had nearly smothered her, and it was time to let it go. All of it. Time to forgive herself for her own mistakes. Time to face a different kind of future. Time for a new start.

Snip, snip.

The hair fell onto her hand, then she tossed the tufts into the waves and watched them waft down to the clear water. She cut another lock, then another, until she could feel the breeze on her back. The sound of the waves seemed to roar the ocean's delight at her offering. The weight of her guilt fell off with the weight of her hair, and she felt lighter, younger, released.

She dropped the scissors to the ground, then ran her fingers through her thick hair. It barely touched her collar now, and she liked the way it felt.

She turned to face Kevin. "I'm free, Kevin! Free to forget the past, free to move forward."

"I hope that means what I think it does." His hands settled gently on her shoulders, and his gaze searched hers for confirmation.

She soaked in the love radiating from his face, the possessive touch on her shoulders. This was where she belonged, right here with Haylie, Kevin, and Sadie. And there was room for Carol too. "Do you think it's possible to really start over? To leave the past in the past?"

"I know we can. We were always meant to be together, Mallory. You captured my heart all those years ago and have never let it go."

Mesmerized, she gazed at his face, the strong planes and angles, his firm nose, the full mouth that was always ready with a smile and a word of encouragement. This was her man. He always had been, but she'd been too stubborn to admit it. Too set on punishing herself for something she could never go back and change.

She reached up and clasped him around the neck, then pulled his head down. "I'll be yours until the moon doesn't shine anymore."

His breath whispered across her face just before he kissed her. "I'm not sure that's long enough, but it's a wicked good start."

Dear Reader,

Shew, we made it through another book together! It was great fun for me to go back to Maine in this story. Have you ever been there? It's like stepping back in time, and I love that beautiful, wild coastline.

I wanted to explore second chances in this book and how too often we are paralyzed by mistakes we've made. God doesn't want that for us! It's way easier to forgive someone else than it can be to forgive ourselves. If you're in that place right now, stop right now and resolve to let it go. (Cue up music from *Frozen*! ☺) When we're stuck in unforgiveness, we can't be completely free in our lives because we're too worried about making mistakes. But mistakes are part of life. We learn and grow from them. Embrace the journey and make those mistakes. Become better and stronger through them!

I love hearing from you! I read and answer all my own e-mail, so let me know your thoughts anytime.

Much love,
Colleen

www.colleencoble.com
colleen@colleencoble.com

DISCUSSION QUESTIONS

1. Have you ever dealt with guilt you couldn't get rid of? How did you finally resolve it?
2. What is a perfectionist? Is it good or bad and why?
3. Have you ever had a rebound relationship? What drove it?
4. Do you know anyone who is adopted? Did they want to find their birth parents or were they reluctant?
5. Family relationships can sometimes be the trickiest of all. How do you navigate rough waters in a relationship?
6. Who was your first love? Do you have any regrets?
7. Have you ever had to deal with a surly teenager? How did you handle it?
8. Have you ever done something to symbolize a decision the way Mallory did when she cut her hair?

ACKNOWLEDGMENTS

I received great help on this book from some Maine friends. A special thanks to Rachael Farnsworth-Merritt, who gave me great Mainer tips. Thanks so much, friends!

I'm so blessed to belong to the amazing Thomas Nelson dream team! I've been with them for twelve years, and it's been such an inspiring time as I've learned more and more about the writing process from my terrific team. This is the first novel where I've collaborated with editor Amanda Bostic and publisher Daisy Hutton, both brilliant minds with great insights into story. The journey couldn't have been more wonderful for me!

Marketing director Katie Bond is always willing to listen to my crazy ideas and has been completely supportive for years. Fabulous cover guru Kristen Ingebretson works hard to create the perfect cover—and does. You rock, Kristen! And of course I can't forget the other friends in my fabulous fiction family: Becky Monds, Jodi Hughes, Kerri Potts, Heather McCulloch, Becky Philpott, Karli Jackson, Kristen Golden, and Elizabeth Hudson. You are all such a big part of my life. I wish I could name all the great folks at Thomas Nelson who work hard on selling my books through different venues. I'm truly blessed!

Julee Schwarzburg is a dream editor to work with. She totally gets romantic suspense, and our partnership is pure pleasure. She brought some terrific ideas to the table with this book—as always!

My agent, Karen Solem, has helped shape my career in many ways, and that includes kicking an idea to the curb when necessary. And my critique partner, Denise Hunter, is the best sounding board ever. Thanks, friends!

I'm so grateful for my husband, Dave, who carts me around from city to city, washes towels, and chases down dinner without complaint. My kids—Dave and Kara (and now Donna and Mark)—and my grandsons, James and Jorden Packer, love and support me in every way possible, and my little Alexa makes every day a joy. She's talking like a grown-up now, and having her spend the night is more fun than I can tell you. And you know how I love coffee! My son-in-law Mark has a coffee roasting business now, CaptainDavysCoffeeRoaster.com, and he sends me the most fabulous IR roasted coffee. ☺

Most important, I give my thanks to God, who has opened such amazing doors for me and makes the journey a golden one.

About the Author

Photo by Clik Chick Photography

RITA finalist Colleen Coble is the author of several bestselling romantic suspense novels, including *Tidewater Inn*, and the Mercy Falls, Lonestar, and Rock Harbor series.

Visit her website at www.colleencoble.com
Twitter: @colleencoble
Facebook: colleencoblebooks

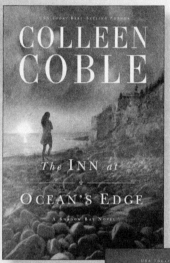
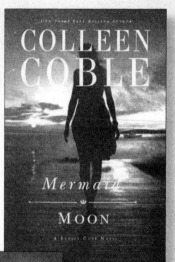
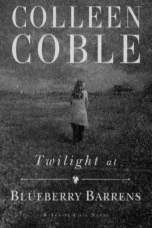

If you loved reading about forensic artist Gwen Marcey as much as I do, pick up the Gwen Marcey books by Carrie Stuart Parks. *A Cry from the Dust* and *The Bones Will Speak* are available now. I think you'll be as hooked as I am!

Colleen Coble

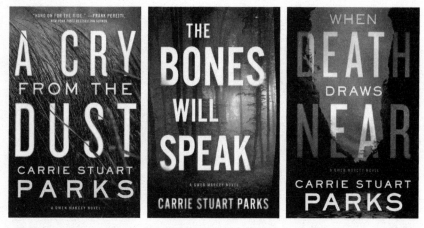

Available in print and e-book.   Available in print and e-book.   Available in print and e-book August 2016.

The *USA Today* Bestselling Hope Beach Series

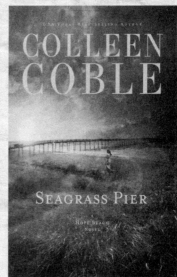

> "Atmospheric and suspenseful"
> —*Library Journal*

Available in print and e-book

COLLEEN LOVES TO HEAR FROM HER READERS!

Be sure to sign up for Colleen's newsletter for insider information on deals and appearances.

Visit her website at www.colleencoble.com
Twitter: @colleencoble
Facebook: colleencoblebooks

THOMAS NELSON
Since 1798